Dark Wine

Library of Congress Control Number 2015930616
Hardback: 978-1-937356-37-8
Trade: 978-1-937356-38-5
ebook: 978-1-937356-39-2

Publisher's Cataloging-in-Publication Data

Shannon, Beth Tashery.
 Dark wine / Beth Tashery Shannon.
  p. cm.
 ISBN: 978-1-937356-37-8
 1. Vampires—Fiction. 2. Cairo (Egypt)—Fiction. 3. Gothic fiction (Literary genre), American. 4. Sex addiction—Fiction. 5. Erotic stories, American.   I. Title.
PS3619.H3549 D37 2015
813.6—dc22
                    2015930616

Cover and interior design by the Frogtown Bookmaker
Frogtownbookmaker.com

Cover images: Sunset from al-Azhar, photograph by Arria Belli,
Abendstimmung vor den Pyramiden, painting by Georg Macco (d. 1933)

Published by BearCat Press
BearCatPress.com

Dark

Wine

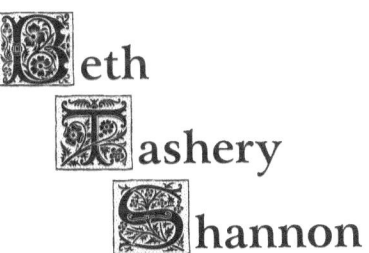

Beth Fashery Shannon

BearCat
PRESS

San Francisco

Also by Beth Tashery Shannon

Tanglevine
(the first story in a quartet, *Windland's War*)

and writing as Elizabeth Adair

The Sun and Stars

For Gayle and Richard,

whose love

and belief have

sustained my writing always.

ne

El-Orouba Road, Cairo
March 1986

rimson blooms flowed past the taxi window. Violet and saffron streamed by too fast for shapes, throbbing rhythms against green. But in the gaps between the leaves, a desolation of sand and rocks stretched away to the sky. Leaving Egypt. The dark Nile sliding through emerald fields, the pyramids incandescent at dawn, the call to prayer interweaving above crumbling balconies and shuttered windows, the minarets and high rises of Cairo fading into dust, like all the mirages we call our lives.

Relinquishing Egypt, where time flows in more than one direction, and the desert floats white on the horizon, like a dream on the rim of the waking mind. Giving up the evening laughter in the bazaars, cinnamon, cumin, mint in the spice sellers' stalls, the constantly honking traffic and a song floating up from the river at dusk. Losing the dark vortex of his eyes. Relinquishing the tender destruction of his touch.

Escaping with her life.

Was it futile to hope that putting distance and seas between them might save her? That knowing she lived might save him?

"Love will save us, will it?" His remembered whisper brushed hot against her ear. "More fools we. You say I've escaped time, that loving me is a glimpse of infinity. Love may take us to the edge of eternity, but it leaves us there. To glimpse eternity is ecstasy. To inhabit its edge is hell."

Was this the beginning of her hell? She could not return to her friends in California or her family in Kentucky. She must learn a new identity. She could never use her real name again, or take up her old work. He knew her too well. She must disappear without a trace.

If only she could disappear to herself too, she would gladly relinquish every shred of her identity, every atom of her memory. She would give anything to be free of the thought of him.

She glanced back again, but no nondescript car with black windows pursued, only Cairo in its golden haze, dwindling into the sunset. Or was it growing? Fading or igniting? The bright curve of the windshield was a mirror, turning the road back on itself, contracting and expanding, opening with promises of the unknown.

**WO**

El-Orouba Road, Cairo
October 1985

pening with promises of the unknown, the road shone in the afternoon haze. "Egypt!" Terry smiled at her, his gold hair blowing in the breeze. "What do you think, Cat? Is it home that's far away, or us?"

Catherine smiled back. It was one of those Terry questions that didn't call for an answer.

Two hours ago the plane's wings had pierced the rose of a Mediterranean dawn. Now it was afternoon. Twenty hours of planes and airports had left fragments of impression iridescent as colored glass. The vast, pale forehead of Africa curving against the dark sea. The slate colored vein of the Nile Valley fanning out to its delta. An airport guarded by policemen with rifles strapped to their shoulders. A young customs clerk peering closely at their passports as if eager to refuse them, then stamping and handing them back with an unexpectedly warm, "Welcome to Egypt!" And now, beneath this chaos of glaring chrome and roaring engines, an unfamiliar smell, strangely alkaline.

The scent of the Sahara.

Horn blasting, a truck hurled straight at them. Their driver honked and swerved casually. The line down the center of the road might have been painted there only for decoration. Nobody seemed to believe in brakes. Terry laughed a little nervously. "*Kwayyis*," he told the driver. "You're a brave man."

"No problem." The driver glanced at them in the mirror. His dark eyes had long, thick lashes. "To Maadi? Very good for visit, Maadi. How long in Egypt?"

"*Ehna mish sana—*" Terry began painstakingly.

"You speak Arabic," the man congratulated him. But taking accurate measure, he continued in his better English, "So. Not tourists. You come to work?"

It was Terry he looked at in the mirror. Egypt did not bar women from driving, or most professions, or the vote, but she'd been told that as a Western woman she'd be neither fish nor fowl. Her independence would be accepted, even assertiveness, but she should not expect equality.

In other words, it wouldn't be that different from home, only more up front about it. What had given her more pause was the widespread poverty, and finding themselves suddenly among the disproportionately privileged. For Egyptians the American coin had two sides. American tourism contributed significantly to the economy, but American support contributed just as significantly to an oppressive regime's stranglehold on power.

Part of Terry's charm was his ability to infect others with his enthusiasm, and he was already eagerly describing the mural he'd been commissioned to paint, part of the innovative architecture of the Hotel Lyndore being built on the bank of the Nile. The driver displayed ruinous teeth in an interested smile.

Fighting the sleepiness of jet lag—it was nearly midnight back home—Catherine tried to follow the conversation. The bottle brush trees with their crimson blooms had petered out, revealing gritty sand, not the velvety golden dunes she'd imagined from *Lawrence of Arabia*, but a jostle of brownish hillocks littered with rocks. It was like some other planet. Mars. A landscape that had nothing to do with humanity. The highway and its traffic were a precarious trickle in an immensity that belonged to the snakes, scorpions and falcons.

Wind clawed up little dust devils, sending invasions of pale sand fine as powder across the asphalt. She watched it blow under the tires of the car ahead. Stealthily, ceaselessly, the desert was striving to devour civilization. Its ebb and flow was sinuous, hypnotic.

Buildings sprang at her, jolting her from her doze. Palm trees fronted the bisque cubes where men in suits or jeans strolled along pavements, and women in long sleeved dresses. Egyptian women did not conceal their faces, but most covered their hair with white or beige scarves and very few wore jeans.

Gradually the suburbs thickened into urban tangles and elevated highways. Billboards advertising cars and vacuum cleaners crowded among garish artwork of weeping young women, cobra-eyed seducers and men with guns. Ads for soap operas? Movies? Still listening to the driver, Terry squeezed her hand, boggling at the lurid caricatures of virtue and evil.

Lanes of houses ran below road level, stone with carved fronts. Some had picturesque domes, painted ornamentation, wrought iron flourishes, but some were falling into ruin. Lines of drying laundry stretched between sculpted stone and rusty corrugated iron. Children in faded clothes played among sandy drifts of refuse.

In the mirror the driver saw her looking. "City of the Dead," he explained. "Old, but not ancient. Hundreds years only."

"They're tombs?" In a lane beside a rickety wheelbarrow a cat slept on a broken plastic chair. "People live there."

"Too many people come to the city. Better life here, they think. But not enough houses, not enough money. These families are lucky. Long time, they clean and guard the tombs." He lifted a hand from the steering wheel, turning it like a shrug. "Stone makes good houses. Cooler in summer than brick."

Jet lag and gas fumes made her dizzy. The glaring sky menaced. Catherine swallowed down her nausea. The City of the Dead gave way to a new snarl of highways and nondescript urban buildings. Among them rose a graceful minaret. Its pale stone was carved as delicately as lace.

The rushing traffic dipped into Cairo in earnest. Between dusty high rises, old side streets offered views of fancifully arched doors and overhanging upper stories. She glimpsed turbaned men lounging with water pipes in an outdoor café, and on a street corner an old woman in black from head to foot selling tomatoes and huge, beautiful cauliflowers. Rusty bicycles and donkey carts wove among the cars.

"Hey!" Terry poked her. "A camel!"

There, head and hump above the traffic like the periscope and hatch of a submarine, it promenaded. Less a beast of burden than some supercilious alien, it surveyed the mere earthlings, batting long, pale lashes with scorn.

The driver grinned at Terry. "No camels in New York City, eh? You want to ride one? My cousin Lutfi has camels. You ride them around the pyramids. You want his address?"

"Absolutely." Terry pulled out the charcoal pencil he was never without and scribbled it on the envelope of his plane ticket. The driver smiled, knowing nothing about Terry's flutters of paper, how they accumulated, how they drifted everywhere except when they were wanted. But if Terry did keep hold of it, when they went to Giza he would find Lutfi. Terry was going to make as motley an assortment of friends in Cairo as at home and he'd love every minute of it.

Terry was a mayfly, a genuinely free spirit. Catherine loved him for it, though it meant she was the practical one. Because someone had to be, not because she wanted to be. Once, her dreams had guided her as Terry's were guiding him now. Once, the future was a choice between beckoning adventures.

Maybe Terry was right that it was just as well she'd been granted no work permit. Unemployment was high in Egypt. Work was nearly impossible for foreigners not already employed on arrival. It might do her good to drift awhile, to remember how to dream. She wasn't even sure what her dreams were anymore.

Lyndore had made things easy, too. The corporation had furnished an apartment in the international suburb of Maadi, saving them the search that Pete Burge, Terry's project manager, said was horrific in this overcrowded city. Since Terry's contract forbade either of them to get involved with any community action organization—there might be political ramifications—maybe she'd get hold of a guitar again. Maybe join a rock and roll band.

"Look," the driver said. "*El-Nil.*"

The Nile. Catherine turned quickly, expecting feathery papyrus tufts, lotus blossoms floating, maybe even the ruins of an ancient temple. Between office buildings she glimpsed a patch of grey water. Unreasoning disappointment took her.

Terry glanced at her. "You didn't sleep on the plane, did you?" He'd snoozed like a baby through half the flight, but she never could. "Want to sleep? I'll do dinner."

She appreciated his thoughtfulness. "No, you rest. You've got a big day tomorrow. I can sleep then."

Terry shrugged. "Just a little paperwork, Pete said. A few formalities. Are you still up for the pyramids in the afternoon?"

Her eyes opened. "What do you think?" He knew how much she'd always yearned to see the pyramids, and to go into one. The Great Pyramid itself, she hoped. She didn't know why, but all her life she'd visited them in dreams. Maybe now she'd find out.

Smiling, she let her eyes half close. The dusty office buildings pulled back like a curtain, and at last a wide, slow river was revealed, a bright shimmer on olive green depths. Palm trees fringed its banks. Bulrushes, Moses. As a child, her favorite Bible pictures were the ones with starry Egyptian skies. She parted the reeds and saw lily pads floating and blue lotus flowers. The water rippled with secret life.

hree

our street," the driver announced. Catherine tried to pull herself awake. Palm trees lined the streets, poking out of the pavement at regular intervals. The tall buildings were nearly identical, with buff plaster, stacks of narrow balconies and the boxes of air conditioners. "Are we in L.A.?" she mumbled, bewildered.

"Just like America," the driver agreed cheerfully.

Blinking her sight clearer, Catherine saw Terry looking like a child who'd been promised ice cream and given spinach. "Wow, great," he managed with an effort.

Uncomfortably aware that the driver probably dreamed of living on such a clean, new street, they smiled as he helped them get their luggage out. Terry tipped him double what they'd been advised to. They parted with Terry's promise to look up cousin Lutfi at the pyramids.

Nothing about the bland hallway felt Egyptian. For months they'd imagined to each other an old building with assorted angles and curves, arched windows and maybe tiled alcoves, on a street dense with blooming trees like the one they'd seen in a photo of

Maadi. Even the name Maadi was redolent with dates growing on trees and views of desert sunsets.

The elevator doors opened on a plain beige hall. They found the door with their number. At least it was Arabic, a two like a backwards seven, the zero a dot, the five like a zero. Catherine unlocked the door and Terry pushed it open.

In the middle of a dim room, lumps huddled like sleeping bears. She put down her luggage, crossed to the drapes and pulled the cord. A fine powder of dust rose. Through it beige walls emerged. The bears became a brown plaid sofa and matching chairs facing a large television.

"Just like America," Terry murmured dolefully.

"We have a balcony," Catherine offered, opening the sliding door. It held a small table, two chairs, and enough room for the potted tree that almost offered privacy from the apartments across the street. "It's a lemon tree, we'll grow our own lemons."

Down the hall she found a windowless bath and two small rooms, each with what loud furniture commercials back home called a bedroom "suit." The kitchen had lots of cabinets, washer, dishwasher. She opened the frosted glass window above the sink, but the view of a row of garbage cans made her shut it again.

"I know the lease says we can't ditch the furniture," Terry took his turn encouraging her, "but there'll be old carpets in the bazaars. And hanging brass lamps, and cushions in colors."

They ate a dinner of instant soup and dried fruit by the light of a stub of candle Terry found in a drawer. He reached for a raisin, his slender arm gleaming in the flickering light. Unexpectedly in this unfamiliar place, Catherine was reminded of the first time she'd seen him. Long, golden hair shone through the smoke and colored lights, a rapt face was revealed in flashes, long arms moved gracefully. From the little club's stage she watched him. Slamming was what was cool back then, but this tall, slender man smoothly wove as if the bass line she laid down was turning itself into his body. She played for him. Music and crowd blended into a blurred spiral and he its helix.

Terry was gazing at the frosted window as if he could see into the Egyptian night. "A pharaoh's palace once stood on this very spot."

"Really?" Catherine asked, surprised.

"Maybe, you never know. Just think, King Tut's tomb, Luxor Temple, they're out there waiting for us."

Catherine tucked a foot under her. "And your mural will join the landmarks on the Nile."

"While it lasts. Didn't those old side streets we passed in the city make you feel temporary?"

Yawning, she strolled onto the balcony. Traffic roared and horns beeped not far away, but their street was quiet. The night breeze trailed an elusive fragrance. Honeysuckle? Did honeysuckle grow here?

In the streetlights the palm trees cast feathers of shadow over the asphalt with bright pools between them. When she focused on those, all else receded into darkness. But when she looked into the dark, the palm trunks sprang out, and the humps of parked cars, but the puddles of light became glaring nothingness.

It was like Terry's paintings, always changing. When he let his visions tumble out onto a canvas or wall he was a winged adventurer. He trusted where it would take him so much he'd never finished college. Her dreams had never been that strong. Only her determination. When time came to write her master's thesis on top of teaching a section of comp, she'd given up band practice and the late night gigs. Terry's vision was the one worth fighting for, she'd always felt.

But it was that vision, its chameleon aliveness, that had prevented the recognition he deserved. You couldn't pigeon-hole his style, critics couldn't give it validating labels and clients couldn't comfortably predict it. He'd made the side of a building in downtown Oakland a window on time, showing the streets beyond not as they were, but as they'd been a century before. That mural, a community project, was so loved that even the neighborhood graffiti sprayers left it alone.

But across the bay in San Francisco he painted a wall at Fisherman's Wharf with soaring shapes dissolving into haze. That was the one that attracted a national magazine article, leading to Lyndore's invitation to submit a design for their ultramodern hotel to be built on the Nile. This commission could, finally, be the beginning for him.

"Cat? What's that wonderful smell?" Terry joined her on the balcony. "Even with the streetlights, look how many stars."

Between the top of the balcony and the building opposite, Catherine saw them thick as spilt sugar. Terry put his arm around her and she leaned against him.

"Come out from under the desert sky, my lovely Cleopatra," he whispered. "In your palace I have prepared a silken couch." He nuzzled her cheek. "I've never made love in Egypt before."

She smiled into the dark. "Neither have I."

In the cool bed he moved warm against her, his skin smooth over the lean angles of his chest. Drowsiness making them lazy, they kissed and stroked in slow caresses. His hands grazed her breasts and on down. Though he loved her slenderness she knew her breasts were smaller than he wished.

But in this strange place at the end of a bewildering day it was enough to lie in his familiar arms. His presence in her felt sweet and comforting, and her womb responded with a faint, sleepy ripple. She moved with him fondly, luxuriously, and cuddled him when he softly cried out.

Afterward, she lay spoonwise with him, drifting in nebulous realms between Egypt where she needed sleep and California where it was early afternoon. Anxieties tickled her exhaustion. The work permit she couldn't get. The dreams she was supposed to pursue, the ones she'd pushed aside for her steady paycheck that had allowed Terry to follow his dreams.

Music was fun, but it had never been an obsession. She liked reading, but had no particular urge to write. What if beneath the practical humdrum of her life she found nothing?

Then, there was the Lyndore contract. It included an option on a second commission. That sounded good, but for two years Lyndore's corporate office owned Terry's imagination. They could dictate what he painted, and how. That had given him pause. Lyndore's insistence on that point had almost made him decline the contract.

Terry didn't care much about money or fame. He just wanted walls big enough to hold his visions. Catherine suspected the final push to sign the contract was the sofa fight.

It had begun innocently. Their sofa was saggy. Though they couldn't really afford a new one, they planned to go on a weekend sofa hunt together. She knew Terry remembered that because he joked about getting a jeep and pith helmets for the occasion. The Thursday before the hunt, Catherine came home from work to find a brand new sofa in the living room.

It wasn't that she disliked the one he'd chosen. But in that first shocked moment she reacted, "How can you spend all my savings without even asking my opinion?"

Without a word Terry got up and left the apartment.

My savings. Even now, the word made her wince. Terry worked hard. When he had a commission he hurled himself into it like a tornado. But here they were, thirty-two years old apiece and still not able to afford a house, or kids. Neither of them ever mentioned that, but Catherine knew Terry wrestled with it.

She sighed and turned over. If playing Mr. Breadwinner and Mrs. Housewife for a year or two was what it took to restore balance, she would. If it meant she had to face her own demons, even if it turned out that in sacrificing her dreams for Terry's she'd sacrificed nothing much, better to face that truth.

Only, in this unfamiliar darkness, the possibility of that inner emptiness terrified her. She pressed close to Terry, but he was sound asleep.

our

xhaling exhaust, the taxi meandered to a stop between two brick walls. Not ageless mud brick. Red bricks carelessly laid with dried mortar oozing like peanut butter between crackers. "*Hinna*." The driver pointed down a sloping alley. At its end was a blind wall.

This driver was as taciturn as yesterday's had been friendly. They'd passed derelict pieces of boat, an old man repairing a fishing net, but this didn't look like a commercial landing. Terry asked him to wait. "*Eshreen ginehat*," he answered. *Twenty pounds*. Far too much, but Terry paid him. The cab scratched off in a sputter of grit and gas fumes.

As its noise faded Catherine heard a radio playing brassy quarter tones. From a window above a child with snarled curls was watching them, but when he saw her looking he hid. "The river must be down there," she supposed.

They walked slowly, alert. Not that it would help if they'd been delivered into a nest of thieves or worse. Where the alley bent a large dog lay. It bared its teeth. They gave it a wide berth.

Abruptly the narrow way opened on a world transformed to silver. The Nile glistened huge and bright, breeze patterning its glitter. Feluccas bobbed along the bank, long, slender masts towering above cockleshell hulls. A man in a blue and white striped galabieh heaved burlap sacks into one. Beyond were several men involved in some discussion. Children who in America would be in school on a Wednesday morning were diligently tying ropes and trotting under smaller loads. One boy shouted at another, who answered with a rude gesture. Both burst into uproarious laughter.

They passed a tethered donkey munching a pile of clover. The green shoots smelled sweet in the sun, but the donkey's hips stuck out painfully beneath its dirty white coat. Flies pestered its eyes. The children did not look starved, but their galabiehs were tattered. One boy had a bluish white blind eye.

Everybody paused to watch them approach. The sudden silence and guarded faces were unnerving. Terry spoke his best Arabic greeting. For a moment no one moved. Then one of the men answered, and Catherine was relieved at the dignified courtesy of his tone. A halting discussion followed. "The landing we want is miles back in the direction we came from," Terry told her, disgusted with himself. "He says everybody knows where it is. The driver brought us here to get a bigger fare out of us."

"Or to punish us for being Westerners," Catherine murmured. "So, we've been had." She might have been amused if there'd been any cleverness to the scam.

"Well, maybe one of these guys might like to make a few pounds." Terry spoke to the man, who answered with an inviting gesture at the line of boats.

The felucca he led them to had planks for seats. Bits of straw and old burlap littered the bottom, but it looked river-worthy. Catherine nodded. "Better than a tourist boat."

Terry grinned agreement and tried out his bargaining. In the end both he and the boatman seemed satisfied. They perched on the planks, a boy came running, and the sail snapped out in a taut curve. Catherine propped her elbow on the rim. She loved sailboats, their gliding motion, their harmony with water and wind. The Nile flowed languidly against the prow, opaque green and softly splashing. The little landing floated away.

A haze obscured the far bank. Early morning mists twirled around the sail. The boatman and his son hunkered together in the stern, talking in throaty tones. Terry squinted at a misty apparition ahead. "That must be Gezira Island." Catherine made out tall, narrow houses connected by garden walls.

"Zamalek will be on this end." Terry craned to see through the fog. "Where's the Lyndore?"

Horns hooted overhead. A bridge emerged from the mists right above them, traffic speeding over it. Then they were in the shadows underneath, sailing past massive, damp stanchions.

"There!" He pointed.

A white rhomboid slanted like some futuristic pyramid, or the sail of a gigantic ship about to traverse the Sahara. In the clearing mists the Hotel Lyndore gave an illusion of completeness. Only its stark whiteness was unfinished, waiting to take life from the mural. Terry studied it, elbows sharp on his thighs.

The sun brightened as he gazed. Catherine felt its warmth on her skin. Whatever he was thinking, he wasn't ready to say it yet.

Abruptly he spoke in Arabic. The boatman and his son hauled the ropes, steering across the current. Catherine held on lightly, skimming on a windblown feather. *Look at me,* she thought, *sailing the Nile under the rays of Ra.* The golden downpourings trembled into silver and the water mirrored them skyward in a glorious dizziness. The hull's splash echoed with vanished temple harps, and in the water's slap, dancers' hands clapped.

"*Hunak,*" Terry directed quietly. Huge sail shifting overhead, the felucca angled and drifted on the current. Observing from this new vantage, he frowned.

With a patience it had taken years to learn, Catherine waited silently. She gazed back at the east bank where Cairo's minaret needles rose among blocky oblongs, the nearer ones clear, the distant ones increasingly softened by veils of hanging dust. The ceaseless honking, someone's song, a grind of machinery and bray of a donkey floated over the water, middle ages and future colliding and merging. Parched and crumbling as Cairo looked, it seethed with energy.

Opposite the city's haphazard vitality the Hotel Lyndore looked pristine, abstract, inhuman. When it opened, tourists would pay dearly for the privilege of isolation from the place they'd come to see. Lyndore CEOs would make deals. Cousins of Egyptian officials would land vending contracts. But to the boatman and his son the Hotel Lyndore would only be a symbol, conspicuous against sky and river, of all they could never have.

Terry's frown made it all too clear he was seeing that too. He spoke haltingly and the current carried the felucca toward a busy landing on the Cairo side. He turned to Catherine. "I need to rethink the whole thing."

Catherine tensed. "Whether to do the mural?"

"No." Terry looked back over the water at the blank rhomboids. "The design. I planned it on paper. In my head. Somebody in Denver accepted it. Maybe that person, or committee, was never even here."

"It's a beautiful design."

"It's the face of the whole city I'm monkeying with. That design's not in synch with this place. Can't you feel an energy totally different?"

She didn't want to admit how right he was. "It's contracted for."

"The paperwork and scaffolding will take a week to finish, maybe two. That gives me time to come up with a better design."

"Pete and the Powers That Be in Denver hired you for the one you submitted.

"I'll convince them. What I need is to get out among people, hear their stories, try to understand what Cairenes feel about Cairo. When they look across the Nile, what do they want to see?"

Catherine gazed doubtfully at the Cairo skyline. Maybe Egypt cared whether Terry listened to it, maybe not, but what he imagined as some kind of *open sesame* might be self destruction. What if Lyndore decided he lacked the steadiness to carry through? She didn't think Terry meant to sabotage himself, even subconsciously. He wasn't afraid of success, only of achieving less than he was capable of.

Foolish impulse or brilliant one, he'd go for it. He had to. That much she understood.

Egypt, she silently entreated. *You're crumbling away, pushing up like an anthill, seething with conflicting layers of hope and misery, history and wrangling civilizations, oppression and dreams. Ramshackle Cairo, you're messy, ugly, indestructible, beautiful, unfathomable. Please, open a few of your secrets to Terry.*

The honking, the clatter of construction, or maybe demolition, the smells of car exhaust, rotten vegetables, and the indefinable scent of sun-warmed Sahara dust, swallowed them as the felucca neared the shore.

You must have so many secrets, Catherine's thought added unbidden. *Please, open just one of them to me.*

 ive

ater cascaded down her breasts. Nile water—by way of treatment plant, city pipes and faucet. Catherine squeezed the washcloth, closing her eyes to the window-less white walls, white porcelain and white tiles.

In their bathroom in California, Terry had painted a garden pavilion with clusters of wisteria and trellises where birds roosted among fantastical flowers. Maybe he'd find time to relieve this bathroom's sterility.

But not now. Terry's doubts about the design were knotting him up, and the "few formalities" of his first work day had dragged out to a week of standing in lines in a cavernous govern-mental maw called the Mugamma, which he described as the circle of hell devoted to bureaucratic self-perpetuation, where the damned brought sack lunches and camped on the floors waiting for officials who might or might not show up. He finally got what he needed, a small stamp glued in each of their passports. Then the scaffolding materials arrived, but they weren't what he'd ordered. He hadn't even managed to shake loose half a day for the pyramids.

After dinner he spent hours in the studio they'd made of the spare bedroom, and every night he went to bed exhausted but dissatisfied. He spent most of his early mornings at a sidewalk café with his watercolor pad, trying out his ideas the Cairenes who frequented it. At least he enjoyed himself there and was making friends.

He'd found one ally at Lyndore. Judy Bakhir headed public relations. She'd lived in Egypt for much of her life and agreed with Terry that the mural should harmonize with the city. Satisfying the corporate office in Denver was Pete Burge's sole objective, Judy had clued him in, but that could be good. Why or how, she was being intriguingly mysterious about. "Just come up with a design that feels right, and we'll see," was all she'd say.

Catherine hoped that was more than bluff. If the Lyndore staff were anything like their wives, everything was corporate politics. Marilee Burge seemed to feel that membership in the bridge club and country club provided as full a life as anyone could want. Maybe so, if staying on top of gossip and one-upping rivals was your career. If you were with Lyndore for the long haul. Marilee and the other wives who'd taken Catherine to lunch understood that she wasn't, and had kept to topics they thought of general interest, shopping in Cairo and other cities, the impossibility of Egyptian TV which was all reruns or else in a "foreign" language, the superiority of all things American.

They were nice to her. They drew her out about restaurants in Berkeley, and shoe styles in the San Francisco Nordstrom. They also advised her about servants. They all had servants. Lazy, ignorant servants they suspected of dishonesty. They insisted Catherine needed one. A maid should be enough for their apartment, unless Terry wanted a driver, Cairo driving being what it was, and servants after all being so cheap here.

Catherine's response that she had plenty of time to do her own housework changed their tactics. At least one servant was essential to Terry's social standing, which reflected on Lyndore's. Also, the Egyptian government expected foreign companies to create jobs. That people needed work and she and Terry could afford to supply it was an argument Catherine couldn't counter. She resigned herself to giving up her privacy.

She interviewed the two women Marilee recommended. The first was motherly and overbearing. The second was nineteen. Samira Ahmed told Catherine in halting English she had been a maid in a Canadian household until her employers left Egypt. She had a three year old girl and a baby. They lived with her husband's parents in a four room apartment. Short and plump, Samira had a round face, emphasized by a headscarf that made her neat features seem smaller than they were. Her eyebrows were plucked to thin, anxious lines. As she talked her hands gripped each other so hard that pale marks showed on her light brown skin. She watched Catherine, close to desperation. "When can you start?" Catherine asked.

"Today, Madam." Samira leaned forward, still not certain she was really hired.

"Catherine. Or Cat. What about tomorrow?"

Lights shone in Samira's eyes as she smiled.

Catherine's toes were wrinkling. Quit sitting like a knot on a pickle, she reprimanded herself. Do something useful. But what? She'd unpacked all the boxes they'd shipped. Samira did the cleaning and shopped for food. Nothing needed doing.

She could always explore more. Though she'd made a pact with Terry to wait to see the pyramids together, she'd been investigating the medieval mosques, the Khan el-Khalili, the Citadel. She found mazes of unpaved alleys not in her guide book. Redolent of the scents of unfamiliar cooking, tobacco, dust and close-packed humanity, they twisted in bewildering chiaroscuros of sun-washed plaster and shadowed doorways. People stared at a foreign woman venturing off the beaten tourist track, and she felt a vague, but exhilarating apprehension. Anything might happen here.

She dried off and dressed in a mid-calf skirt and blouse of light fabric but with elbow length sleeves. Too much bare skin was considered immodest. When the summer heat came, light, loose coverage was said to be the best protection. The ancient Egyptians hadn't thought so, but a lifetime in the sun had accustomed their skin to it.

Though the pyramids were out of bounds, she'd made no promise not to explore the rest of ancient Egypt. The Cairo museum had the best ancient Egyptian collection in the world. Still, she'd hoped to share it with Terry.

Catherine brushed her hair, quickly did her eyes, and frowned at her peeling nose in the mirror. Rubbing it, she went out to the living room. She eyed the all-too-predictable suspense book on the coffee table. Where to find books in English besides the few best sellers in the hotel gift shops? The Lyndore wives hadn't known. Maybe she should investigate that today.

Samira padded in with a dust rag, flip-flops smacking the soles of her feet. She saw Catherine and hesitated. "Come on in," Catherine told her. "I'm about to bounce off the walls."

Her maid gave her a puzzled look, but began wiping the pale dust that kept collecting on every surface. Her flip-flops had huge, day-glo plastic flowers on top. Perversely, Catherine imagined wearing them to a Lyndore wives' gathering. "I like your shoes. Where can I find some?"

"*My* shoes?" Samira asked in surprise. "The Mouski."

The Khan el-Khalili was the rambling old marketplace where tourists bought souvenirs from stalls that glistened with brass, silver and colored lights, but nearby was the less decorative Mouski, like a vast flea market. "Maybe I'll go look for some," she mused.

"Why? Nothing good in the Mouski, not good for you, Madam Cataron."

Nothing for anyone who could afford better, Catherine wondered, or was Samira warning her it wasn't safe for her to go there alone?

Samira blotted the perspiration from her forehead with her sleeve and bent to dust the inlaid octagonal tables Catherine had placed among the dull chairs. No wonder she was sweating, working in her long sleeves with her head and neck swathed in rayon, like a medieval woman in a wimple. "Do you wear a scarf at home?"

Samira silently repeated the words, lips moving, until she came to one she did not recognize. "Skarif?"

Catherine gestured to her own head.

"At home? No, Madam Cataron."

"Please, just Catherine."

Samira looked unhappy, maybe thinking it was a criticism of her pronunciation.

"Or Cat."

Samira giggled and would not repeat it.

"Would you be cooler working without it? That would be fine with me."

Samira's eyes widened. "Mr. Terry."

Terry, a strange man, might come home and lust after her naked hair. "Oh," Catherine said, at a loss for any other answer. At least, any that would make sense in both their worlds. "And you still won't let me get the groceries?"

"No," the young woman answered firmly. "What will the other ladies say? They must respect you."

Catherine sighed, weary of not knowing the major social rules from the minor ones. From what she could tell, Samira had an equal horror of breaking either.

Samira decided to take the ignorant foreigner in hand. "You go buy the dress, and the things for Mr. Terry. Go with a Lyndore lady."

ix

inus a Lyndore Lady, Catherine stepped from the taxi. Hot dust whirled around her. Horns blared and buses bumbled, crammed with people, and more people clung to the outsides thick as pollen weighing down bees. One slowed and some jumped to the pavement. Passengers pushed out past others pushing in. Some gave up but some boys and men made flying leaps for any hold they could grab. Off the bus chugged carrying its human burden. The likeliness of fingers slipping, bones crunching under wheels, made Catherine shudder. Why didn't the government run more buses?

"*Mubarak's administration is pretty good,*" Terry had imitated Pete Burge's booming bass. "*They keep the place safe for tourists and commerce.* Pete blamed the faulty scaffolding materials on the Muslim Brotherhood.

The pandemonium of Tahrir Square ended at a tall wrought iron fence. Within was a garden. Running along the rambling pink front of the Egyptian Museum, the haven of walks and greenery was studded with statuary. A central walk led past a fountain to a massive entrance surmounted by an arch and two sculpted queens. To Catherine's eye, their Art Nouveau poses and vaguely Grecian drapery clashed with the dignity of the genuinely ancient Egyptian sculpture in the garden, yet they and the doorway looked oddly familiar. The notion itched her that she'd been here before.

Not in this life, she thought with a wry smile. She was not a believer in reincarnation, but it was not the first time she'd been assailed by stray feelings that she belonged here somehow. Then another memory came, and she laughed. Grey celluloid moonlight illuminated Zita Johann pounding on this door, hypnotized by the evil love spell of Boris Karloff. *The Mummy!* In her teens she'd loved old horror movies, and that one had been a favorite. For a whole summer she'd tried like crazy to imitate the elegant S curve of Zita's back. She grinned up at the Art Nouveau queens and got in line.

Ticket in hand, she passed the long fountain planted with stiff arches of papyrus. A street cat perched on the rim, blinking in slit-eyed awareness of being a goddess. The French speaking couple who paused to snap Her Worship's picture realized it, too. Catherine entered the familiar door.

The galleries were pleasantly cool. Voices and footsteps echoed as if in a deep well, and enigmatic carved faces invited on all sides. Catherine pulled her guide book from her shoulder bag. Tutankhamen, upper floor. She climbed the stairs two at a time.

Tour groups crowded the Tut exhibit, guides lecturing in several languages. Catherine tried to be wherever they weren't. She saw golden thrones, gilt shrines covered with magic spells, and creamy translucent alabaster cups. Looking terribly young and fragile, Tutankhamen and his queen hunted ducks in a Nile marsh. They strolled in a palace garden, she offered him flowers or poured him a drink. The ostrich feather fans stirred air scented with myrrh, and courtiers' sandals whispered among murmurings in a language now dead. What were their thoughts, these vanished people? Did this young couple really believe themselves gods? Or were they two children alone, terrified of conspirators, afraid maybe even of their own army?

And the craftsmen who carved the jewels and ebony, what thoughts ran through their minds as they worked? Ceremonial daggers gleamed, cryptic symbols writhed with snakes, goddesses stretched protective arms, all vivid, yet all achingly remote. In a case by itself was the young king's exquisite golden burial mask. He faced death with enigmatic composure. His obsidian eyes gazed back at her, black as holes into eternity.

Unsatisfied, Catherine wandered back to the first floor. To touch, yet not touch, that was all her stay in Egypt was so far. Even Terry seemed to have moved just out of reach, amusing her with tidbits from his days, but locked into his obsessive quest for his design and spending his free time in an old fashioned coffee-house where women weren't welcome.

It was almost closing time. The tour groups ebbed. Catherine found herself in the cavernous central hall. Overlooked by a balustrade, it housed enormous statuary. She had it to herself except for a guard dozing on a bench. Her steps reverberated among looming pharaohs of black basalt who watched her without moving their eyes.

She came to a pyramid-shaped black stone. What could it be? Outstretched wings were carved into the granite, and two long-tailed Egyptian eyes. The feeling of being watched grew. Not by those eyes. Stronger than that. Catherine glanced at the guard, but a truck could have pulled in and hauled out the heaviest statue in the place without disturbing his soft snoring.

Creepy.

All right, Cat, she told herself. All the mummies are locked snug in their cases. Nobody sees you, nobody cares. Maybe that's exactly what you don't like about Egypt?

She tried to shrug the feeling off. The black granite thing had a label in five languages. According to it, this was a pyramid. A capstone from one, anyway. The very tip-top of one. The eyes were there to guard the burial of some king forever.

Only, it hadn't. Here it was, torn away from its place and purpose, gawked at by people like her who didn't begin to understand it. Did she understand anything at all? Was anything understandable, or was it only the daily trivia of job, habit, all the circumstances we mistake for ourselves, that mask the vertigo of meaningless isolation? Was she anything at all?

Catherine backed away from the stone. From those eyes that saw too much, and saw nothing. Watching. She glanced up at the balustrade. It was empty, of course. "I'm not here," she murmured into the silence. "I've lost myself, and for my next trick, I'll lose my mind." Starting with talking to myself, she thought. She lowered her glance.

And almost missed the man shadowed between two stone sarcophagi, staring at her.

Or, he had been. Soon as she looked, he turned away to study the carved symbols on the stone. Who did he think he was, snooping on her private panic attack? But maybe her embarrassment made her defensive. Maybe he'd heard her, thought she was sick or in trouble, and only wanted to make sure she was all right.

Like hell he did. She wasn't so off kilter she'd misread that intrusive stare. For a split instant it had pierced hot as some coal, a darkness igniting molten crimson. Seductive. Presumptuous. Predatory.

As if he felt her indignation, he turned and gave her a small, mocking smile.

Catherine turned away, ready to kick in her own teeth for falling for that trick. Museums were among the worst pickup joints in the world. He was pale. A newly arrived tourist. A well dressed one, European by the cut of his suit. Traveling alone and so on the make.

She put the large glass case in the center of the gallery between them. It wasn't his interest that irked her, it was its sheer arrogance. That mocking smile, as if he imagined all he had to do was look and women would come running.

She gazed up at a limestone pharaoh with what looked like an empty flower pot on his head. Only her own footsteps sounded in the cavernous silence. His footsteps hadn't left the gallery. That made her uneasy. He still watched her, she was certain of it. She wanted to leave, but she'd be damned if she'd give the asshole the satisfaction of running her out. She strolled only gradually toward the colossus at the end of the gallery. On either side, stairs led to daylight and a glimpse of a farther gallery.

The colossus was massive, a man and woman throned, in pale buff limestone. You could tell they were a couple. The label said Amenhotep III and his Great Royal Wife Tiye. As Catherine stepped up to the bottom stair she was scarcely on eye level with the queen's big toe. Tiye's arm was wrapped affectionately around her husband's back. Both smiled with a tranquility so benign that she couldn't help wondering what they'd really been up to.

"Monstrously wholesome, aren't they?" remarked an English voice.

Catherine's neck prickled. She wheeled.

He stood near enough to touch her, gazing up at the colossus. How had he got so close? She'd heard not one footfall. "Crafty old hypocrites," he continued. "Some say Amenhotep was dissolute and diseased, and Tiye an iron willed tyrant."

She considered not answering, but it was very close to what she'd been thinking. "They do look like two cats who've each swallowed half a canary," she allowed.

That amused him. "Quite." His eyes posed a question his voice did not reflect. "You are an American on holiday."

"My husband and I are from California."

Not an eyelid twitched. "What brings the two of you here?"

"Terry's a muralist. He has a commission here."

"Not the Hotel Lyndore?"

That knocked her off balance. "How did you know?"

"I take an interest. I deal in art. The Lyndore is the only important mural commission in Cairo of which I'm aware." Formally he reached for her hand. "Geoffrey Harrow."

"Catherine Lanier," she answered reluctantly. His touch was warm and dry. His eyelashes flicked as his eyes lowered and he turning her hand slightly, wrist up.

Why? But the motion was so slight that maybe she was mistaken. He met her eyes.

She supposed he'd make a wonderful find for some woman if he could live up to the intensity of his eyes.

He released her hand and glanced at his watch. "It's nearly half past four. The museum closes soon," he remarked. "I'd like to hear about your husband's work. Can I interest you in tea at the Nile Hilton?"

Catherine gave him a polite, final, smile. "Thank you, but I need to go."

"The Hilton is right in the Midan et-Tahrir. It's an easy walk." She would not have to get into a stranger's car, he meant.

"I really don't have time."

"No time?" He glanced ironically up at the ancient statuary. *'Time is a river which sweeps me along, but I am the river; it is a tiger which mangles me, but I am the tiger; it is a fire which consumes me, but I am the fire.'"*

"Borges."

He stepped back. "You know Borges, do you? And do you enjoy his games?"

"His mirrors, labyrinths, tricks of seeming and reality. Deceptions."

"What isn't a deception?"

Catherine regarded his pale face, his arched eyebrows, his eyes, their mockery now playful. Was that what she'd lost? The ability simply to relax and play?

"If you hope to pump me about what the mural will be like, it won't work. Terry and I are both sworn to secrecy."

"No matter. I'm curious about his other work."

She'd made it clear she was no pickup, and he'd accepted that. If all he wanted now was to be a step ahead of the rest of Cairo's art scene, no harm. If he could connect them to that scene, this chance meeting might be her best stroke of luck so far. The Lyndore crowd was hopelessly uninterested in anything of the kind. Despite the prickly beginning, this man's interests and wit made him seem a more promising friend for Terry and her than any other they'd met so far.

"All right," she told him. "You win, there's time. Even enough time for tea."

even

et's go then, shall we?" He sounded as if now that she'd agreed, he no longer wanted it. They walked through the galleries in silence.

To break it, she asked, "Do you deal in paintings?"

"Antiques."

"European or Islamic?"

"Both."

"And ancient Egyptian?"

"That would be illegal."

Pausing in the foyer, he took a pair of sunglasses from his pocket and put them on. In profile his nose made a perfectly straight line, strong and graceful. As he took stock of the garden and people in it, the sun reflected from the impassive black lenses. Probably he thought they were cool, but they made him look like a gangster. Then, despite the heat, from his other pocket he drew kidskin gloves. Catherine looked away to avoid staring at the affectation. She most definitely disliked Geoffrey Harrow after all.

She let him step into garden ahead of her. Daylight burnished his hair mahogany. The Nile breeze stirred fine, soft ends that wanted to curl slightly. All right, he was handsome. No doubt he went through life trading on it.

They left the green garden for the dusty oven of braying traffic. Beyond the forging stream of metal stood a sidewalk of store fronts and a broad curve that must be the Hilton. A traffic light changed color, but no one paid attention. "So near, yet so far," she said.

"It's a game of dare," Geoffrey answered. "Stare them down." He stepped out and an oncoming car screeched its brakes. Catherine tried to imitate his brazen calm. Maybe that was why the shades. That unreadable black stare had a daunting effect. She stayed close, giving a driver who bore down on them her evilest eye. Horn blaring, cursing out the window, the man jerked to a halt, but a bus beyond sped up. Geoffrey pushed her out of its path, shielding her with his body. They plunged to the curb laughing. "Let's do it again," she joked, her heart beating light as rain.

"Courting death is your notion of a good time, is it?"

"You wouldn't talk if you could see the smile on your face."

He was still holding her arm. He let go. "*Touché.*"

"Thank you for coming between me and that bus," she said seriously.

He didn't answer. She wondered if the moment of closeness startled him as much as it did her. He walked on. Not startled. Troubled. But why? The shop fronts threw shade over most of the pavement. Walking along the sunny part, she asked, "Have you lived in Cairo long?"

"Twenty-two years." He kept to the shade.

"Then you must know the good book stores."

"I must." His voice bit, astringent as the limestone taste of the dust. But he suggested, "Try the Anglo-American Bookstore."

The Nile Hilton's courtyard made a sheltering oasis from the scramble of the street. Shiny blond stone and neatly arranged trees and flowers gleamed dustless, and the plate glass fronts of the hotel shops were topped by huge hieroglyphs in pastel tiles. Catherine smiled. "Out of the frying pan into the mall?"

"Not the effect your husband will aim for?" Geoffrey asked casually, slyly.

"They're what Terry has a horror of perpetrating." Even his old design wasn't bland kitsch, of course, but he was afraid of a more sophisticated version of the same thing. "Prettified Western stereotypes of Egypt, reinforcements of American and European complacency."

"The Ministry of Tourism can hardly sell crowding, poverty and worry that speaking out too strongly will land you in prison."

"No, but do they have to sanitize Egyptianness, to remake it into a toy in our own image?"

With old fashioned courtesy Geoffrey pushed open the revolving door for her. "Whether Disney or da Vinci, whatever a Westerner paints will be a Western perspective."

"He can try to reach out. Not everywhere is America."

Muzak burbled through the lobby. Men and women in business suits perched on sofas chattering in the accents of Brooklyn, London, Tokyo. Geoffrey gave her a small, ironic smile. "Isn't it?"

He led the way to the coffee shop. A waiter started to seat them by the window, but Geoffrey indicated a booth secluded in a corner. An exotic brass lamp hung over it. On the table beneath stood a paper Thanksgiving turkey.

Geoffrey had the grace not to remark on it. Finessing off his kid gloves finger by finger he continued, "I've seen the Lyndore, of course. That striking sweep of one surface above the other."

She smiled. "That won't work. My lips are sealed." But she described Terry's Oakland mural, the one at Fisherman's Wharf, the ones on a Montana library and a New Orleans coffee shop. From Geoffrey's responses, he knew far more than antiques.

"You must spend time in Europe," she said. "Or New York."

"I subscribe to art journals. I have a lot of time on my hands."

"I thought time was an illusion." But as she pulled the tea bag from her pot she admitted, "I've never had enough time to go where I I've wanted, or do what I'd like."

As if reminded, Geoffrey took his teabag out, too. "What keeps you so busy?"

"I directed a university tutoring program. It was just a shoe-string operation, but we made a difference."

"You gave it up unwillingly."

It was not a question. She thought she'd hidden her reluctance better than that. She'd have to be more careful around Terry. But with a stranger, it was a relief to say it out. "Freedom isn't as simple as I thought. I was good at my work. Without it, I can't think what to do with myself."

Geoffrey's glance hinted that he could think of things to do with her. But then he turned his attention to his tea.

So, he knew the boundary between flirtation and seduction, and he was playing well within it. Good. It meant she could play the game with him. Why not, when she'd never see him again?

In the lamplight his eyes were so dark she couldn't tell iris from pupil, but his features weren't so perfect as she'd thought. Not quite symmetrical. His right eyebrow was determined, even ruthless, but the left began with a subtle lift, giving that side a thoughtful, even a sad, expression. His nose that was so classic in profile had odd little planes and angles from the front. His nostrils were too narrow. A funny nose, in a civilized way. His upper lip curved in a clearly defined bow, at odds with the austerity of the lower lip. From the lines around his eyes, he was older than she'd thought. Not late thirties, middle forties.

"Uprooting, beginning a new life, is never easy," he said. She heard the understatement in his voice. He must have experienced the mix of loss, restlessness and resentment she was feeling. He's lonely too, she thought.

"Why did you uproot?" she asked. "Business?"

"I wanted a change." He lifted his cup to his lips, but frowned as if scorning the easy answer. "Europe and America have become too orderly, don't you think? Egypt is controlled by too few greedy people, but that isn't order. I find Cairo rather—invigorating."

"I wouldn't take you for a rebel."

"I'm not one, unless you count rooting for the underdog in action films. I probably spend too much time at the cinema."

"A movie addict? So am I."

He met her eyes. "I begin to feel you are dangerously perfect, Catherine."

"Except for being married."

"Does that matter?"

"Yes," she told him firmly. "It does."

"Well, that's something, I suppose," he replied.

Was it relief she heard? He put his cup down, still full. He hadn't bothered with his pastry, either. Probably the coffee shop's food wasn't up to his standards. Despite his gallantry maybe neither was she.

Though she was sorry the interlude was ending, she knew that had there been any real possibility of it continuing she wouldn't have indulged in this little imaginary seduction. In all, it had been a rare treat. Not many men would have understood the game's subtleties. She took her cue. "Time, again. How late is it?"

He showed her his watch.

"I should go."

He stood at once.

That hurt, but she hid it. "Is there a cab stand?"

"At the front door." But then he said, "Let me give you a lift."

She smiled. "I'd guess we don't live in the same part of town."

"And what part is that?"

She didn't want him to know. Instead, she let her smile linger.

"Very well," he returned with an amused hint of spite. "Then I won't tell you the name or address of my shop." He walked her to the front entrance. She saw the taxis at the curb. Beyond, the Nile gleamed in the sunset, a copper surface with veins of amethyst. Geoffrey put on his sunglasses and gloves.

He'd hurt her vanity, and she couldn't resist needling his. "Isn't it a little dark for the cool shades?"

"No." But he relented. "I have an allergy."

"To what?"

"Light."

She was too startled to answer. Anyway, she knew he wouldn't want sympathy. "Goodbye, Geoffrey," she told him. "I enjoyed it."

"Did you." It was neither a question nor a statement. He walked out the door.

She waited until she was sure he was gone. As she got into a taxi, she smiled to herself. If I ever do give in against my better judgment, she thought, let him be less complicated than Geoffrey Harrow!

ight

"Is that you, Cat?" Terry called out from the studio. She found him leaning back in his chair, long legs propped on his stack of unpacked boxes, his battered sketchbook in his lap. "The gang at Fareed's Coffeehouse praised my latest try. I've found a style they like as much as I do."

"Hey, great."

"I'm close, I feel it. So close." He held up his pad. Suggestions of shapes had stolen into the delicate wash of colors, a hint of Cairo skyline floating high, a suggestion of a face with Egyptian features, not a model or movie star face, a person's face, looking toward the Nile. And a cloud, or perhaps a bird breaking into flight. Hope. Catherine took it from him to admire. Terry watched her, rocking the chair back on two legs. He grinned.

"What now, show it to Pete?" She tried to hide her doubt. She'd had faith he'd find the design he was looking for, but would Lyndore really accept any change this late?

He sighed. "I'm not sure." He took back the pad as if she was the one trying to deny him.

For an instant it crossed her mind to wonder if Geoffrey Harrow knew people with the influence to get Lyndore to consider it. But even if he did, even if he agreed to, even if she wanted to owe him, since when did hotel CEOs give a horse apple what art critics thought? "What do you want for dinner?" she asked. "A stir fry?"

She'd taken over all the kitchen duties with the rest of the housekeeping, but old habits died hard, and Terry washed and sliced the vegetables as she cooked, chatting about the trials and tribulations in the saga of the scaffolding. When the stir fry was sizzling, she said, "I went to the museum. I hope it's ok that I didn't wait."

"It's only fair. At this rate the Lyndore will be as old as Karnak Temple before I can grab a day off." He picked a piece of zucchini off the cutting board and poked it into his mouth. "Oh, I almost forgot. Judy asks to meet you for lunch Thursday if you're free."

"'Course. Give me her number and I'll phone her. You'll want to see the museum."

"Definitely." He crunched a strip of raw onion between his teeth.

She slid the cut onion out from under his hand into the pan. "Don't, you'll have dragon breath."

He reached for a piece of cauliflower instead. "What was the best thing you saw?"

"Everything. Too much to tell. I met an Englishman who knows art."

"See? We'll find friends if we look.

Mischievously she added, "He tried to pick me up. He was good looking and had a wonderful accent."

"Yeah, you and English accents."

Glad he was not taking it seriously, she added, "Have you ever heard of anyone being allergic to light?"

"Albinos?"

"Nope."

"Eczema. Hey, isn't there a ripe lemon on our tree?"

She headed to the balcony for it. There was no reason to be put out. Of course Terry was right not to be jealous.

When she returned with the lemon, he began telling a joke he'd heard from one of the construction workers. It turned on an Arabic pun, and he could already follow well enough to think it was funny, but he fumbled trying to get it across to her in English.

Catherine sliced the lemon, trying to think what impression of the ancient Egyptian art she'd seen would interest him, but all that came to her mind was eyes. Tutankhamen's obsidian eyes. The slit eyes of the cat on the fountain rim. The winged granite eyes in the gallery. Geoffrey Harrow's eyes, a fathomless darkness, a fascination she had escaped.

The thought grazed her with unexpected regret.

Catherine pawed through her drawer for socks. She was curious to meet this Judy Bakhir. She and Terry had grown thick as thieves. Though nominally from Chicago, Judy was an archeologist's daughter and had grown up just as much in Egypt. She'd studied modern Islamic culture, married in Cairo and carved out a career as a liaison for American and European businesses. When Terry told Judy about the brainstorms at Fareed's café, she saw it from a fresh angle. "Me and the guys," he'd enthused to Catherine, "we're not slackers daydreaming when we should be at work. We're multicultural collaboration. We're what can happen when people bust through separatism and work together to accomplish things. Judy thinks Mr. Beet might see possibilities for Lyndore in that."

"Mr. Beet" was the site workers' name for Pete Burge. Terry delighted in their pronunciation and the construction workers were just as delighted when he told them what *beet* meant. All traces of gloom had disappeared from his moods. They swung between high and higher. He was so full of Judy says this, Judy says that, Catherine wondered if maybe Terry had a crush on her.

She wondered if she'd mind if Judy turned out to be cute. She and Terry had an open marriage. At least, they'd begun that way.

Commitment, they'd promised, did not mean limitation. They respected each other's freedom to feel and live.

But it had been years since either had acted on that freedom. Since then, idealistic social experimentation had been followed by a conservative backlash. AIDS had also become endemic. Or maybe it was just that they were no longer wild kids.

But if Terry was attracted to this Judy, there was no reason to feel guilty over fantasizing about Geoffrey Harrow.

Maybe it was the mystery she'd deliberately woven around the attractive, moody Englishman, and that even if she'd wanted to, she didn't know where to find him. Maybe it was some rebellious part of her reawakening now that she'd slipped free of the role of helper and authority figure to college students. Maybe it was her imagination reviving.

Could imagination be separated from passion? But was that what she needed, at loose ends and off kilter as she was?

No. The last thing she needed was to fall in love with a fantasy.

But when she stopped herself, the fantasy went underground into her dreams. Asleep, she felt the tender skin at the back of a male neck, damp with the sweat of arousal, the soft tendrils of slightly curling hair soft between her fingers. Not golden hair, dark. She dreamed of a stranger thrusting into her core, forceful, tender, perilous. She woke in the grey dawn with pleasure and alarms resounding through her body.

No, she told herself for the umpteenth time. No more of that.

Two hours to kill before lunch. Judy had suggested Groppi, an ice cream parlor near Tahrir Square, a meeting spot for foreign residents and Cairo intellectuals. Catherine picked up the letter she was writing to her sister and went out to the balcony.

Though the view wasn't much, the lemon tree had a faint, pleasant scent, and if she sat quietly, birds sometimes landed among its glossy leaves. She loved their chattering. Catherine picked up her pen. *Wherever trees grow,* she wrote, *song birds gather thicker and more melodious than at home.*

Gwen, raising two kids in Kentucky, envied her Egyptian interlude. The least Catherine felt she could do was offer her sister and her friends in California the pleasure of imagining the adventure they thought she was having. She sent them descriptions of the narrow, winding ways where men in pinstriped galabiehs and girls in flamboyantly hued dresses tended piles of oranges, fragrant melons, little bananas on the stalk and cages of pigeons for the pot.

If her life was falling apart, it was not Egypt's fault. Everything her writing celebrated was real. On dusty, shaded corners caleches loitered, hooded like baby buggies, the horse drowsing, the driver's sandaled feet propped on a pile of vivid green *bersim*, a sort of clover, for the horse's lunch.

Sometimes the man coughed alarmingly, or the horse's ribs showed, and she wrote that, too. She described how Egyptians walked arm-in-arm with their friends, showing their affection with a lack of embarrassment she envied. Even pairs of policemen sometimes patrolled hand-in-hand. She yearned for the companionship they shared.

At first, she'd thought she'd only missed the old closeness with Terry since the Lyndore whirlwind had caught him up, but how long had it really been?

Overheard conversations haunt me, she wrote. *Talk is more poignant when only the tones of voices can be understood. Some of the humor comes through. Egyptian humor delights in the absurd.* Catherine admired the strength they drew from mocking the ridiculous, to withstand difficult lives. Their outbursts of laughter were quick, and if their anger flared easily, forgiveness was often close behind.

But it all excluded her. Though tutoring second language students had taught her the lack of words could be deeply isolating, how different it was to experience it herself. She felt she lived on a surface as transparent but impermeable as glass. It was like pressing her nose against a window pane she could see through, but never get past.

Wandering by twilight in the old quarter of the city, I heard the call to prayer. How to describe that? *The rise and fall of the chanting interwove from all directions as the muezzin of each mosque timed himself individually to the nightfall, each minaret a needle piercing the dusk, sewing its thread of summons across the sky.* How to convey those changeful patterns of harmony and dissonance? Invisible layers of depth and distance thickened the near voices like ropes flung from the rusty public address systems, the far ones laced the air, tenuous as cobwebs. She'd paused, listening as an abrupt, sharp yearning rose in her.

For what? She had no idea, except that for a clear moment she'd known that Egypt and she had, somehow, intimately to do with each other. Then, as swiftly, the certainty vanished.

She put down the pen. Nonsense. If she had unsatisfied needs, she'd better find out why. At least, she lectured herself, stop moping and do something constructive.

She shut her writing pad and went inside.

 ine

 alconies and turn of the century flourishes overlooked busy Talaat Harb Square where many streets intersected. On a corner like a pie slice Groppi stood alone, its door and plate glass sheltered by a deep porch and decorated with a mosaic of creamy pink and deep carmine roses on midnight blue. Through the window Catherine saw cases of pastries, veined marble, high ceilings and twirling Singapore fans.

She entered to a sweet fragrance. Cakes and candies bright as stained glass nestled in big, old glass-fronted wooden cases. She'd read of the confection shops so stylish a century ago, and San Francisco was beginning to sprout painstaking Art Noveau replications. Those served organic food and boutique coffee. Groppi's cakes were white flour, their icings glittering with refined sugar. Its slight dilapidation possessed the grandeur of the real thing.

In a second room patrons lunched on ice cream and sipped coffee. A low hum of conversation mingled several languages. A woman waved. Catherine smiled and headed toward her.

Judy was older than Catherine had imagined. Her short brown hair was plainly cut and her wire rim glasses were thick. She stuck out a hand. "Cat Russio? I'm Judy Bakhir. Welcome to Egypt! How are you settling in?"

"Slowly but surely, I hope." Catherine sat across from her. Judy's broad shape gave a comfortable impression. Her nondescript khaki suit was dowdy, but did a good job disguising the ever-present Sahara dust. So. Terry had not a crush but a mother figure. "It's Cat Lanier," she added.

"You kept your own name?" Judy put a menu in front of her. "I would've too, but mine was Deutelbaum." Her friendly grin invited a laugh. "How's Terry? He seemed a little green around the gills yesterday."

"Fine, he says. I don't think he wants to admit when Egyptian food doesn't agree with him."

"Mummy tummy, eh?" Judy clucked her tongue sympathetically. "I don't like to tattle, but Terry trades lunches with the construction workers. Not all of Cairo has proper water treatment. Not that Egyptian food is dirty, you understand. The species of microbes are different, that's all. When I go home, American food makes me sick now."

Catherine glanced over the menu, trying to think of banana splits and parfaits, not what might be swimming invisibly in them. "Your home is Chicago?"

"The South Side. My father taught archeology at the Oriental Institute." She noticed the waiter and gave her order. She changed Catherine's coffee to Arab coffee. "You must try it. You may think it's too sweet at first, but you'll acquire the taste, I promise."

Catherine had tried it. She avoided sugar and the ice cream sundae already sounded awfully sweet, but she didn't want to be rude. Judy was generously guiding Terry through the pitfalls of Lyndore politics, and that might mean everything for the new design.

"My whole family came to Egypt on my dad's excavations. I wanted to follow in his footsteps, teach in America, work here, though I chose modern history. Then I met Ibrahim. Another dissertation fallen by the wayside, I'm afraid, but we have a son and daughter, and I like my work."

The ice cream came, and the demitasses of thick, black coffee. Judy attacked hers with gusto. "Ibrahim's a professor at Cairo University. His family's from Cairo. How do you like your ice cream?"

"It's different," Catherine answered truthfully, "but good."

Judy nodded in approval. "*Gamousa* milk."

Egyptian buffalo. Interesting. But the red glop on it tasted so artificial she pushed it aside. They ate in silence for a few moments. Though their small talk felt a little forced, they were allies. Catherine moved on to a real question. "Terry says you see a potential in his new design?"

Judy nodded, swallowing. "The design's nice. What grabs me is how he came by it. Pete's not much interested in art, but he's understandably concerned that corporate in Denver feel he's in control of a smooth operation. He can't look indecisive." She smiled impishly. "Pete worries about keeping Terry—and me—in hand. He thinks we're rebels, and there's a war going on."

Catherine frowned. She'd seen power struggles at UC Berkeley and knew what they could do to projects like her tutoring center, or Terry's mural.

"You see, Pete is in charge during construction. Once the Lyndore opens, Gawaz Farhad will manage it. That's a clear division. But they're squabbling over who controls publicity— that's me."

"Sounds touchy for you."

"Ah, but there's the opportunity. Gawaz's trump card is his knowledge of local culture. So what stronger coup for Mr. Beet to pull off—yes, I know Terry and the guys at the site call him that— than Terry's collaboration with his Egyptian coffeehouse buddies?"

"Publicizing Lyndore on a multicultural cutting edge? East and West working together."

"We could, you know, if we'd drop our prejudices and listen to each other. We have more in common than at odds. Corporate has been promoting something close to that image." Judy counted off her points with her spoon against her dish. "New luxury hotels are springing up along the Nile like mushrooms. Competition is fierce. Denver's going for a young niche, affluent but progressive. Whatever the murkier aspects of multinational businesses in 'developing' nations—strange word for a culture thousands of years older than ours—Terry's collaboration is honest. It's truly a shared creation between a Californian and Cairenes." She scraped the last of her syrup, but let the spoon rest with a clink in the dish. "You've got to admit your husband is great media material. Articulate, good looking. This could make him famous."

Between Judy's tutorial, the sweet coffee and sundae, Catherine felt a little rattled. She was grateful for Judy's energy and savvy, since she suspected Terry was out of his depth in a sea of corporate politics. "I wish I could offer useful insight," she admitted. "I feel like a clueless outsider."

"Hang in there, I'll do my best and let Terry do what he does best. You and Terry are hardly alone. Most expats are outsiders, misfits by nature. That's why we left home."

Judy seemed anything but a misfit. Catherine sipped her coffee, though she knew it was aggravating her unsettled nerves.

"Backwaters attract oddballs," Judy warmed to her subject. "Egypt isn't a happening place economically. Hardly Dubai or Hong Kong. Maybe that's why it has an especially peculiar collection of expats. "

"Like in *The Alexandria Quartet*?" Catherine tried not to sound too eager. "I'd love to meet some of them."

"Never read it. Doesn't Laurence Durrell live in France now? But look over by the window, that redhead puffing like a smoke-stack?"

Catherine nodded. She'd noticed the cigarette smoke since she'd entered, and that a lot of it was pouring from one woman sipping from a demitasse and scribbling on a steno pad.

"That's Antonia Boyer, remember the *New York Times* libel suit last year? The *Times* fired her. Now she's shadowing a certain ambassador. Word is, she's onto a scandal big enough to restore her credibility."

Catherine grimaced. "I don't need to know her."

Judy grinned. "It gets better. That old man behind me, the one eating candied orange peel? He's a New Age guru. His disciples believe he was Imhotep in a past life. You know, the architect who built the first pyramid? He's harmless, fun to talk with if you're in the mood. I'll introduce you if you like. But not to that one, over there by the wall. Not harmless. Shady character name of Harrow. He's an antiques dealer and sells on the black market. Including to a prominent European museum."

Catherine started. Slowly, she turned. There sat Geoffrey Harrow, reading the *Illustrated London News* in his shades.

Judy peered owlishly at her through her glasses. "You know him?"

"I met him at the museum."

Though his suit was much whiter than the dust, it was impeccably spotless. A dashing hat was angled low. It and the shades hid most of his face, but his clear cut lips were set in a bored expression as he turned a page, the perfect picture of neocolonial decadence.

Too perfect. Catherine suspected him of parody.

"He's more than a little strange," Judy said.

"Strange, how?"

"Neurotic. A loner, has phobias about his food, won't eat in restaurants or other people's houses."

For an allergy sufferer, that wasn't necessarily neurotic. "You don't like him." Catherine wished he'd take off the shades. She wanted to see of his eyes were as compelling as she remembered.

"No reason to. Even if his ethics weren't questionable, he has a superiority complex bigger than the colossi of Memnon. His shop—Antiqa, near Garden City—is interesting, but I'd be careful about buying anything pricey from him. I'd get a second opinion."

"He sells fakes?" No more than a con man? That would be too disappointing.

Judy shrugged. "European furniture, they say. A fine old piece should have a paper trail, past sales, estate appraisals." She shrugged. "But whenever his pieces have been questioned, experts say they're genuine, so if he is a forger he's too clever to get caught with his pants down."

Catherine smiled. "There's a thought."

"Geoffrey Harrow, sexy? Hmm, some might agree with you. Can't say I would."

"He's a womanizer, then?"

"Not that I've heard. As I said, he's a loner. No rumor I've heard has ever connected him romantically with anyone, man or woman—rats! He's caught us talking about him."

Catherine didn't risk another glance, but Judy's distress grew. "Oh no, here he comes. I can't antagonize him, Pete wants our interior decorator to consult him on the Sultan Suites—You're a Kentuckian, tell me, are you interested in the horse show at the Gezira Sporting Club?"

White filled the corner of Catherine's vision. "Hello, Judy."

Geoffrey's voice was colder, more precise, than she remembered. He turned the black lenses of his shades onto her. "Catherine," he added, surprised.

en

udy put an admirable face on it. "Won't you join us?" Geoffrey Harrow's expression was aloof. For a moment Catherine imagined he would refuse Judy to embarrass her, but he thanked her and pulled out the chair between them.

Fantasy hadn't added to his grace, or the impression of athletic power. A light sensation brushed her knee. His knee. The touch sent unforeseen pleasure straight up the inside of her thigh. Before she could react, he moved his leg away. Not far. She still felt his warmth through the fabric of their pants.

So. He wanted to continue their game.

But she didn't. Not if there he'd be consulting for Lyndore, not an enticing stranger but an acquaintance of hers and Terry's. Especially not now, while their marriage scrambled for balance.

"Am I interrupting?" he asked.

He knew damn well he was. He was playing with them. Beneath, she sensed an edge, like a cat's sadistic play with its prey. He knew good and well they'd been gossiping about him. But Judy made the flimsy denial that was her only polite option. "We were discussing Cairo's expats," But Catherine had to hide a smile when Judy couldn't resist adding, "Talking about what a peculiar bunch they are."

"Peculiar?" Geoffrey repeated innocently. When neither of them took the bait, he remarked, "If this were my country, I would see the presence of so many American—and British—corporate creatures in a less benign light."

Like Judy, he meant? His comment wasn't just insulting. It struck at all the good intentions and beneficial results she obviously prided herself on. His revenge for her calling him dishonest? But he couldn't have overheard that, he'd been too far away. At most, he'd seen them glance at him as they talked.

His blow had gone home. Judy opened her mouth to answer, but closed it again. She couldn't vouch for all the motives of Lyndore, or any the corporations she liaised for. Who could draw a paycheck without being implicated in some way?

Catherine couldn't let him get away with it. "Well then," she asked him, "Are you going to come out with it and ask what we were saying about you?"

He paused, startled. Then took off his dark glasses. "If you like." Shadowed only by his hat brim, his pupils snapped to points. The irises weren't the black she remembered, they were rich brown. "Yes, I know you were discussing me, and yes, I am curious."

Mischief goaded Catherine. "We wonder if you sell fakes."

He turned to Judy. "No, I don't." With an ironic smile, he added, "Though I'd say just the same if I did, wouldn't I?" He looked at Catherine. "If I did sell forgeries, I doubt I should try selling one to you." Hints of amber flickered in the brown if his eyes, transparent as the edge of a flame. Beneath the table she felt the brief touch of his knee.

The waiter approached with the full cup Geoffrey had left at the other table. Geoffrey asked the man to take it away, and Catherine took the opportunity to draw a slow, calming breath. She made no answer. His move, still.

But his glance fell on what remained of her sundae. As he considered it, she noticed the indentation of a small scar beneath the corner of his mouth. Its crescent echoed the curve of his lower lip. "The juice of cherries is usually dark, I believe," he mused. "Curious how people prefer their flavorings scarlet, as if a craving for something quite other than the blood of a fruit hides in the recesses of the human brain."

"*Ya Geoffrey. Es-salam 'ale-kum.*"

Turning, Catherine saw a young man with curly hair and slim shoulders. The light from the windows fell on a face like an ancient sculpture, narrow, with lean cheeks, full lips and large, expressive eyes. Terry would love to draw it.

But Geoffrey's eyes narrowed slightly. "*Wi ale-kum es-salam, ya Mounir.* I expected to see you later at the shop." His switch to English couldn't have been courtesy to Judy. Her Arabic must be fluent. He didn't sound pleased to see the young man.

The Egyptian smiled apologetically. "As I passed I saw you through the window. I have it with me. May I join you?"

Geoffrey gave way, though not with the best of grace. "I can't give you a full appraisal here and now."

"I know. I just wonder if you think it's interesting." His client took the empty chair. "Mounir Abdel Razak," he introduced himself to Catherine and Judy, since Geoffrey hadn't done so.

"Judy Bakhir." Judy shook hands with him.

Catherine offered her hand. "You say you have it here?" Geoffrey prompted before she could say her name.

Mounir glanced at her, but reached into his jacket pocket and withdrew a white cardboard box. He put it on the table. Casually, Geoffrey swept it to him and lifted the lid. Catherine heard his indrawn breath.

Pillowed on cotton lay a figurine of creamy stone, opaque at its center but warmly translucent at its edges. About four inches long, it was a man or woman with arms crossed over the chest, each hand holding an ankh. It was broken off at the knees, but otherwise the subtle carving was undamaged.

Gently Geoffrey lifted it, examining it back, then front again. Its face was long, with softly modeled eyes that seemed to gaze inward under heavy lids, open but dreaming. Catherine wondered if Mounir realized it could almost be a carving of his own face.

"How did you come by this?" Geoffrey's tone was carefully noncommittal.

"You've heard of John Pendlebury? My grandfather was a basket boy with his dig. Mr. Pendlebury gave it to him for his outstanding work."

"Did he write a note? Record the gift in any way?"

"I don't know. My grandfather might remember.

"And the registration number, to verify that the Antiquities Service allotted this object to the EES."

"What is it?" Catherine asked.

"A shabti," Mounir Abdel Razak explained. "Our ancestors buried these with the dead. Say a magic spell and the shabti wakes and serves its owner in the afterlife. Or so they believed." He smiled. "Anything hard or unpleasant, the shabti jumps up and does it for you."

"I'll take a few."

"It only works after you are dead," Geoffrey told her. He turned back to Mounir. "In all my time I've never held a shabti like this one in my hand before. I regret that I can't make you an offer without proper documentation."

Misreading his frown, Judy spoke kindly to the young man. "The face is lovely, almost impressionistic. Look at the eyes, all light and shadow with no sharp lines at all. There's so much expression. It's a beautiful mixture of ancient and modern styles."

"Not your field," Geoffrey returned with a trace of smugness. "The Amarna style is unlike traditional work. Its contemplation, its emotion, all that seems the most modern about it, are its most Amarna qualities. This looks like the real thing. That is why I must refuse it unless there is proof of legal possession. A shabti of even an ordinary person from the reign of Akhenaten is rare. But if this is what I think it may be…"

"Nefertiti," Mounir answered with certainty.

"I agree that it seems a royal person. Amarna art is annoyingly androgynous—annoying for identification, at least. It may be Akhenaten. May I photograph it?"

"Why?"

"For reference, of course. I don't want the shabti itself on my hands without papers."

It seemed to Catherine he was protesting too much. She wondered if these scruples were an act for Judy's benefit, and if the conversation might go very differently in the privacy of his shop.

"There may be documentation. If I decide to part with it, that is." Mounir took back the shabti, laid it on its cotton and replaced the lid. He put the box back in his pocket.

Geoffrey sat back in his chair, watching Mounir's face. "Take good care of it. Perhaps where it actually belongs is in the Egyptian Museum."

Whatever Geoffrey was watching for, Catherine saw no change in Mounir's expression. "You'd call her such a treasure?"

"If it's genuine. More so, if it is Nefertiti."

"I hope you'll help me find out." Mounir's hand went to his jacket pocket. On his finger and thumb Catherine saw old calluses. He noticed her looking. "Farm work," he said. "I'm an administrator with the Ministry of Health, but my family are village people, Miss—"

"Cat Lanier."

"Pleased to meet you, Miss Lanier. " He reached to take her hand again.

"Mrs.," Geoffrey corrected him, reaching across to shake his hand instead. "If you'd like an appraisal, bring the shabti to Antiqa where my reference books are. Until then." It was a dismissal.

Mounir switched his inquisitive glance to Geoffrey. If he was offended he didn't show it. He rose, wished them a good afternoon, and left Groppi with long, smooth strides like those that Catherine had noticed in country and desert dwellers who wore galabiehs.

"A nice young man," Judy said pointedly. "I'd have liked to talk more with him."

"As you well know, his interest in Ms. Lanier was improper."

"Because he comes from a village? He was simply being welcoming to an American in the American way." Judy's unspoken accusation was plain. *Racist*.

"He was also trying to palm off an illegal antiquity on me, in case you hadn't noticed." Geoffrey returned. "Why would he do that in front of witnesses?" He put on his shades and stood. "A pleasure." Leaving enough to cover his coffee and tip on the table, he walked out.

When he was gone Judy gave a put-out sigh. " I do hope Pete doesn't use that man as a consultant."

So did Catherine. In under forty-five minutes Geoffrey Harrow had managed to be rude, vindictive, jealous and suspicious. But her heart was drumming as if she'd been running.

leven

A tomato. Drowned in sunlight and fed by the Nile, scarlet, ripe and fragrant. Its skin resisted her knife only slightly, then split, releasing juice like a relieved sigh. Each slice fell from her blade whorled like a sculpture, spilling seeds. Catherine licked her upper lip.

Samira lowered the heat and laid out a paper towel. The little balls she was frying gave off a crispy, beany scent. Falafel. Only, Samira used less spice than the American instant mixes, and she called it *ta'amiya*. "Next Monday, Terry's work friend and her husband are coming for dinner," Catherine said. "Can you stay a few hours late that night? I'll pay you time and a half."

Samira faced her, frowning. She never liked to say when she didn't understand, but Catherine was learning the difference between her silences that meant *no* and her puzzled ones. "If you can work until nine, we'll pay you for the extra time, plus half."

"Oh! Yes, Catherine, I can work," Samira answered eagerly. The sounds in Catherine's name, especially the "th," seemed alien to her. So long as it wasn't "madam" it was fine, but the only other person who called her by her full name was Geoffrey Harrow.

Not that she'd seen him again, or was going to. Did she love to hate him, or did he fascinate her? Whatever Judy said, at least some of his rudeness to his client had been male competition. She was sure of it. The only question was, did she want Geoffrey's attentions?

"It'll be dark by the time you're finished," she continued aloud, "So one of us will take you home. That is," she amended, "I will."

The one time Terry had offered Samira a ride, Samira had refused, embarrassed. To her, a woman who would ride alone with a man who wasn't her husband was little short of a prostitute and deserved whatever happened to her.

Catherine watched Samira fish the *ta'amiya* from the spitting oil and space the balls on the paper towel. In some ways the confinement of Samira's world had kept her childlike. It was hard to believe she was the same age as the beer guzzling, frequent flying students she'd tutored at UC Berkeley. In other ways, hard work and necessity had made her more mature than some of those sophisticated Californians would ever be. "How are Amina and Karima?"

"Good, but Karima cries." She pointed to her mouth. "Tooths."

"Teething?" Karima was a tiny, delicate thing with the hugest eyes and longest lashes Catherine had ever seen. Too delicate, she worried. "And your husband?"

"Fawzy is good, too." Proudly Samira added, "Soon he is... *rais*."

"What's *rais*?"

Samira raised a hand to gesture, then spread both in the futility of explaining with signs. "Good job."

"That's great." A fly circled Catherine's head and she shooed it.

"Yes, but who knows when."

"Oh." Catherine wasn't sure if she meant the promotion, new job, or whatever was definite or only hoped for. Samira yearned for an apartment of their own. Fawzy's mother looked after the children by day but demanded Samira repay her by doing housework late into the night, and her old fashioned father-in-law was always on Fawzy's case, trying to make him order Samira to wear shapeless black on the street, from head to ankles, like a village woman.

Or a medieval nun. Terry had told Catherine a construction worker's joke about the prudery of the *saidi*, country people from up the Nile like Samira's family. *Why doesn't a* saidi *kiss his wife when they make love? He's too busy holding up the hem of his galabieh with his teeth.*

What was Samira's life like, struggling between the drabness of endless work, the tyrannies of her in-laws, and the contradictions between the strictures of her village upbringing and the freedoms of the women she'd worked for, or the actresses and pop singers Cairo idolized?

Catherine sliced a cucumber, thinking. She put the pale green rounds with the tomato slices under a wire and net plate cover. That was almost second nature now. Though the apartment's window screens were in perfect repair, the smell of cooking drew hordes of flies.

"Your village," she asked, "does your family still live there? Your parents, I mean."

Samira was quiet a few moments. "Yes," she answered. "Father, mother, uncles, aunts. But my brothers are in Cairo." Bringing the *ta'amiya* and tahini, she sat down at the table.

"What's your village like?"

Samira passed her the food first. "Not like here. The Nile, the..." she pointed at the vegetables on the table. "We grow many food. But there is not much...place. Little land, big desert."

"Was it fun, playing in the desert?" Catherine remembered, in Kentucky where she'd grown up, crossing the creek on teetering stones, playing pioneers with her sister, hiding in the cane thickets to ambush the neighbor kids. What would it be like to have the verge of the Sahara for a childhood kingdom?

"The desert? We did not play there. Father—" She vigorously beat an imaginary child.

"I see." A bloated fly made a kamikaze dive for her *ta'amiya*. Trying to wave it away, Catherine accidentally batted the sluggish thing. It flopped like an overripe baseball. "Ugh!" She jerked back.

Samira grinned, then was embarrassed she had.

"Why weren't you allowed?" Catherine asked. "Poisonous snakes, wild dogs?" When Samira looked puzzled, Catherine mimicked a slithering snake with her arm, then growled. They both laughed.

"Snakes," Samira repeated, storing up the word. "Snakes. And bad men from other village." She mimed shooting a rifle.

Catherine wondered if she was exaggerating, or if parents told girls such tales to keep them from straying out of their control.

Samira saw her doubt, but said nothing. It struck Catherine there might be good reasons to keep girls from straying. "In the desert," Samira reached for the English, then gave up. "*Deeb.*"

"Bad men? No? An animal?"

"No, no. Not the man, not the animal. *Deeb*. Bad *thing*. Black, with the tooths of the dog, but not the dog." Her shudder was play acting, but her hushed voice was not.

"Some kind of demon?" Catherine asked, intrigued.

But that word was unfamiliar to Samira.

"How often do you get home to see your family?"

"Maybe soon," Samira answered wistfully.

She sounded as if she'd never been back. "If you could, you'd rather have stayed?"

"No jobs. No money. Fawzy says mud houses are dirty. He says village life is bad." She looked sadly at Catherine. "Like Mr. Terry, he must go to Cairo. You and me must go with them."

Realization silenced Catherine. All the while she'd been thinking of herself as the stranger, and that Samira, because she was Egyptian, was in her element. Now it occurred to her that Cairo might seem as far from home to the young village woman as it did to her. "Yes," she answered Samira's unspoken yearning, and the bond it made between them. How terribly frustrating to have their communication confined to scraps of baby talk! It made the loneliness all the more palpable.

The phone rang.

"We talk of the husbands. Mr. Terry—his ears burn." Samira smiled, proud to show off her English witticism.

Catherine smiled back and went to the living room to answer.

"Hello, Catherine."

For a moment she couldn't breathe. She'd never given Geoffrey her number. But he knew who Terry was, so there were ways to get it.

"I'm driving to the country on business tomorrow. It's a village near Saqqara, a very different sort of place than Cairo. Would you like to ride along?"

"You're breaking the rules."

"Yes," he admitted, knowing exactly what she meant. There was a pause. "What if I promise to be on my best behavior?"

"So you can charm me out of mine?"

"No." He sounded strangely serious. "I enjoy your company, if you must know."

He wanted friendship? Judy had said he was a loner. But that didn't mean she should trust him. "Let me think about it."

He told her his phone number.

After hanging up, she looked at the number she had written. She hadn't put his name on it, and she'd already torn it off the pad. To keep Terry from finding it? She stuck it in her pocket and sat on the sofa with her arms crossed, then noticed what she was doing. Self-protection, or the anticipation of an embrace?

In their adventurous early days, there'd never been secrecy. She and Terry had trusted each other. They'd trusted that what they shared was strong enough to be honest and generous with each other. Maybe their love was no longer strong enough to withstand complete honesty.

Maybe it wasn't love that held them together but habit. In earlier days, no one could have shaken her whole universe with the touch of his knee. It was ridiculous, stupid. Yet that touch had aroused her so outrageously that if his thigh had met hers she might have made love to him right there on a table in someone's banana split.

In the secure past, Terry would have laughed at that admission. It might have turned him on. Now her instinct was to fear it. That it would devastate Terry to know how she really felt. She took a breath, deciding. If the attraction between Geoffrey and her became irresistible, time enough then to decide how to handle it. Whether to talk it over with Terry or just tell Geoffrey no.

So, she was considering telling Geoffrey yes?

That shook her. She faced the truth that it was no game. Never had been. She wanted Geoffrey Harrow.

And if acting on her open marriage was enough to seriously shake that marriage up, maybe a shaking-up was what it needed to get back in balance again.

Or, destroy it.

Don't phone Geoffrey, she told herself. He was a proud man. If she didn't call him back, he wouldn't come running after her. He'd let it drop.

Behind her eyelids she saw the shaley bed of the creek where she'd played at adventures, a sway of willow branches reflecting on its surface in gold and green flecks of brightness. She saw the colored lights blinking to the rhythm of her fingers on the bass strings. Heard the quarter tones of Egyptian music throbbing from a high window into a thin blue twilight.

Catherine took out his number. She looked at it. Just squiggles. Meaningless. As unfamiliar as the Arabic 0 that meant 5 and dot that meant 0. She crumpled the slip of paper to throw it away.

She opened it, picked up the phone, and dialed.

welve

erched on the arm of the chair, Catherine watched out
the window. She had set Samira to a task in the back of
the apartment, telling her only that she was going out
to look at an antique. Samira assumed it was a shopping trip with
a woman friend, and Catherine let her. The sun kindled an early
mist in the street below. It blazed for a lingering moment before
a breeze from the distant Mediterranean consumed it. She could
smell faint sea salt in the air. She had a bet with herself that
Geoffrey's car would be either a Mini or a Jaguar. A black one, of
course.

She'd still said nothing about this growing friendship to Terry.
Because who was to say it would be any more than that? For all
she knew, Judy had mentioned to him that they'd run into
Geoffrey at Groppi, but Terry hadn't brought it up. Beneath her
bright mood she felt an undertow of longing, but that was her
own business and was more than Geoffrey. How long since the
future had been a complete unknown?

She almost didn't notice when a dusty Toyota ambled into
sight. Its windows were tinted dark grey. Only when she saw that
did it occur to her this nondescript sedan might be Geoffrey's.

Arriving in unforeseen ways began to seem a specialty of his. At least she'd been right that his car was black. As he got out the morning light found bronze in his hair. She hurried down.

The sun flashed off his shades as he turned to her. Without wasting time on a greeting he got back in the car and opened her door from the inside. Whatever Judy said about him being a loner, he seemed practiced at discretion. Catherine distrusted what that implied.

Shielded by the smoked glass, he took off his shades and glanced at her skirt and long sleeved, button-down blouse. Perhaps he thought her primness was a message to him.

"Since your client lives in the country I guessed he might be conservative," she said.

"Thoughtful of you. Yusef has lived in America, but he's an old traditionalist at heart." He started the car. "He has been a client of mine since I first came to Egypt. He's the *omda*, the mayor, of his village and owns a chemical plant in Cairo. When he finds out you're American he'll want to discuss baseball."

"I'm afraid I'll disappoint him. I'm not much of a sports fan."

"Spectator sports do lack a certain excitement, don't they?"

She glanced quickly, suspecting a double entendre, but he was attending innocently to the road. He left the quiet streets of Maadi behind, heading downriver along the crowded Cornishe. The glare of raw new high rises was muted by the tinted windows. "Now that you have been in Egypt nearly a month, what do you think of it?"

Catherine returned his glance long enough to acknowledge it, but not long enough to make any promises. "Terry's preparations are going well, and the Lyndore wives no longer feels duty-bound to ask me out shopping so often."

"Lyndore wives?" He smiled. "Any relation to the Stepford wives?"

"I wouldn't be surprised. They think Terry is a cute little airhead and they're disappointed that I refuse to be one."

"I'm curious about your husband."

"Curious enough to meet him?"

"No," he answered, to her relief. Rows of sugar cane and beans passed, and far away, at the pale edge of the desert, a building under construction. Or maybe it was an old, crumbling turret of rock. In the haze it shifted like a thought, defying definition. He asked, "Is Judy Bakhir a good friend of yours?"

"Terry's friend. Why do you dislike Judy so much?"

"She's a gossip."

Catherine smiled. "What else has she said about you?"

Geoffrey glanced at her, but volunteered nothing.

"Judy's been great to Terry," she continued, amused at his conceit, "but no, I can't say I'm that drawn to her. Of the women I've met so far, I like Samira, my maid, but her English isn't good and my Arabic is worse."

"So much for the people round you. What about you?"

Catherine shrugged. "I'm fine," she said, meaning it. "I always am. I write lots of letters, I stocked up at the Anglo-Egyptian Bookstore as you suggested. I've been exploring Old Cairo and the Mouski, and except for that one trip to the museum I haven't even started on ancient Egypt yet."

As implacable as the voice in her own head, Geoffrey asked, "Is sightseeing enough?"

She opened her mouth to tell him she was perfectly happy with her life, but in honesty she couldn't. "I'm not exactly burning up the world," she admitted.

"Not all of it, perhaps." He said it so quietly she barely heard him over the motor. He refused to look at her, but playful amusement showed in the quirk of his mouth. The outline of his upper lip was as clearly defined as a wind-blown ripple in the sand.

Keeping her voice light, she confronted him. "You never let up, do you?"

"Do *you*?"

"I'm not doing a thing," she protested, feeling almost as blameless as she let on, if not quite.

"So the fault is all mine?" Dust blew up suddenly, obscuring the road ahead, but he spared it little attention. "You, of course, are not enticing me to distraction."

"Don't try to flatter me. I'm not that beautiful. Or that gullible."

"No?" It was not clear which he was contradicting. "Then perhaps I have a penchant for the truth spoken in a soft voice."

"Compliments like that I might not mind." She paused, then warned him, "*Might* not."

Darkly through the windshield she saw a man leading a loaded donkey. As suddenly as it had risen, the dust died away, leaving verdant fields crossed by irrigation trenches. Catherine saw no lone farm houses, but occasionally they passed villages of mud brick clustered densely to waste as little as possible of the cultivable land. Desert rimmed the horizon, its whiteness more distant than the sky.

"So you are filling in time," Geoffrey resumed. "Even without a work permit you could always give private English lessons."

"If I wanted to fill in more time."

"I see. The question is more fundamental than that."

"I think so." She glanced at him but did not reveal more of her tangled hopes and fears. His interest in her might be no more than a tactic, lasting no longer than his sexual curiosity. Letting him know how vulnerable she felt might be setting herself up for a hard fall. She watched his hands turn the wheel with precisely controlled energy.

What might their touch be like? And that skeptical face when he gave way to passion? A grove of palms closed around them, its dense shade blue through the smoked glass. Geoffrey rolled down his window and the rattle of the fronds surrounded them like rain. Catherine had been careful to leave the tinted glass up against the sun, but now she lowered it and leaned out, breathing the fertile scents of green growth, flowers, mud and manure. A shrill metallic rasp reminded her of summer in Kentucky. "Cicadas," she said. "I never heard them in California."

"Tell me about California."

"You haven't been there?"

"Not for years. Where did you live?"

"In Oakland, by Lake Merritt. It's not really a lake. It's saltwater, a backwater of a backwater of a backwater of the Pacific ocean, Terry likes to say."

"Brackish."

"Smelly," she admitted. "If you live by it, you try not to dwell on the pollution."

"Proof, if more were needed, that humankind are a porcine species."

"Maybe, but the reflections of the city lights on the water at night are beautiful. I like the Bay Area, the creative people, the tolerance for differences. I woke early to watch the water birds. Egrets, terns, gulls. Pelicans soaring like pterodactyls. At sunset you might see a heron standing. You know that no-neck profile they have against the twilight?"

"Yes."

"And evenings at the corner coffeehouse. Espresso and passionate discussions of politics, or movies, or art exhibits, with whoever drops by."

"As incurably gregarious as Egyptians, Californians. And just as Quixotic. But you're not really one of them."

"No," she mused, startled at his perceptiveness. "California is a chance gathering. I feel like a guest at a party. I don't feel the deep, gut-connection to the place that I do in Kentucky."

"Egypt is a very long way from Kentucky."

"Yes," she agreed wistfully. She was quiet for a while, listening to the pulsing rasp of the insects that sounded not farther from home than California but much closer. The palms gave way to fields laid open to the thick honey of the sun. Geoffrey rolled up his window. Reluctantly, Catherine started to do the same.

"Keep yours down if you like."

"The light won't bother you?"

"Your side is away from the sun."

"An allergy to something as inescapable as sunlight must give you a rough time. What is it, exactly?"

"A nuisance, not worth discussing."

"Then tell me what is," she turned the tables on him. "Where's your home?"

For a moment she thought he would evade her again. But he answered, "Wiltshire. I grew up in a village not far from Salisbury."

"What's it like?"

"Green. Peaceful. I left to study at Cambridge, then went to London, but like you, I sometimes feel regret."

"For the creeks, the woods, the hills," she said, thinking of Kentucky.

"For the streams, the forest, the downs," he agreed.

"And the willows."

"Yes, the willows. They grow here. See, by the canal?" He pointed out a clump of twigs straggling from the bank. Their thin leaves did look willowy. "Though hardly the great weeping willows at home."

"No," she agreed. "So, what keeps you away from yours?"

"I no longer belong there. But here we are. This is Yusef's village."

 hirteen

 igzagging and dusty, the narrow lane to the village crossed the canal on an iron bridge. Girls in fluorescent prints were washing clothes below the bridge. Through the open window Catherine heard the bright spatter of their talk. Their reflections in the muddy water turned to watch the foreigners go by.

A dirt lane climbed the bank to the village. The car bumped over potholes, raising a thick dust. Dogs came barking, yellow ones with their tails curled over their backs, surly and ill fed. They bared their teeth as if they wanted to leap, but Geoffrey put on his sunglasses and rolled down his window, so she sat back, bluffing the snarling animals into thinking she too was unconcerned.

As they drove at a crawl into the cluster of mud brick buildings, children came running. Two bigger boys drove away the dogs with rocks. The younger ones trotted alongside shouting, "'Allo, 'allo!" When Catherine helloed them back their answering 'allos rose to an uproar.

"They know all about tourists," Geoffrey said. "They imagine they have netted two stray ones."

"For what?"

"Photos, directions, lunch, it scarcely matters. Everyone knows foreigners are made of money and not very bright." The lane twisted tightly between the flat roofed houses. Whenever they reached a bend Geoffrey honked a warning to whatever people or animals might be beyond. The fronts of some of the houses were painted white or turquoise, but the sides were brown mud brick. Solid wooden shutters hung on hinges, but there were few window panes, and through the open doors wandered toddlers, swarms of flies, and long-haired goats. Beneath the odors of compost and packed earth came an undertone of butane and children's urine.

As they passed a well, two women stopped talking and turned to watch them without upsetting the large containers balanced on their heads. One woman's was pottery, the other's plastic. In the countryside of Catherine's childhood it was customary for people in cars and at the roadside to wave whether they knew each other or not, but the women stared impassively at Catherine's smile and lifted hand. Whether it was shyness or deep disapproval she couldn't tell.

A thin donkey ambled into their path and Geoffrey paused, blowing the horn. The gaggle of children caught up with them, now clamoring for cigarettes. With a curt Arabic warning Geoffrey drove on. Catherine saw other women scrutinizing them from dark doorways. "Imagine this village being your whole life," she said quietly as they left the children behind.

"For most of humanity, throughout most of time."

"Yes." The thought oppressed her.

"Now, if they like, they can leave their villages for shanties in the Fustat garbage dump." He smiled. "Isn't progress a wonderful thing." Tooting the horn, he rounded a corner. "There's Yusef's."

Surrounded by palms and flowering bushes was a larger house. Its creamy yellow front gleamed. The side was the same plain mud brick as the others. Shaded stairs climbed to a porch with a waist high wall topped with columns. Geoffrey parked under a clump of mimosas. "Lock your side, will you? I don't want to come out and find a goat has been put in my car."

As they climbed the stairs Catherine felt the slight touch of his hand on her back. Her nerve endings realigned to it as involuntarily as filings to a magnet. The dark lenses held her gaze. Then he reached out to knock on the door. Before he could, an old man in a blue galabieh opened and greeted Geoffrey by name in Arabic. They followed through a cool, dim hall to double doors painted vermilion. The old man swung these wide and with a sweep of his arm invited them in.

From nowhere, apprehension seized Catherine. Maybe she was a fool to come to this remote place with a stranger, no one knowing she was here. Trade in women was no joke in this part of the world, and what did she know of Geoffrey, except that Judy called him shady? With a scarcely perceptible pressure at her back he guided her through the door into a large room with velvet chairs lining the walls. A magnificent cut glass chandelier hung from the ceiling, and on two coffee tables, one carved wood, the other Chinese lacquer, were brass trays of flat bread, skewers of grilled meat and vegetables, and thin yogurt. A samovar sat near the hearth. Through the screened, unglassed windows she saw a garden where lotuses floated on a pool.

"Ya Geoffrey, sabbah el-kheir!" A stout man came through the door. He looked in his late fifties, his face broad and his hair grey. Above his large, expressive eyes, protruding brows gave him a formidable look. His clothing was Western, sport slacks and a plaid shirt.

"Sabbah i'noor, ya Yusef. Is'salam aale kum." Geoffrey shook his hand, and to her surprise they followed with a brief embrace. Catherine knew Egyptian men hugged, but she hadn't imagined Geoffrey doing it. He introduced her to Yusef.

"Pleased to meet you," their host said in a strong Boston accent. "Are you English too?"

"American," she answered, aware of Geoffrey watching her.

"Ah, my second home. Do you keep up with the Red Sox?"

Catherine caught Geoffrey's amused glance, feeling ridiculous for her fears.

"No?" Yusef shook his head. "Too bad. Well, please have a seat." He paused, looking alarmed. "How forgetful of me." He swung the wooden shutters closed and switched on the chandelier. Geoffrey relaxed as he thanked him and took off his dark glasses.

They sat in a corner where the lined-up chairs met, Geoffrey next to her, Yusef at right angles. If the chairs had been only slightly narrower Geoffrey's thigh would have touched hers. He gave her a brief smile, sharing the tension and savoring its small torment. The servant poured hot tea into juice glasses and offered the food. Geoffrey, she noticed, took only tea. He and Yusef made small talk in English about Yusef's son, a military officer stationed in the Sinai.

Though she tried to eat her kebab, Geoffrey's nearness deprived her of ordinary hunger. With an act of will she turned her attention to their host. The gulf between the luxury of this house and the poverty of the village made her skeptical of Yusef, but he responded to Geoffrey's caustic wit with a ready sense of fun, and she could see why they got along. His smiling animation had an easy dignity. Geoffrey's was different, but no less absolute. Yusef rested on his composure like a cushion. Geoffrey wore his like a cloak. Through its occasional partings you glimpsed him flashing like a concealed jewel. Or, the jeweled hilt of a dagger?

As Geoffrey described his adventures shipping an eighteenth century sideboard from Rome to Alexandria, the quiet resonance of his voice wove a spell that distanced all else. It was enough to listen to his understated ironies that made the mishaps more amusing than they could possibly have been at the time, and to watch his hand sketch graceful descriptions in the air.

The subtlety of his attraction fascinated her. Each time she studied him she saw more, the harmonies and dissonances in his features, the luminous reflections of the chandelier in the darkness of his eyes. The fineness of his facial structure became all harsh angles when he turned his head only slightly. Sensuousness and austerity warred in the shape of his lower lip. The very glances that stirred her spoke also of self-denial. Behind the swift alterations in his expressions she caught fleeting hints of something else. Sadness? No, it felt sharper than that. Some unrevealed grief that only a strong will held in check.

Ridiculous, she scolded herself. Every cynic must be a tormented Byronic hero? Lust after the man all you want, Cat, but keep a dash of common sense. Around this one you'll need it.

"Have another kebab," Yusef urged her.

"Thank you." She leaned forward and took one since Yusef's courtesy made refusal impolite. Before she could settle back, Geoffrey moved his thigh to the edge of his chair. He remained expressionless as a sphinx, but the invitation was clear. Arousal pulsed between them, vivid as a scent. Or else his scent was part of the intoxication, some faint but heady spice with an undertone bitter as smoke. She could almost identify it, but it kept eluding her. All she knew was that it lured her, potent with mystery and sex.

It's just aftershave or soap, idiot, she told herself. But she wanted to press her thigh against his in the intimate contact of an irrevocable *yes*.

Unaware, Yusef bit a grape off the bunch he held and savored the juice. A sardonic twitch played for an instant on Geoffrey's lips. Jewel, she thought, or hidden dagger? She leaned back in her chair, refusing to quite touch him.

Yusef frowned at Geoffrey. "You haven't taken so much as a single bite, or even a sip of tea." He turned to Catherine. "For twenty-odd years I've known this man, and never will he eat one crumb! I think he finds my hospitality poor."

Geoffrey's long-suffering eye-roll was far from the Byronic depths she'd been about to cast him into. "You know it isn't so."

"As strong as you are? Special diet!" Yusef wiped his hands in a disdainful gesture.

"It's because of my diet that I am so strong," Geoffrey returned with what looked suspiciously like more of his private amusement. Catherine could not imagine what diet, however exotic, could make the statement so entertaining. Flavoring his English with mock-Arab-style poeticism, he continued, "Your repast would tempt the jaded palette of a pharaoh, and your tea is more fragrant than roses blooming by evening. You know very well your hospitality is the finest in Egypt, so let's be sensible, shall we?"

Yusef frowned. "Hmph!"

Geoffrey caught her eye. Clearly it was a recurring argument, and this was always its end.

The meal over, they got down to business. Taking them to another room, Yusef showed them a large drop leaf oak table. Geoffrey studied its top and legs, then crawled underneath to examine the joints. From that vantage point he began telling their host about it, but his talk was technical, and Yusef had trouble following it. Geoffrey switched to Arabic. So he was skilled at the language. Catherine listened to the richness of his voice as the back-throated *kh*'s and *gh*'s flowed without a trace of the notorious British mangling of other people's languages.

If she couldn't follow the talk, she found plenty of interest in the view. His behind was trim and firm, and when he backed out from under the table the muscles were temptingly outlined. As he emerged he tried to catch her looking, but she was faster.

He lifted a brow, acknowledging the entertainment he had accidentally offered, and that she had won that round by keeping him guessing whether she'd noticed. All the while he discussed the table in textures now silk, now cool crystal, now the scimitar edge of whetted steel. She coveted the delicately probing touch he wasted on the beveled edge of the wood.

Yusef turned to her. "You've been very quiet, Catherine. What's your opinion?"

"The grain of the wood is striking. It's a lovely table, but I'm not qualified to judge it."

"Oh? I thought you must be in the business too. Well Catherine, I bought this table on a whim, and now our friend Geoffrey tells me that for the price it's the wisest purchase I've ever made. Any other dealer would have offered to take it off my hands and tried to cheat me."

"The difference is that I know you're too sharp to be taken in," Geoffrey answered.

Yusef showed his none too perfect teeth in a grin. "I try to be. Geoffrey's an expert on the European antiques brought to Egypt before our independence, but he also knows Islamic art."

Geoffrey was just as genuinely pleased. Until today she had never seen him show warmth to anyone but her. He seemed in his element trading courtesies with Yusef, old fashioned politenesses that affirmed the liking between them. Yet Catherine guessed those same formalities kept all within limits. Old friends they were, but business friends. She didn't like the similarity to the games he enjoyed playing with her. Don't hope for too much from him, she warned herself again, but knew she was ignoring her own advice.

"The two of you will stay for the soccer game? It's just some villages on this side of the river against some on the other bank, but the competition is fierce!"

"Thank you, but it's time I got back."

"So soon?"

"I'm afraid I must." Geoffrey went to the other room for his sunglasses.

When he was gone Yusef turned to her. Lowering his voice, he asked, "May I speak with you, Catherine?"

Curious, she nodded.

"We both think highly of Geoffrey, eh? Then let me tell you this. He's brought in experts before, specialists to consult, but he's never brought a pretty young lady."

"What do you mean?" she asked innocently.

Yusef frowned at her left hand, but the rings made for Terry and her by a friend in Berkeley, each set with a sea-green crysoprase, did not look like wedding bands. He was uncertain. "If you're not already married, consider. Geoffrey is wealthy, and though he fusses over food, he's strong. I've seen him haul furniture like a twenty year old. He could father many sons to replace the one he lost. Sons would do him good, and a woman could do much worse for a husband. I say this not to interfere, but because I wish him well." He stopped abruptly.

Geoffrey had come in silently, but from his expression, his mind was on his own thoughts. "Ready, Catherine?"

When he had gone out Yusef gave her an avuncular wink. "Consider it."

ourteen

illage children waved and followed as they drove back, but knowing them Yusef's guests, no longer pestered. The women watched with the same stony reserve, but Catherine hardly noticed. So Geoffrey had once had a son. Maybe the submerged pain had not been imaginary after all. She'd gotten the impression he had spent his years in Cairo more or less on his own, but presumably he'd been married. Or still was.

He stopped where the lane met the road. "I apologize for the lack of air conditioning. Roll your window all the way down if you like." Taking off his coat and tie he laid them neatly on the back seat, then opened his collar and the next button.

More than he needed to. But as he drove Catherine couldn't resist a glimpse of the newly revealed territory. The hollow and tendons of his throat made pleasing contours. Just visible at the bottom of the opening, dark hair caught the light, fine and soft. That surprised her. With his smooth hands she'd pictured a chest like pale marble. She preferred smooth chests, but she was curious whether the hair covered his upper chest or just the center, and how far down it went. And whether his nipples were the brown hinted by his hair and eyes or pale to go with his fair skin. He glanced out of the corner of his eye. Of course. Deliberately she looked away, but had to smile. He sped up, and the breeze with its heavy, fecund fragrance swept through the car.

She didn't want to stir up grief, but she did want to know him. "Yusef said you lost a son."

"What?" Geoffrey asked, preoccupied with skirting a pothole. "Yes," he answered as it sank in. "I had a son. Richard. But he died a long time ago." She heard regret, but no fresh grief. Either the wound was much older than she'd thought, or he and his son had not been close.

"How did he die?"

"Pneumonia." Calmly he passed a truck, offering nothing more about it.

If he wanted to keep his feelings to himself she was not going to pry, but she did need to know one thing. Point blank she asked, "Are you married?"

"I was. Twice, as a matter of fact, but both marriages are over." He glanced at her. "Why did Yusef mention Richard?"

In mischief, she told him. "He thinks I should marry you and give you other sons."

"Does he?" The words were lightly amused, but his hands tightened on the steering wheel. "Tell me Catherine, do you want children?"

She couldn't resist pretending confusion. "Whose?"

He did not smile.

So she answered seriously. "Someday. Not yet."

"But you have other ambitions."

"Doesn't everyone?"

"I'm not asking about everyone."

"When we get home, Terry and I want . . . "

He glanced attentively at her.

She thought of her hopes that first night in Egypt, that Terry's success would sweep away the resentment that had accumulated as quietly unnoticed as a drift of snow. That passion would return, and adventure. But she wondered if they were even possible between the two people she and Terry had become. "I don't know what I want. I'm not certain I belong in my marriage any more than I belong in Egypt," she astounded herself by adding aloud.

To her surprise, Geoffrey did nothing to distance himself from her unexpected emotion. He only listened.

"I put all of myself into building the tutoring program. A small ambition maybe, but I cared about it. I didn't want to leave it, or my friends. But this is Terry's big break."

"You could have stayed in California while he worked here."

"I brought up that idea. He said he couldn't cope without me. Terry isn't very practical." She sighed. "There were just too many reasons I couldn't leave him in the lurch."

"Such as?"

Terry's sense of self-worth and the sofa fight were not things Terry would want shared with an outsider. "Guilt," she answered. "Money and security were never important to him until I made them important. Under different circumstances I could have loved Egypt, but I have no life of my own here." Relieved to let it out at last, she said, *"I don't want to be here."*

Geoffrey pulled the car to the shoulder of the road. He took off his sunglasses. The light made him narrow his eyes, but he let her see them. "I want for you to be here. Very much." She looked into the warm brown the sunlight made of his irises. The intensity of his gaze drew her not by the sex, but by the heart.

Coldly he added, "I can just as truthfully say I wish you had never come to Egypt, I wish to hell I'd never met you, and I wish you'd go back to America and stay there."

If he had backhanded her against the car door the blow would have been no less. She kept her mouth shut, drawing measured breaths as he restarted the motor. When she trusted her voice, she said tightly, "Would you be so kind as to tell me why?"

"As you say, you have hopes for the future. I prefer not to change that."

Elation flared at the thought of her future including him, astonishing her as much as his conceit. "I hardly know you. What on earth makes you imagine I'd change a single one of my hopes because of you?"

She expected him to puff up with masculine pride. Instead, he smiled. "Point well taken."

She raised her eyebrows. "You'd better believe it."

"I want to."

"What's that supposed to mean?"

"There are complications on my side as well as yours. I prefer not getting too involved."

"Fine by me."

They passed through the weals of palm shade and sunlight in silence.

After some miles, he began talking about antiques. She wondered what 'too involved' meant. If he only wanted to get laid, he had a strange way of going about it. He'd bottled up every trace of sexual nuance. If he meant he did *not* want to go to bed, he had an even stranger way of showing it. At last, smoking factories and bitter dust smudged out the fields. "Shall I take you home?" he asked. "Or to the shop and see those ceramics?"

If she said home maybe she'd never see him again. She wished she wanted that. "I'd rather see the sculpture you mentioned."

"That's too valuable to keep in the shop. It's in my house."

The idea of taking her there bothered him. That gave her satisfaction. "So?" she dared him.

From his silence she thought he was taking her to Maadi, but he continued along the Cornishe until Garden City, south of Tahrir Square. She was a little surprised. She had walked in Garden City, enjoying its picturesque mixture of *belle-époque* and Arab architecture, but she'd imagined Geoffrey living in Zamalek like most wealthy English residents.

He drove through winding streets cooled by flowering trees. Archways and fanciful ornamentation gave each building its own character. Garden City had all the charm she had once imagined of living in Cairo. He pulled up in front of a large, grey stone house set farther back from the street than most. A high wrought iron fence surrounded it. Sycamore figs threw feathery shadows across a balcony, and the windows were screened by wood carved in intricate patterns.

"This is wonderful," she admitted as he unlocked the gate. She was still wary of him, but the house did suit him. Certainly more than that nondescript car of his.

In the dim entrance hall Geoffrey let out a breath of relief and took off his dark glasses. As her eyes adjusted Catherine made out a Harraniyya tapestry on the wall and a staircase with banisters carved like twining vines. "This way," he said. She followed to a high ceilinged parlor. Some of the furniture matched the house in age, some looked older. Above the fireplace ran a mantel of black granite, satiny like the pyramid capstone when she first saw him in the museum.

Geoffrey let her look at his private world as she pleased. On the mantel stood a jade Chinese sculpture. Beside it, a boat was paddled by little wooden oarsmen with long eyes and white kilts. The wood was dry and cracked in places, ancient Egyptian.

On a table stood a sculpture in translucent white stone, a slender nude in an ecstatic dance, her body and flying hair forming a crescent like a cold flaming moon. Caught by its beauty, Catherine crossed the carpet . It looked European though its sensuous grace reminded her of India, a vibrant eroticism with a core of pitiless fierceness. For all the compassion in her face, she was a moon goddess, incapable of mercy. Yet exquisite. The white flesh seemed so alive Catherine reached out, then the probable value of the sculpture stopped her.

"That's the one I mentioned," Geoffrey said behind her. "It's the best piece in the house. Touch it if you like."

Feeling him watching, she followed the arc of the ribs down to the hip with her finger. The stone was like cold silk, and she shut her eyes to intensify the sensation. Like a silky heat she felt the brush of his fingertips across her wrist. It invaded her skin, flowing like molten electricity. She opened her eyes. His were close, a point of light in each. His lips, more exquisite than any sculpture, parted slightly as they met hers.

Their softness surprised her. Catherine opened her lips, and the tip of his tongue swept lightly across the tender inner skin. The chill surging through her had a heart of incandescence. His hands shaped themselves to her back, and his mouth opened her farther, as if he wanted to drink. She tasted him in return, a cool freshness underlain by a very faint harshness, like spring water with a hint of rust, but not unpleasant. They lingered, drawn gradually into the intimacy of breasts against chest, thighs meeting at last through the thin barriers of cloth. He pressed against her with subtly growing insistence, scarcely moving yet claiming her, and his arms tightened around her, stronger than Terry's, a stranger's arms. She pulled free.

At once he released her. Taking a shaky breath, she stepped back. "Geoffrey, I don't know."

He regarded her gravely. "Perhaps you are less interested in me than merely feeling restless."

He knew better. "No," she called him on it. "I'm afraid I'm much too interested in you."

He paced away. At last, without turning, he said harshly, "Time for you to go."

She controlled her expression, but this time it took longer to manage her voice. "I think I'd better," she struggled to keep it level. "Only, tell me this: What exactly do you gain, playing with me like you've done?"

Swiftly he turned. Whatever she had expected, it wasn't the pain she saw. Shocked again, she asked, "Why do you do this?"

"Because," he answered, his voice hard despite the suscepti- bility in his face, "if you don't go now, I shall ask you to stay."

"Is that so terrible?"

Acknowledgement that he wanted it grew in his eyes, but also some other emotion that made him tense as if he feared it. From her own depths an answering fear rose, of vulnerability, of opening as never before and not being loved in return. Or, a rational corner of her mind asked, is it that I'm afraid I *will* be loved? Suddenly, despite all she shared with Terry, she felt as if she never had been.

"I'd like to stay," she said.

iilfteen

ow it seemed less that Geoffrey was afraid than that she watched two cravings struggle. *Whichever wins*, she thought without knowing why, *he will be defeated.*

She saw his defeat. "Yes," his voice was harsh. "I want you." He took her in his arms. This time his kiss was an impulsive plunge. His arms tightened, shattering the shell of habit that had protected and imprisoned her for so long and letting nameless longings rush in. Eagerly she twined her tongue with his, holding him as fiercely as he held her. At last he let her go, and they looked at each other, alarmed and inflamed. "Come upstairs," he said.

Crimson walls, a high bed with tall mahogany posts, a massive wardrobe of dark polished wood, marvelously carved chairs with feet like hawks' talons and deep wine cushions, a Persian carpet patterned like stained glass in garnet, amber and midnight blue. Afternoon light through crimson draperies cast a rose haze on the white bedspread. Catherine tried to calm the pounding of her heart. "Sexy," she remarked with a detachment she did not feel.

"You have a taste for red, do you?" A sardonic light reflected in his eyes as he drew her to the bed. A sexual predator if I ever saw one, she thought, but then gasped at the heat of his breath on her throat. His lips grazed her neck, finding the softnesses and hollows with a delicate, very deliberate leisure.

However carried away he had been downstairs, he was obviously in flawless control now. He paid skilled attention to each sensitive spot, exploring with soft pressures of his lips and moist swipes and ticklings of his tongue. She caught her breath at the subtle variations of his touches, but they were not the passion she craved from him.

"Geoffrey," she began, and he raised his head. He knew what she wanted and was unwilling to give it. Leaning to her again, he centered his lips on her pulse and circled with his tongue, sucking gently. Chills swirled like cool water, dissolving her resistance. She let him have his way for now. Tilting her head back she stroked his hair. It felt even softer than she had imagined, and she let it run slowly through her fingers. His lips parted more and without warning he closed his teeth on her throat in a sharp nip.

She cried out, pulling away.

He lifted his head. Still shivering from the mixture of sensations, she met his gaze and found cool amusement overlying flame. Before she could answer it, he opened the buttons of her blouse and traced a path with his lips over the ridge of her collar bone, then slowly down to the top of her breast. With her fingertips she explored the planes of his back through his shirt, and followed his spine. She leaned closer, breathing in his elusive bittersweet scent. He unfastened her bra and brushed it and the blouse from her as if they were dead husks, freeing the living kernel of her. Breathing quickly, she waited for his touch on her breasts, but it did not come. Hoping he was not disappointed, she opened her eyes.

He was looking at her, his face appreciative. "I knew you would be lovely."

"Small."

"Delicate and beautifully shaped." He smoothed her shoulder. "Your slenderness is perfection, Catherine. I would not change a single thing about you." If he was a predator, he was a generous one. "If it weren't for your husband I would kiss the blood to the surface and deliciously mark you. Here." He cupped her breast, and she drew a quick breath. "And here," he whispered. He closed his lips over her nipple, spiraling his tongue. Needing to touch him in return, she found his forehead and traced down the ridge of his cheek. Her whole awareness was reduced to the sense of touch as he flicked his tongue over the erect point of her nipple. Again he drew back, and for a long moment gazed at her without a word. Then, his expression unreadable, he brushed his fingers lightly over her other nipple and watched her response.

His enjoyment was as sweet as the sensation, and she let him know with a soft sound. He bent to the other breast, sucking lightly at first, then stronger and faster. Reaching under his shirt she stroked the bare skin of his back, and he answered with his teeth, not hard this time, biting just enough to heighten the sensation. Afraid that if he thought her a conquest already made he might lose interest, she tried to hide the power of her response to him. Softly she teased, "You're very oral, aren't you?"

"You could say that," he replied with such solemnity that she suspected he found her remark exquisitely amusing.

"You and your secrets," she said. "Now it's time to reveal them all."

"All?"

"All. Then we'll see what happens to your smugness." She sat up and kissed him, playing tag with his tongue, exploring its underside, retreating then advancing to lightly touch his teeth. She opened her eyes at his abrupt withdrawal. "All right then," she said. "Lie down."

The crimson of the room reflected in his eyes as he complied, silently daring her. She undid the buttons of his shirt, taking her time and purposely leaving the edges overlapped until she finished. Slowly, she drew them apart. Geoffrey's chest muscles were lithe yet compact. In the dim light his skin was luminous, and the hair did spread over most of the upper part. A finer growth faintly shaded his stomach, gathering at the center in a dark rivulet that ran down to his navel. After liking smooth bodies for so long she was surprised at how sweetly carnal she found this soft shadowing. His nipples were a lovely warm color, more coral than pink. She savored the soft tickle of the hair, the heat of his skin, the tautness beneath. She breathed in his bitter, intoxicating spice, teasingly familiar yet still not quite identifiable. The skin overlying the rippling of his ribs was satiny-fine. With the merest fragment of a smile he invited her to linger, but her curiosity was too urgent. She unfastened his belt and trousers and edged the zipper open.

She felt his heartbeat quicken. Her liked her aggressiveness, that she went for his sex before he uncovered hers. Even baring his feet was a sexual act, the shape of each toe ridiculously provocative. She smoothed her palms up his calves to his thighs, over the deliciously fine skin of his hips, down his firm belly to his scanty black briefs. "You didn't wear sexy underwear today for a particular reason?" she asked, and heard her voice throaty with anticipation.

His lips curved slightly. "Why should I do that?"

The outline of his sex was plainly visible through the black cloth. Slowly she reached out, desire dizzying her like a drug. Ever so slightly he arched his hips, revealing more clearly the semi-erection that pressed the cloth. Her own sex throbbing, she touched him. With a swiftness that startled her he put his hand on hers, closing her fingers around him. In a welter of eagerness, and misgiving about where such a powerful attraction might lead, she stared into his eyes, and saw his own heat and reluctance. Slowly she drew down his briefs. His cock lifted, nearly hard but still weighed by its heaviness, the tip protruding from the foreskin that enveloped the rest.

She stopped in surprise.

"Is anything wrong?" Irony blended with his desire.

"I've never had an uncircumcised lover before."

"Getting rare these days, I suppose." He paused, then added

by way of explanation, "I wasn't born in hospital." When she didn't answer he asked, "Will it do?" Beneath his dry mockery she heard a defensive edge.

She closed her hand around him, sliding the foreskin in tentative, curious strokings and watching the head emerge, flushed deep rose. She investigated with her lips and tongue and felt him relax. That pleasing her mattered so much to him pleased her still more, and she took him in her mouth, letting him know how perfectly he would do. He drew soft, quick breaths, and she urged him on until he gathered with a different tension, the flared ridge of the head exposed, the shaft straining. Its veins were prominent, and the shape of the head gave its thick, slightly curved strength an elegance that suited him well. Her own sex was tender and swollen in answer, her juices flowing.

Rolling onto her, he reached under her skirt and beneath the lace of her waist band, inquiring by touch before he revealed her. Parting her as carefully as if opening the petals of a flower he spread her wetness over the throbbing center. She sighed, powerfully attuned to his touch, but every nerve sang with a different need, and he sensed it. Quickly he stripped away her skirt, hose and pants and raised over her, his face and body tense. She positioned him. Looking into his eyes she waited to plunge into ecstasy with him at last.

But he remained poised above her, his eyes opaque in the semidarkness. With the tip of his cock he touched her opening just enough to make his holding back intolerable. Controlled skill was not what she wanted now, and she tightened her fingers on his back. silently asking him not to shut himself off from her. His jaw tensed, and with a single small movement he thrust quickly into her, a sensation as swift and subtle as the dart of a snake's tongue. And just as perverse. Instead of going on, he raised again, his body not touching hers. Frustrated with this new game, she tried to roll them over and gain control, but he pressed her shoulders down. He entered her deeply. A sweet pang speared through her and she gasped.

"You like *this*, do you?" On the *this* he pierced her, held off, then penetrated again, dipping into her in sporadic bursts, playing with her expectations, withholding then invading, not building a steady rhythm to his own orgasm but concentrating on her responses. She accepted the bright waves of pleasure he gave her, trying not to care that it was artistry not abandon, wanting him too much to refuse what he insisted on having only on his own terms. Greedy for the sweetness, she closed her eyes to the bitter sight of the restraint in his.

At last his arms tightened and he thrust fast and steady. His driving sent a new orgasm through her, long and sharp. His heart beating hard against her, he stilled, his body tense. He drew a single breath, tight as if with pain, and sighed. At first she thought it was his climax, but his tension did not ease. Waiting, she held him close. Gradually his hardness in her subsided.

It felt wrong. Though he stroked her as if in after-tenderness, his muscles were rigid. Slowly he withdrew and rolled away, face turned up to the ceiling. His eyes were closed, his profile a contained calm.

Softly, she said, "You didn't come."

He opened his eyes. "How very observant of you." His voice grated.

"You're the one who said it's risky trying to sell me a fake."

Now he looked at her. "So I did."

"Then why pretend?"

He did not answer at once. Finally he replied, "The trouble is not with you."

That wasn't enough. Not after he had nearly opened to her. But it was not too late. She had almost reached him, and might yet. "Tell me what you want."

"Nothing," he answered too quickly.

"There's something." She stroked up his thigh, making it a challenge. "I can tell."

"Don't touch me, Catherine."

Startled at his sharpness, she withdrew her hand. "Geoffrey, what's wrong?"

His eyes reflected the dim light more brightly, but he turned them away. "You would rather not know."

"Look, if you have some taste that's a little — unusual, I'm harder to shock than you may think. I'm open to most anything — short of being beaten."

With a speed that astonished her, Geoffrey rolled over, grasping her shoulders. "I shall never strike you, Catherine," he said, eyes wide. Then they narrowed. "And if anyone else does, I'll kill him."

She pulled away, staring at him. For the first time she felt real fear. Not of involvement. Of Geoffrey himself.

He sat up, looking sadly at her. "If I gave you pleasure, it's enough for me."

She kept her distance but told him the truth. "You did. But it'd give me just as much to do the same for you."

"Possibly." He gathered his clothes and left the room.

That was one way to end a conversation. Slowly she dressed, examining the frayed knot of her emotions. She'd believed that even if it complicated things with Terry, making love with Geoffrey would clarify her own feelings. Instead she was lost in a maze of contradictions. Remembering his allergies, she wondered if he was more seriously ill then he let on. Why hadn't she even thought of protection? Maybe she'd just committed the most disastrous carelessness of her life. But none of those fears explained his opening, then withholding. No, she began think he had problems all right, but not physical ones.

Time to get out of it now.

She wished she wanted to. She wished she could believe he was some sadist manipulating her for cold fun. Turning away from that would be easy. But her pain caused him no pleasure.

She stood, struggling against weary defeat. Soon it'll hurt less, she promised herself. I'll go home. I'll plan an Egyptian Thanksgiving feast. I'll appreciate what Terry and I have. I've learned my lesson. Next time I'm tempted, I'll know enough to let fantasy stay where it belongs.

ixteen

"*akud kaam men hina lel-haram,*" said Catherine.

"*Takhud,*" Samira corrected.

"*Takhud,*" Catherine tried to pronounce the harsh-soft sound in the back of her throat.

"Good. Now I say in Arabic, 'Where is the bus stob?'"

"Stop. Does Arabic have p?"

"Stob," Samira attempted it again.

"It's like a b, except you sort of spit: — p."

"Bab! Bap!" Samira tried, and they both laughed. "Pah!"

"That's it! Good."

Samira grinned. "Where is the bus stop: *Fain mahatet el-autobis?*"

Catherine tried to be as careful with the clipped consonants as Samira with her p. "*Fain manatet el-autobis?*"

Samira giggled.

"What?" Catherine asked, miffed when she thought she'd done such a good job.

"Not *manatet*! *Mahatet.* You say the—what you jump in the pool!"

"'Where is the diving board to the bus?'" Catherine burst into laughter with her. "Speaking of bus stops," she said, reminded, "is it dark when you walk home from your bus? Maybe you should get off at that big terminal at Tahrir Square and let me pay taxi fare from there."

"No, when I walk home the sun is gone, but there is still light."

"All right, but be careful. Did you see today's paper?"

"The man, dead? I hear the womans talking on the bus."

With embarrassment, Catherine realized that even if Samira's family could afford newspapers, she might not be able to read. By law at least one child in each family attended school, but not all could be spared from the farm work. Undaunted, Samira jumped up for the *Egyptian Mail* that lay on the dining area table.

Catherine turned to the story. True crime and gruesome murders. Lovely. But better than obsessing about Geoffrey. In the four days since she'd seen him she'd made no decision. Or, too many. She resolved to break it off only to remember his kiss seeking the sharing he dreaded. She longed for him to let down his guard, only to distrust his hint of some urge he wouldn't reveal.

She felt guilt qualms, too. For Terry's sake she'd made an eclectic Thanksgiving feast of turkey stuffed with *ta'amiya* in tamarind sauce, but though that turned out well, her heart wasn't in it, and Terry's mind wasn't on it, either. As he gave her the latest rundown on corporate politics her mind strayed to Geoffrey. His razor wit. His understanding. It was Geoffrey who'd become the friend she needed so badly. Could they just be friends?

But remembering the strong grace of his body, tense with the secrets she had not, after all, uncovered, set her heart hammering. She had never been so absurdly infatuated. At least she kept enough perspective not to call it love. To love someone you had to know him.

Catherine spread the paper on her lap. "'Murder Victim Drained of Blood,'" she read the headline to Samira. "'Habib

Abdel Sabour, an accountant with a Cairo engineering firm, was discovered dead last night at a bus stop on Shirif Street.'"

"What is 'discovered?'"

"They found his body. 'According to a police spokesman'—the police say—'the thirty-seven year old man had a severed jugular vein. The instrument of death is as yet undetermined'—somebody cut his throat, they don't know what with. 'The police are investigating whether Abdel Sabour's death occurred at the stop. His co-workers say he often took the bus after working late.'"

"'Investigating?"

"It sounds like they don't know if he was stabbed there, or if the body was dumped. Either way, I don't want you getting mugged at night."

"On the bus they say this man's money was not gone. Only his blood. Maybe he wasn't killed by—mugs."

"Who, then?"

Samira searched for the English, but gave up. "*Masas ed-demaa,*" she answered darkly.

Catherine had heard random killings were rare in Egypt, but family violence and feuds were both common. "What, an argument? Some enemy?"

"At night, the things that bite the neck and eat the blood."

"Dracula?"

Samira looked stubborn. "Fawzy laughs too."

"I'm not laughing. I just think a human killer is more likely."

The phone shrilled. They both jumped. Samira grinned, but Catherine waited for the second ring before picking it up.

"Cat? It's Judy. Do you mind postponing our dinner plans? Pete's just scheduled a late meeting on Monday."

Monday. Judy and Ibrahim. Dinner. She'd forgotten. "Oh... Maybe later in the week?"

"I'm sorry to upset your plans. I knew we were closing on the land for the next site, but not that I'd be involved. You know how it is." Being the competent one, she meant, expecting Catherine to know the feeling.

But Catherine only felt as addled as if someone had shaken up her brains and poured them back in her head. "No, that's fine, really."

"What's the matter? You sound funny."

"Oh, Samira and I were telling vampire tales."

"*Ed-Dracola*, eh? The office is full of it, too. I called a friend who reports for *al-Ahram*. They're holding back details to avoid a hubbub, but it gets creepier. They didn't identify a murder weapon because there was none. The poor guy's throat was cut by *teeth*. Possibly, an animal's. Weirder yet, there's not a trace of blood at the supposed crime scene. Not even on his clothes."

"Very weird."

"Well, maybe you'd better not tell your maid that. There's bound to be some explanation, and I doubt it's the undead. I'll check with Ibrahim about dinner and get back to you."

When Catherine hung up she found Samira had gone back to work. Breakfast dishes rattled in the kitchen as they were taken from the drainer and put away. "Sand must be clogging my brain," she told the room.

Sand? Its emptiness mocked her. More like, man. Forgetting things wasn't like her. Any more than inability to make decisions. Geoffrey had her tied in knots. Was he worth it? The question was that simple.

If only he wasn't such a good listener. If only talking with him didn't cut through her confusion about the direction her life was taking. She smiled at the recollection of how beautiful he made her feel, and his endearing anxiousness about whether she liked his cock.

But she remembered his grip on her shoulders. *I shall never strike you, Catherine. And if anyone else does, I'll kill him.*

"Hey Cat, are you home? We've hit on the absolute, the stupendous, the most perfect idea. Cat?"

Catherine turned down the oven and went to hug Terry. He gave her a kiss, still talking. "Believe it or not, it's Mr. Beet's idea."

She followed him to the bedroom to sit cross-legged on the foot of the bed and listen as he poured out his hopes and frustrations, their new homecoming ritual.

"The coffee committee collaboration, it'd be good media stuff, right?" He took off his shirt. "Open the dirty clothes?" Catherine leaned over and lifted the lid. Terry wadded his work shirt and fired it into the hamper. "Two points. Where's my rhinoceros tee shirt, have you seen it?"

"I sent it out with the laundry. You wore it four days straight."

"Oh. Well, listen to this. How about a TV documentary? Fareed's café, dreaming up the design. Painting the mural with the coffee committee's help. Lyndore leads the way to global art!"

Catherine smiled. "So, Mr. Beet thinks that's his idea?"

"What?"

"Nothing."

"The timing's perfect. This weekend Mr. Big flies in from Denver. Beet and Big are going to Sharm el-Sheikh, on the Red Sea. The next Lyndore's gonna be a scuba dive resort." Terry threw his decrepit no nukes shirt over his head and looked for his jeans. His legs were skinny as a crane's, she thought absently, trying not to compare them with the lithe muscles of Geoffrey's. And the shadows outlining his calves, tinged crimson by the light through the curtain.

"Mr. Beet will pitch the idea to Mr. Big. If it's yes, we'll 'move decisively on it,' as we say in the World of Busyness." He put on his jeans. Catherine smiled at the Lyndore universe Terry was creating, filled with cartoon characters and fantasy settings.

"After all," he jumped back to the present as he headed down the short hall, "it isn't really a different design, just an 'update.'"

Catherine followed to the living room. "Dinner's ready. Are you hungry?"

"Almost." He slung his long frame onto the sofa and grabbed their trusty old solar calculator from the coffee table. "I want to lock in the contract for the Scuba-dore. Imagine living for a year on the Red Sea!"

Catherine curled into a chair and picked up her book as he immersed himself in square feet and ratios of color mixtures, happy as a clam.

At least, she supposed clams were happy. Clams didn't have to decide what to do about Geoffrey. She was beginning to wonder if she'd have to, either. Five days and no word from him.

It's for the best, she told herself. Whatever he was hiding, it could hardly be good. Yet, it hurt that he'd leave her without even a goodbye. Whatever had gone wrong, the tenderness they had shared surely meant something?

Against the glow of the lamp Terry's profile had a clarity that had always looked Elvish to her. Not cutesy elf. Tolkien elf. She remembered the first time she'd thought that, hiking in the hills above Berkeley with the sunlight and leaf shadows slipping over his face. It made her sad he had no idea what was happening.

Early in their marriage, in more free-spirited years, they'd each had a fling or two, for lust or comfort or friendship. Catherine remembered nights in the dark, pillows propped, feet nestled together, Terry listening to her feelings and telling her his. She should tell him now. With understanding and patience, maybe they'd come through this with a stronger bond than before.

She had no illusions that her feelings for Geoffrey would be easy for Terry to handle just now. Her timing stank. She knew Terry well enough to understand that his bravado covered fear. If Mr. Big didn't go for the scheme, it panicked him that he'd be trapped for a year grinding out a painting he didn't feel right about. But what scared her was how far apart they were drifting.

"Terry," she said.

He looked over at her.

"There's something I want to talk about."

"Sure." He put the pad and calculator on the coffee table.

"Do you remember when I went to the museum?"

"Hey, museum — I meant to tell you— Just a minute, Cat, I want to hear, but it's what sparked the whole scheme. The Brooklyn Museum wants to film us for PBS. Judy says they'll approach it as art, not commercialism, praise Allah. Isn't that great?"

"Great," she said coldly, unable even to try hiding her hurt at his utter self-centeredness.

"Sorry I cut in. What were you saying?"

If that was all he cared, if the whole world revolved around Terry Russio and his damn mural, fine. "Never mind." She opened her book.

"Hey Cat, what's wrong?"

"Nothing."

"I thought you'd want to know." He sounded aggrieved. For a moment he said nothing else, then he sighed. "I know I'm wrapped up in my own stuff lately. I haven't been the best listener." He faced her earnestly, his grey eyes like shallow water after the depths of Geoffrey's. "I feel like I've leased my soul to Lyndore. But it's only leased, not sold. This is temporary."

"I hope you're right."

"I am. Please accept my apology and tell me what you were going to?"

"I'm not angry anymore," she answered, meaning it. All she felt was utterly alone. "I don't feel like going into it now. It'll keep." She started reading. She heard him sit still for a moment. Then he picked up his calculator. The small tappings were like the thud of a heavy door between them. She was not sure whether she was shut in or out, only that where she was it was grey and cold.

 eventeen

 uge and billowing, a paper banner proclaimed: MAADI RECENT PHARMACY. What might it mean? A new pharmacy? A modern one? Or maybe, Maadi's late, lamented pharmacy?

Whatever pharmacy it was, maybe it was open. Terry's stomach was acting up again. Catherine parked the car, which she was driving comfortably now, if not yet amid the rampant whirl at Cairo's center, and went inside.

The place was new. Recent! And brightly lit, with an entire shelf of cures for digestive ailments. She found the pills Terry said decimated the baddest bugs. This was no time for him to have the mummy tummy. Mr. Big was arriving from Denver tomorrow.

Luckily, stronger remedies could be had over the counter in Egypt than back home. She got to the check-out as the man ahead was finishing his purchase. He took his sack from the clerk, glanced at her and paused.

"Ms. Lanier? We met at Groppi. I'm Geoffrey Harrow's client, the one with the shabti."

Even before he spoke she recognized the lean curve of his cheek and long, elegant nose. "Of course." She smiled, wishing she weren't so pleased to encounter even such an indirect connection to Geoffrey. "Good to see you again."

"Mounir Abdel Razak," he reminded her.

She wanted to ask him if Geoffrey had appraised his figurine, if Geoffrey was well, if he was very busy. But she remembered the tension between Geoffrey and his client. She didn't want to pry if the deal had soured for lack of legal documentation. She paid the clerk, giving the young man a chance to say goodbye and go.

But he waited for her. "Antiqa as been closed for three days," he said. "Do you know whether he's out of town?"

That hadn't occurred to her. A sudden business trip, not a cold dismissal. "No idea," she answered. "I don't really know him that well." True, as far as it went.

The young man opened the door for her. "Just as well. I probably couldn't stand parting with my shabti. I want an appraisal, though. I want to know if it was really made for Queen Nefertiti."

The afternoon sun sparkled through the mimosas shading the parking strip. Fern-like shadows swept the sand with each breeze. The sky arched blue. "A magic figure." Catherine smiled. "Nefertiti brought back to life?"

"Speak the right spell and she returns, beautiful and joyful again." Mounir smiled sadly. "I wish that could be."

What a romantic this young man was! "Your village was in the ruins of Amarna? What's left of Akhenaten's city?"

"The remains of walls, worn down by the wind. The British are slowly excavating it. In our teens my friends and I worked for them. My friends wanted to go to Cairo and get rich, but to me, Amarna was the most beautiful place in the world. Do you want to know about it? We can get a Coke over there. A little bit of America for you."

He gestured toward a Pizza Hut with motor scooters parked outside. "Not my favorite bit," she answered. "A childhood with

Akhenaten and Nefertiti should be told in a café by the Nile, not a teen hangout."

"Not my favorite American influence either." But he smiled to soften the criticism. "It's not that I don't want change, but often I feel I was born into the wrong time. I want to look forward, but I keep finding myself looking back."

"Maybe you should have been an ancient Egyptian."

Cairo's top 40 blared as they opened the door. A dozen teenagers lolled in plastic booths, international, bluejeaned and resentful of adult intruders into their lair. Mounir ordered a Coke at the counter, Catherine got tea, and they sat by the front window, a zone avoided by the kids. "Ha," she said. "They don't want their parents spotting them."

"Especially the Egyptian girls. They've said they're at a girl-friend's house, not hanging out with boys. Some put on their jeans once they're away from home, others' families think this is fine. Egypt is crazy, mixed up with too much old and new." He sipped his Coke thoughtfully. "Villages like mine are still very traditional, of course."

"Though Akhenaten and Nefertiti were rebels. Are you descended from their followers?"

"No. We were Bedouins. Our ancestors, the Beni Amran clan, found it deserted and called it after ourselves, Amarna. We knew little of Akhenaten and Nefertiti until Europeans crazy enough to climb the cliffs deciphered the hieroglyps in the old tombs. But you're right, the ancient people do seem very close when I'm there." He put on a stern frown. "Don't revere them, they were not people of the book," he intoned. "That's what our muezzin used to say. Maybe not, but they were people of the light."

"They upset the old priesthoods, who retaliated on them?"

"Nefertiti and Akhenaten died young, but it's a mystery how. Some say a palace coup. Some think a plague killed Nefertiti, or maybe it was Akhenaten who died. All we know is that after they were gone it was a policy to discredit them, even to wipe out every memory of them. The city was abandoned to the sand and wind."

"Moments of beauty," Catherine mused. "Why are they so often ended in destruction?"

A louder song played, a singer pouring out her heart to the catchy five-beat of Egyptian pop music, boom-boom...boom-boom-boom! A kid in a leather jacket got up and strutted to it. Mounir glanced at him and shook his head, but his smile was indulgent.

"I don't know," he answered her. "But when I was their age I hoped to be the one to discover the answers. So did Nefissa, a girl I grew up with. We dreamed we'd be great archeologists. —That is, when she wasn't dreaming of being a queen. Nefissa, Nefertiti, all the same, she claimed."

"Did Nefissa work with the excavations?"

"Her parents wouldn't let her, and Dr. Barry didn't hire girls. Nefissa was so mad at me for getting to that she wouldn't speak to me for weeks."

"Well, it's not fair."

"No, it's not. On Fridays, my day off, we attended mosque, but then Nefissa made me show her where we'd worked that week, and tell her what we'd discovered. Oh, how she bothered me about it, but I'd have done anything for her."

"I hope she became a famous archeologist and showed up everyone who stood in her way."

"I wish she was away at Cambridge now, or some American university." He was stirring the melting ice in his Coke with his straw. He pressed his full lips together hard, as if some thought hurt him too much to let out.

Catherine lowered her gaze to her tea and sipped. She waited, for him to say more if he wanted, or not.

"I did everything for her," he protested, then added, "Except give up hunting."

"You quarrelled about that," Catherine guessed.

"Yes, but I was no different from the other village men in that. Gazelles are wonderful creatures, graceful and gentle, but my mother and sisters welcomed the meat. I think, maybe, Nefissa also envied my freedom to wander alone at the feet of the desert cliffs pursuing them. That was joyful, a chase through a maze of rocks, washed by the sun, and the cliffs gleaming against the blue sky. Tracking a gazelle, you suddenly find yourself in places of great silence. No sound but sand grains blown against the stones, and just beyond your reach, a gazelle, bounding from rock to rock."

The song ended. The boy who'd been dancing fell noisily into his plastic seat. "I talk too much, sometimes," Mounir said. "Thank you for letting me."

But Catherine had a strong feeling he hadn't said what he yearned to. "Did Nefissa marry?" she asked gently. "Is she still in the village?"

"No," he answered sharply. "Her family moved to Cairo, and I followed. We got engaged. But you must have things to do, and I should go back to the office. I have a report to finish. I hope your husband's mural goes well. Thank you for listening," he repeated, rising and picking up his sack of whatever he'd bought from the pharmacy. "Do be safe."

That had an oddly cautionary ring. Catherine watched him go, wondering what he was so reluctant to tell, and what had come between him and his Nefissa.

As she let herself into the apartment the phone began ringing. "I'll get it," she called to Samira. Dropping her keys in the chair and one of the bags of groceries she'd bought on the sofa, she grabbed the receiver with her free hand and stuck it between her shoulder and ear. "Yes, hello?" She set the other bag on the table.

"Have I called at an inconvenient time?" Geoffrey asked.

A subtle catastrophe shook her. He had not abandoned her.

But if not, why string her along for so many days? "I was only trying to hold onto too many things at once."

"Oh?" She heard his cool amusement. "None of them slippery, I hope."

His presumption was beyond belief. "Only one," she flashed out.

There was a pause. "Point taken," he answered at last. "Will you let me make amends? An afternoon at the cinema, a chance to talk?"

Put a stop to it, she commanded herself.

She opened her mouth to tell him it was over.

But she imagined sitting close to Geoffrey in a dark theater, bantering insights shared afterward, the sound of his voice and bright points of light in the darkness of his eyes as he delivered some delicious irony. How could she be missing someone so terribly when she'd spent scarcely eight hours all told with him?

"Tomorrow at one?"

"Yes."

Now you've done it, she thought after she hung up. Who was she fooling? Not herself. Was seeing him one more time really worth the trouble she was asking for? Worth the full-fledged affair that she knew Terry would be unhappy with, that might even endanger their marriage?

No, she answered the incandescence that licked delicately at her bones. It's not wise, not sensible. And yes, Geoffrey's worth it.

But through her elation came Mounir's parting words. *"Do be safe."*

Eighteen

A date to the movies. Catherine suspected Geoffrey of choosing the most disarmingly wholesome activity he could think of. A little necking in the dark maybe, but no chance of being alone together? That was fine with Catherine. Usually she relied on her instincts about people, and usually her instincts were reliable. Why Geoffrey Harrow continued to baffle them was a mystery it was time to solve. His car pulled up in the street below, and she reached for her shoulder bag.

"Black windows." Samira's admiring voice sounded behind her.

Catherine jumped. She'd thought Samira was in the kitchen. Before she could ask whose car it was, Catherine said, "If you finish the cleaning, take the rest of the afternoon off. I may not be home till dinner time."

"Thank you, Cataron!" Samira beamed. Time to herself, that her slave-driving mother-in-law didn't know about, was so precious to Samira that Catherine tried to make sure she got a little every week. But that wasn't her only reason. Samira assumed that behind the smoked windshield she admired so much was some woman friend like Marilee Burge or Judy Bakhir. In Samira's world, nice women didn't traipse around alone with men. Geoffrey had not opened his car door. Thankful for his discretion, Catherine hurried out, slid in beside him and shut it.

He was a shadow. Night black from turtleneck to boots, he was graceful as some predatory feline. Catherine took a quick breath, but only allowed, "So, today you're a panther."

"If you like." His answer was a low purr, but his eyes were guarded.

"I do like," she replied, but casually, a compliment but not an invitation.

He started the car. She hadn't foreseen wanting him so immediately, or so much, as if being close to him rubbed out every doubt she had.

"Since you're looking for good books in English, I brought two for you to borrow," Geoffrey said. "They're on the back seat."

Catherine reached for them. Both were fiction by authors with Arabic names.

"Two of Egypt's leading writers, in translation." He cut a sharp turn onto the Cornishe. "Naguib Mahfouz is a Nobel Prize winner. 'Midaq Alley,' is his best known, but I like 'Miramar' better. The other is a novel by Nawal el-Saadawy. Unlike Mahfouz, she is *not* universally loved. Her outspoken feminism has cost her time in prison. I thought you'd be interested."

"I am," Catherine said, surprised. But then, one of the few predictable things about Geoffrey was the impossibility of classifying him.

Searching for the right words, she watched him thread nimbly through the traffic. If he sensed it, he gave no sign. His clear cut profile was composed.

"I came close to telling Terry about you."

"Because you're having second thoughts."

"Like you are."

"Yes." After a moment he asked, "Why didn't you?"

"First, I want you to know that if I had, it wouldn't necessarily change much. Terry and I aren't monogamous. It's been a long time, but I'm not unfaithful to the vows we made. It's my not telling him that I feel is wrong."

"A modern marriage," Geoffrey replied. "All as civilized and above-board as the meat on the table."

She felt the sting. Was it disapproval, or jealousy? "Love and possessiveness are not the same thing," she countered.

"I wouldn't know. I haven't your purity of heart."

"Or do you just love secrecy for its own sake?" When he didn't answer, she added, "No marriage is simple, but ours can't be all that incomprehensible."

"It is to me."

"Good. I'd hate to think I'm ordinary."

"Passion balanced by an honesty just as deep is not ordinary," he replied quietly.

Startled, Catherine turned to look at him, but he refused to glance at her. He set his lips more firmly. "I'd still rather your husband didn't know," he said at last.

"If we go on," she reminded him.

He nodded, acknowledging. "If not, it's none of my business."

To the left the Nile lay beyond a strip of park. The sun shone so brilliantly that even through the grey glass the water was jade green. "Have you been to the movies in Cairo yet?" he changed the subject.

"No," she followed the change with relief. "I was warned against going alone."

"With good reason. Prostitutes work the cinemas. It would never occur to some men that a woman alone might simply want to watch the film." He glanced at her with the hint of an ironic smile. "I don't include myself in that company, but you're in for an experience."

"Why?"

Amusement glinted in his eyes. "As I delight in unnecessary mysteries, I shall let you find out for yourself."

"Do you ever wonder if life might be easier if you were less impossible?"

"Or far more difficult." Geoffrey turned onto 26 July Street, away from the river. "Do you like Meryl Streep?" he added with a hint of his velvety undertone.

"Is that appreciation of her acting I hear, or lust?"

He smiled. "Both."

"Then, what if I said I'd rather see Tom Cruise?"

"You fancy him, do you?" Geoffrey asked, interested.

"Not especially." She smiled at his curiosity whether it was true.

"Then, who?"

"That's *my* secret," she returned, thinking: Geoffrey Harrow.

But the Meryl Streep film was sold out. They settled on a Japanese police drama at a nearby theater, since the ticket seller assured them it was dubbed in English. As they walked in, the movie was just starting. Cigarette smoke billowed so thickly the screen was hazy. The audience seemed more interested in their conversations than the film. Before Geoffrey could take off his dark glasses, refreshment sellers converged on them, loudly offering everything from chocolate bars to cow peas still in the pod. Catherine chose an orange, Geoffrey chose nothing, and they found a seat near the back where the smoke was less thick.

On the screen, a police car swerved to a halt and an officer built like a sumo wrestler burst out with a drawn gun. The audience made anticipatory remarks to each other. The dialogue began in Japanese, not dubbed. The subtitles were in Arabic.

"I don't know Japanese," Geoffrey said, "and I promise not to peek at the Arabic."

"Make up our own story?" Catherine smiled.

"You take the crooks. The cops are mine."

They traded impromptu dialogue, saying I told you so when the action seemed to confirm the absurd tale they wove and laughing as their story soared to ever greater outrageousness. Catherine had never heard Geoffrey laugh out loud. The sound held a resonance as different from his ironic edge as noon from midnight. She touched his hand and he closed it around hers. Despite the stuffy theater his skin was cool, his fingers strong and gentle.

"When must you be back?" he asked as the credits rolled.

"Terry's out tonight, and I told Samira to go when she was done. I feel happier knowing she's taking the bus by day."

"Ah, the phantom murderer."

"Paranoia would be silly, but there are other dangers. She lives in a rough neighborhood."

"Actually, I think you're right to urge caution. Since your husband and maid are both taken care of, I'd rather not give you up yet." As if tempting her to great wickedness, he arched a brow. "Another film?"

"Let's," Catherine answered, feeling like a kid sneaking off with the candy box. This innocent mischief was their most delightful companionship yet, forgetting the needs and betrayals of passion, just talking silliness and holding hands.

ineteen

uiet filled the twilit street. "I like leaving movies almost as much as watching them," she told him. "They're another dimension. The door from any theater leads back to our universe, but I have to stop a minute and remember whether it's San Francisco, Kentucky or Cairo. I've been that completely gone."

"Like waking after dreaming?" he asked.

"Yes. Doesn't it seem so?"

"I can't recall." He sounded wistful. "It's been a long time since I dreamed."

"Since you remember it. Everybody dreams."

"I don't. Are you hungry?"

"Not especially."

"Good." Stepping to the curb he waved down a caleche. The driver reined in the horse and they climbed in. The top was still up, and within its privacy they sat, thighs lightly touching. The driver urged the horse to a trot along the narrow straightway of the Shari'a Champollion. Lights were coming on in shops, and people strolled the edges of the street, greeting friends and looking for bargains or amusement. Cairo came alive by twilight.

"Tonight is Baudelaire's '*Le flacon*'" Geoffrey said. "The flask is open, and its perfume fills the air with memories.

"Mille pensers dormaient, chrysalides funèbres,
Frémissant doucement dans les lourdes ténèbrès,
Qui dégagent leur aile et prennent leur essor,
Teintés d'azur, glacés de rose, lamés d'or."

"Translate," she asked, listening to the yearning in the Egyptian folk music that drifted down from some window.

In a voice as still as a twilit pool he answered, "A rather free rendition might go:

"Myriad thoughts slumbered, funereal chrysalids,
Softly throbbing in the dim shadows.
Shaking free their wings they take flight,
Luminescent azure, opalescent rose, incandescent gold."

"Some memory is making you sad," she said softly.

He did not answer. The hoof beats marked off the slowly passing doorways. Wanting more of the sound of his voice, she said, "Arabic, French, you mentioned reading Borges in Spanish. How many languages do you know?"

"Nearly a dozen. But I'm out of practice with some."

"You must have talent for them."

"It was drilled into me at university. In my college, expressing oneself fluently mattered above all else. Hopelessly traditional, I felt. I preferred an empirical approach."

"Straight humanities? Sounds very radical to me, for a Cambridge college in the—what, sixties? Which college was it?"

He paused. "University education is your field, of course. I forgot. Tell me, Catherine, do you know the ancient Egyptian belief about night? By evening the sky goddess Nut comes to Geb, the earth god. She arches her starry body over him, and her darkness is fertility, the darkness of the womb. And of the tomb, which they also regarded as a source of life."

Catherine listened to the depths gathering in his voice, stirred by the sound, the touch of his thigh, but however compelling his subterfuge, he'd again deflected the subject from his past. The caleche entered the Cornishe with its bright streetlights. "Geoffrey," she said.

"Yes?" he murmured.

"Why did Judy warn me against you?"

"That I am 'a shady character?'"

Catherine frowned. He'd been sitting across the room when Judy made her "shady character" remark. They hadn't repeated it to him.

"Better shady than ponderous," Geoffrey remarked with a touch of spite.

"Maybe, but Judy is smart and diligent." She changed the subject. "Did you ever appraise that figurine? I ran into Mounir Abdel Razak the other day."

"Did you?" Geoffrey's voice sharpened.

"So the deal didn't work out? He told me about growing up in Akhenaten and Nefertiti's city. He loves Amarna. No way can I see him running around selling off bits of it on the black market."

"No? He came by my shop and tried to interest me in the shabti again, still without papers. Of course, there is another possibility, isn't there?"

"What, a government agent trying to trap you?"

"It wouldn't be the first time. That's why gossip like Judy Bakhir's can be so damaging when a dealer is too successful. I wonder if Mounir's running into you was really accidental?"

Catherine frowned. "I don't know, that wasn't how it felt. He's..." she searched her impressions. "He's sincere."

"Then he's interested in you."

"Don't be silly, I'm too old for him."

Geoffrey spoke in Arabic to the driver. The caleche halted by the stone railing. Beyond it, the Nile glittered with reflected lights. "A walk?" Geoffrey leapt down and turned to help her.

With his black clothing blending into the darkness, his face and outstretched hand seemed eerily disembodied. Misgiving seized her, but his fingers brushed hers gently. His hand closed cool around hers. With a graceful ease, as if he'd practiced the obsolete courtesy a thousand times, he handed her down from the carriage.

They strolled in silence along the bank. In leafy shadow they paused to watch the wavering reflections of the lights. Geoffrey's hand sought hers again, but his skin now seemed chill in the evening air.

"I've spoilt your mood," he said. "The fact is, I do suspect Abdel Razak of being a government agent. A rather bumbling one, if he approached you. I am not stupid enough to take his bait, and I dislike his prying."

"He didn't ask about you, except whether you were in town."

"Establishing trust first, perhaps?"

"Why are you so cold-blooded?"

"Cold-blooded? Is that what you think?" He pulled her against him and parted her lips, the cool of his mouth mingling with the heat of his impetuousness. Catherine tensed, but stronger than startlement, or eagerness, rose her desire to seize the truth about Geoffrey Harrow. She opened every sense to the tension of his body, the faint, bittersweet musk of him, the quickening of his breathing. With eager yet lingering attention he stroked her tongue with his, now softer, now harder, now softer again. Slowly he withdrew. He looked as startled as she felt, but he did not try to disown what they had shared.

Instead, he gave her his slight, dry smile, a full admission of his vulnerability to her. *I'm in love with this man*, Catherine realized. *Not just in lust. I care for him.*

"You are too tempting a refuge," he murmured. "Too compelling. From the moment I first saw you in the museum I wanted to taste. . . " He turned her hand, running his fingertip down her wrist. ". . . your beauty. Because you *are* beautiful, Catherine. More than your husband, or any of them, know." He caressed her inner wrist, his finger gliding lightly. "Your skin is so transparent I can see the tracery of the veins beneath, blue with the dark wine of your blood." He bent to her, his lips parting to brush her wrist. His tongue swept swift and cool, making her catch her breath.

"Let's go to your house," she said.

"Don't ask that."

"Then a hotel, I don't care. I want you now, Geoffrey."

"Will you not understand that though I can't stop myself from seeing you, from touching you, I do not choose to feel this way?" With some emotion she could not identify, he implored, "Tell me you love your husband, and I mean nothing to you."

"I wish it were true."

With a groan he held her closer.

Abruptly he moved away. "Do you imagine I'm looking for some ridiculous conquest? I've avoided entanglement for a long time. I wish to continue that way. That first day, I asked you to tea hoping you would bore me and I could forget you. I wanted no part of it. Then, or now."

"Why do you do this?" she asked. "Not just to me, to yourself?"

"Because love destroys. I want only to be unencumbered by attachments or regrets."

"What's been done to you to make you so bitter?"

"A more relevant question is what I have done to others."

"I'm listening."

He turned away into the shadow of the trees.

Steadily, she said, "Give me a good reason to break it off."

"Isn't my silence enough?"

"I honestly don't know," she answered quietly, miserably.

He sighed and closed his arms around her. She stood in them, shaking with weariness and fury at him, and at herself for loving him. "This must end," he said. "I'm no good for you, Catherine. Believe me that I will not call you. I don't want you calling me. Stay away, and I promise I'll pursue you no longer."

They did not ride back to the car in silence, they talked about small things, both realizing it was their last time together and neither wanting to waste a moment of it. He drove to Maadi by the most direct route, but not fast. When he stopped outside her building he did not touch her. He studied her face by the dim illumination of the dashboard. She flicked on the overhead light so they could see each other better, looked at him a sad moment longer, then got out of the car. As she started up the walk she heard the car door open. Geoffrey came up to her. "I want you to have the books. Keep them."

A parting gift, a bond between them after he was gone. As she took them he touched her hand. Then the darkness engulfed him. The uneven throb of her heart was so loud that she did not hear the car start, but its lights began to move. With a small cry she hurried toward the door, but instead found herself turning. Too late. He was driving away.

Lights shone in the apartment windows. She steadied herself, then let herself in, deliberately climbed the stairs and with the same resolve unlocked the apartment door. "Terry?"

Instead, Samira stood in the living room. "You're still here?" Catherine asked. "What's wrong?"

Samira watched her put down the books. Her face was as aggrieved as if it were she who had been betrayed. At last she answered, "Problem in the water."

Catherine hurried into the bathroom and found a leak in the pipe between the tank and toilet, and the bucket Samira had stayed long past her usual time to empty so it would not overflow. "Thank you." She searched for what else to say.

"Welcome, Madam," Samira answered, as if to a stranger. "Now I go."

"Not by bus in the dark. I'll pay your cab fare."

"Thank you, Madam."

When Samira had gone Catherine lay in the dark bedroom fighting futile tears.

Twenty

atherine stared wearily down at her fried egg. Her fried egg stared back up at her. "Today'll decide it, one way or the other," Terry said with certainty. Despite his excitement, he yawned. "It took a fifth of scotch and a belly dance show for Mr. Beet and Mr. Big to brainstorm the idea of an American-Egyptian mural, but they finally did. They asked me if I'd mind incorporating some of my coffeehouse buddies' ideas into my work! If I'd mind sharing the credit with them!" But his own glee made him groan. "My head! I need some aspirin, I didn't sleep too well."

"I'm sorry if I kept you awake," she said. "I tried to be quiet."

"You were. The living room light didn't bother me, but I saw it on. What were you doing up so late?"

"Reading." Or, trying to. Halfway through, she still mixed up the residents of Midaq Alley, and it wasn't Mahfouz's fault.

"Back to the old days, huh? Remember how we used to sit up all night, you with your guitar and me with my paint? Why don't you get yourself a guitar? A better one, we can afford it."

She looked across the table at him. He was busily sopping up his egg yolk with some flat bread. It wasn't that he didn't notice anything was wrong. He was trying very hard not to notice. "So, how should we celebrate? Now that it looks as if it's all working out, I'll tell you there were times I really doubted."

"I know," she said, then smiled at him. "But after all your work and worry, it's really happening. Just as you deserve."

"If Mr. Big likes the idea sober as much as he did last night, let's have Judy and Ibrahim over to celebrate. It's as much Judy's doing as mine."

"Sure, if you want."

"Aw, come on, Cat. All's well. I'll have more free time now. We're waiting for one more permit before I can start painting. Let's use the delay to see the pyramids. I tried to phone you about it yesterday afternoon. Several times."

"I was at the movies."

"Oh. See anything good?"

"A cop thing and a comedy."

Since her conversation didn't exactly sparkle, he glanced again at the paper. "Did you see this weirdness? The vampire's moved to Maadi." He sobered. "Well. It's not funny. A woman's been killed. She went out last night and never returned. They found her behind her apartment building. It's like the bus stop murder last week, she was drained of blood. No way, it's just too strange."

Catherine took the paper and tried to focus where he pointed. "That's only two blocks from here."

"You didn't know her, I hope?"

"Her name's not familiar. But I let Samira wait outside for a taxi, and you came home drunk. It could've been one of you."

"Or you," he answered soberly.

She'd been in no danger, she'd been with Geoffrey. But they all needed to be more careful. She put the paper down.

"I thought we'd left stuff like this behind in Berserkely. Remember Ophelia, that girl who hung out on Telegraph Avenue in the slinky black dresses, purple nails three inches long? The teenies thought she was cool until she cut that kid and tried to suck his blood." He finished his coffee. "You and Samira be careful till they catch this loony, huh? Keep the door locked."

"We will," Catherine answered dully. If Samira ever came back, she thought.

Samira arrived at the usual time. She needed her job, of course. But she wouldn't meet Catherine's eyes. *It's not fair*, Catherine wanted to cry out, *Geoffrey and I only said goodbye*. But what Samira blamed her for was true. However briefly, she'd taken a lover, and even if she never saw him again she still loved him. "I've taped up the leak," she said instead, "but it oozes, so the bucket should be emptied once or twice a day until the plumber comes."

"Yes, Madam." Samira saw Catherine had done the dishes and got out the broom. Blue shone at her throat, a small pendant shaped like an open hand. In the palm was a bright blue bead.

"That's an interesting necklace. Does it mean anything?"

"For the evil eye," Samira answered briefly. "For bad things."

"Yes," Catherine answered, "I want you home before dark."

"Thank you, Madam." Samira concentrated on the sweeping.

Catherine missed speculating with her about this second murder, sharing the shock of its nearness, but plainly, Samira no longer wanted to share fellow feeling with her. She was just another promiscuous Western woman, the kind of bad influence Samira's mother-in-law warned her against.

"I'm getting out of here," she said. "If Terry calls, I've gone for a walk."

Samira just looked at her.

The phone rang.

For an instant Catherine thought it might be Geoffrey. But before she touched the receiver the illusion fragmented. He'd meant what he said.

"Catherine?" A man's voice. She didn't recognize it. "This is Mounir Abdel Razak. We have to talk, it's important."

"What? How do you know my number?"

"You told me your husband's name. It's listed. There's something I didn't tell you—I thought—" he sounded desperate. "It's all changed, and you need to know. Please don't think I want anything improper. Will you meet me, I beg you?"

All she felt was weary disillusionment. Geoffrey was right, Mounir had some agenda. He wasn't the innocent dreamer he'd pretended to be. Geoffrey Harrow, Mounir Abdel Razak, whatever they were playing at, she wanted no part of it.

"Can you come to Fishawy? It's a café in the Khan el-Khalili. Any taxi driver knows it."

"Listen—"

But he'd hung up.

She took a cab to the Khan el-Khalili. Not because she trusted Mounir. Or believed Geoffrey's suspicions, either. Government agents didn't work like this. Some other thing was going on, and she needed to know what it was. Or was it that she couldn't let go until she knew the truth about Geoffrey?

As she got out of the taxi the sun felt warm. Boys were already sprinkling water to lay the dust in the lanes of the gaudy bazaar, this biggest tourist trap in Cairo. Tee shirted shoppers wandered among booths of fluttering galabiehs, hanging brass lamps, and silver jewelry. Walking down the alley as the driver had directed, she saw outdoor tables under awnings and entered Fishawy, a maze of small rooms and their mirrored reflections.

Carved wood, scuffed floors, tables crowded into every cranny, the café was thickening with smoke from the hookahs some of the patrons were already puffing on. She spotted Mounir at a table near the door where the air was fresher. He waved.

Government agent, indeed. The young man's jeans and white shirt were crisp, but his dark curls looked mussed as if he'd been running his hand distractedly through them.

"I thought you wouldn't come," he said with obvious relief. "Tea?"

"Arab coffee." She needed the jolt. He signaled a waiter and gave the order.

"What's so important to tell me?"

"What I didn't say about Nefissa."

This was too strange. "Why?"

"Because you need to know. I told you she was my Nefertiti. Proud, beautiful, the woman of the tender smile. She was, but she could be bossy, stubborn, fearless to a fault. I followed her to Cairo, won her love and her family's approval. But she insisted that when we married she wouldn't give up her job. It took her into bad neighborhoods, but she was doing her small part to make them better, she said. She couldn't stand to feel caged, she had to do what she felt was right."

He paused as the waiter brought their coffee.

When he'd gone, Mounir gestured with his hand. "So, I gave in," he said. "Stupidly, wrongly." His hand tightened to a fist. "Sell the Nefertiti shabti that Nefissa found in the cliffs and gave to me? Never!"

"Then why pretend you would?"

"Because they're alike in one more way. Nefertiti just vanished from history. Nobody knows how she died."

"Nefissa is dead?"

"I believe she is. But no one knows, her parents, or me, or the police. She worked for the Ministry of Health, as I do. Opthalmia is endemic here. People don't have to go blind, it's curable. Many women from the villages don't trust city doctors. Nefissa visited them and persuaded them to get help for their children. One evening she went to see a mother in Shubra. She never came back."

Mounir sagged in his chair, fighting to control his voice. "That's why I need an excuse to see Geoffrey Harrow." Steadying himself, he said quietly, fiercely, "Geoffrey Harrow knows what happened to Nefissa."

wenty-one

ome tourists came in and claimed a table nearby, chattering away in Dutch. Mounir gazed at them unseeing, his dark eyes devoid of hope. None of this made any sense. "Geoffrey knew Nefissa?"

"I have no reason to think so. But that may not have been necessary to him. I'm a hunter. I know something of hunters, and Harrow is one."

"What are you saying?"

"I think you're in danger. When I first saw you through the window at Groppi, the two of you were flirting. I didn't know how well you knew him and I even thought you might be his partner in it. I realize now that you're not. You don't know what Harrow is." He paused, and corrected himself. "What he may be. What I suspect he is."

"A killer, you're saying?"

"There seemed no connection between Nefissa's disappearance in Shubra and a so-called 'vampire' murder at a bus stop in a completely different part of town."

"Mounir—"

"For one thing, when a beautiful woman is waylaid—" His hand clenched around his coffee cup. "You know what I mean. But the bus stop victim was a man. I suspected no link, until this morning when I read about the murder in your neighborhood. No, let me finish, Catherine. Harrow was in your neighborhood last night."

This man was stalking Geoffrey, following him around. Catherine wanted to go, but didn't dare.

"And he was in Shubra the night Nefissa disappeared. Two people admit they saw her that night. The woman she went to visit, and an old woman who lived nearby. It was late, but too hot to sleep, and she sat at her open window. She saw a woman walk by on the street below. A woman wearing Western clothes, unusual in Shubra, and a blue and white headscarf. Nefissa wore a headscarf when she went to talk with country women. It had blue and white stripes. Not long after, the old lady saw another unusual sight. A man also dressed in Western clothes got into a parked car and drove away. It was a small black car."

"That's enough evidence to accuse him?"

"The man had dark hair and Harrow's height and build."

"So he must have been Geoffrey? And he happened to be in the neighborhood where Nefissa—or someone else with a blue and white scarf—walked earlier, so he must have killed her?" Utter disbelief at such an irresponsible accusation made her voice too loud. The Dutch tourists stared at them.

"This is why I didn't want to tell you," he said quietly. "I know how crazy it sounds, put like this. There's more, but I promised not to tell that information, or where I got it. I wouldn't tell you any of this if I wasn't afraid you're in danger."

"If you want me to pay attention, you *will* tell me."

"I can't. Will you be satisfied with this? License plate. Last two numbers."

"The same as Geoffrey's? That definitely makes him a serial killer. Listen, Mounir. What if Nefissa isn't dead? You say she did things her own way, that she felt caged. What if she just needed to cut loose?"

"Escape from me?"

"Or her parents," she tried to soften it.

"Of course I've thought of those things. But she wouldn't. You didn't know Nefissa, her pride in her honesty. If she wanted to be rid of me, she'd own up to it." He ran his hand through his hair. "Even if she did, why would she leave her family, her friends, her job? That makes no sense."

Unless, Catherine thought, Nefissa was involved with another man. From Samira's reaction to her own behavior last night, Catherine could imagine all too well what an Arab woman night face if her fiancé and family discovered she had a lover. Maybe just going off with her lover, leaving her name behind and taking his, was simply the easier solution.

"What do the police think?"

"They don't, anymore. It's seven months past, and what's one missing person in this huge city? Why should the police make it harder on themselves? But I know Nefissa is dead. I can feel it. Like a deadness in here." He touched his fist to his chest.

Unfortunately, it did seem more likely to her that he was right than that a woman would leave behind her entire identity, family and friends. Not unless she'd been involved in doings far more radical than Mounir knew about, and had needed to escape the authorities. —Who might have caught her and dragged her off to prison without a trial, or even official acknowledgment.

Or, if some extremist group imagined Nefissa was a feminist threat, might they have taken her out? A horrible thought, but so was a random act of street violence. For Mounir, maybe any answer, even the worst, was less painful than uncertainty.

"You see, it's this," he told her quietly. "This, that you need to know. Last night, when Geoffrey Harrow took you home and drove away, he didn't go back to the city. He drove down the Cornishe, as if he would. But then he doubled back. He drove back to Maadi, Catherine. Then, the woman was killed."

He paused as if expecting an interruption. When she remained silent, he continued, "I'm not judging you. Your life is your own—unless someone steals it from you. A man and a woman have had their lives stolen from them. So, it's not about sex maybe, but both were bled to death and that looks like a ritual. Serial killers invent rituals. Before these two, no bodies were found, but some serial killers, I've read, have a growing need to display what they do. My Nefissa may have been an early killing. Between her and your neighbor last night, there is the common thread of Harrow in his black car. Black in the night, with the windows too dark for anyone to see into."

Catherine shook her head. "I've got to go."

"Did you quarrel with him last night? Did you turn him down? Does the killing of your neighbor mean anything to you, might it be a message to you?"

"This is crazy." She stood up. "I won't listen to any more unfounded accusations."

Mounir only remained where he was, looking up at her as if he understood. "You're right that I don't have enough to take to the police. Not yet. But Catherine, I pray to Allah that when I do, the evidence that finally convicts Harrow isn't your death."

Twenty-two

shall never strike you, Catherine. And if anyone does, I'll kill him. But men made dumb threats like that. Whatever came between Geoffrey and his ability to let go and love, every touch he'd given her, every expression she'd caught in his eyes showed her a complex man, moody, but never a psychopath.

Mounir had constructed a dark fantasy to fit his worst nightmares. Because an old woman saw Nefissa, and later a black car, Mounir had decided Geoffrey was a murderer. When the 'vampire' killings happened along, he'd tacked them onto Geoffrey's bill, too.

"Your skin is so transparent I can see the tracery of the veins beneath, blue with the dark wine of your blood."

Geoffrey had a poetic streak, that was all. He'd done nothing to suggest even garden variety sadism, much less 'ritual' behavior. Mounir's vagueness about all that showed he knew no more about serial killers than she knew from movies.

"If it weren't for your husband I would kiss the blood to the surface and deliciously mark you."

So what? If Mounir really had other reasons for suspecting Geoffrey, why wouldn't he say them? But he must have some source of information beyond what the police would tell a citizen. Especially since, if the police suspected harm had come to Nefissa, her fiancé would automatically be among their suspects. How did Mounir know about the man getting into black car, or that the old lady had seen part of its license number? Would the police share so much even with her parents? Not if they were like the police back home.

In all of Cairo, how had Mounir identified Geoffrey from a vague description and two digits of a license number? He must have had help from someone with access to official records. That made it all the more risk for him to tell her about it. He claimed she was in danger, but on what grounds? What if Mounir was imaginining all of this and it was actually Geoffrey who was in danger from Mounir?

Imagining all this, except for the killer who believed he was a vampire, or who wanted others to believe it. A killer who'd struck last night in her neighborhood.

Where Geoffrey had been last night.

Blue with the dark wine of your blood.

As Catherine unlocked the apartment door she remembered a glimpse of Ophelia sheltering from the sun in the underground BART station. Ophelia, with her secretive little smile.

Her entire life was spinning out of control. It pushed her to the verge of panic. She let herself in and locked the door behind her. "Samira?"

"Here, madam." The rasp of scrubbing began in the kitchen. Catherine put down her shoulder bag and kicked off her shoes without the scrubbing giving any sign of letting up. She sat on the end of the couch farthest from the phone.

One bright morning, walking along the path by Lake Merritt in Oakland, she'd spotted something big and grey-white against the levee. As it floated, bumping the concrete wall, she saw it was a dead manta ray, at least a yard from one tip of its winglike fins to the other. It looked way too big to have washed in through the sluices with the tide. Then it occurred to her it might not have come from the bay at all, but lived its life in the salt backwater of the lake. She remembered the vertigo as her world shifted. Walking by the lake each day she'd seen its surface, no farther down than the birds, and the fish they dived after. For the first time she'd wondered how deep the familiar water was, and what unknown things lurked so near. The bloated greyish thing bobbed in the water, mocking her illusion of a safe, understood world.

She slid across the couch, picked up her address book, and dialed. "Judy? This is Catherine. I have an odd favor to ask."

"Ask away," Judy's voice came over the line, gratingly cheerful.

"It's about that murder in my neighborhood."

"Dreadful, isn't it? I hope she wasn't a friend of yours?"

"I never met her, but it's too close for comfort. Have you heard anything else from your reporter friends that isn't in the papers?"

"Hm," Judy answered thoughtfully. "I know someone I can ask. Let me see what I can dig up. By the way, even ask we speak, Pete and Terry are in a meeting with Hal from Denver. It's about you-know-what."

"I'll keep my fingers crossed. Thanks." Catherine hung up and paced to the window, then back. Grabbing a pillow from the sofa she hurled it hard as she could. It hit the wall with a muted *thuf* and flopped to the floor.

Collapsing on the couch she laughed in exasperation at the futility of all she did. Cut off from her past, her surroundings, from herself, how could she guess whether Mounir's grief had unsettled his mind, or if he was using her in some vendetta against Geoffrey? Maybe it was over black market antiquities after all.

Or why Geoffrey had ended their affair even as he seemed to fall in love with her.

Geoffrey had been married twice. Presumably he'd been hurt, carried baggage, but so did most people. Geoffrey's barriers were so impenetrable there had to be more explanation than that.

Like, that his vehement denial about hitting came from a fear that his most powerful desires really would harm her. Like, that his swings between seduction and coldness were an attempt to scare her away for her own good.

Oh right, and he was also a vampire. Driving home to his nice, comfy coffin he'd changed his mind and decided to stick his fangs into a snack…she stopped her giggle before it turned hysterical.

It took forever for the phone to ring.

"I talked with my friend Mahmoud, with *el-Ahram*," Judy told her. "You're right, there are details they've been told not to print. The authorities are afraid of a panic. The puncture marks weren't supposed to be mentioned, and there are other bizarre details. There wasn't a drop of blood near either body, yet your neighbor left home only thirty minutes before she was found dead. Hardly enough time to drag her off, wait for her to bleed to death, clean up the corpse and deposit it neatly behind her building, eh?"

Judy was enjoying this. "Any theories?" Catherine asked.

"If he—or should I say, they—bled the victims on the spot, what'd they do with the blood?"

"Why 'they'?"

"Mahmoud made a good point. One person can't gulp all the blood in a human body—ugh, what a thought. They'd have to pump it into a container and carry it off. To do it so efficiently, even a team would need practice. Starting on animals, for instance. Journalist theories lean toward a cult. Why would anyone else bother? The police are seeking similar m.o.'s outside Egypt. Well, that's it. Not very reassuring, but the first killing was nowhere near you. If they do it again they'll probably pick some new part of the city. Oh, here's Terry! He looks like he's got news. Terry, it's Cat." Catherine heard the phone handed over.

"Whoopeee!"

"Sounds like yes." Catherine felt a flash of happiness for him.

"Mr. Big's on board, Mr. Beet's taking the credit, and I'm taking my ass over to the site right now. Get some champagne, Cat! Bye."

In doubled relief Catherine put down the receiver. Terry would do the mural of his dreams, and Judy's reporter friend was right. No one could accomplish that grisly act alone so quickly, and joining cults was hardly Geoffrey's style.

Neither was making off with jars of blood, even if the stuff fascinated him. She felt thoroughly ashamed of herself for her imaginings. She felt sorry for Mounir Abdel Razak, but he was desperate for an answer to a mystery that might never be solved. So desperate that he'd taken to following Geoffrey through the city, and spying on Geoffrey and her last night.

Mounir was charming, persuasive, she liked him, but she'd never have gone off the deep end if Geoffrey hadn't hurt her. Part of her must want to believe the worst of him. She felt thoroughly ashamed of herself.

Geoffrey was afraid to love. That much was clear. If the loss of a sweetheart obsessed Mounir, what about Geoffrey losing his son? Yet if he dreaded intimacy, he wanted it. Needed it.

Not that he was blameless. For one who feared pain, he dealt out too much of it. She didn't care for his macho possessiveness, either. But his protectiveness showed he cared.

He was going to find it harder than he thought to escape his caring.

With a steady hand Catherine dialed his number.

Two rings.

"Yes?" Geoffrey answered.

His single curt syllable was so typical she couldn't help smiling. But she let him hear all the quiet force of her faith in him. "It's not over, Geoffrey."

He was silent.

"Do you understand?"

At last he answered. The reluctance and hunger in his voice encompassed all passion, and all promise, as night encompasses the conflagrations of all the stars. "I understand."

Twenty-three

ack your bags, Cat! Big and Beet want me to look at the Sharm el Sheikh site with them. We get a long weekend brainstorming on the beach, and Lyndore's footing the bill. We leave Thursday, back Sunday night."

"The day after tomorrow?"

"Yeah, Mr. Big's into power. Snap your fingers and see the underlings jump. He's a playpen bully, but he'll be gone soon, so just relax, watch the circus, and enjoy the beach."

Four days as part of Mr. Big's entourage, playing cards with Marilee Burge while the guys drank and Terry tried not to mind being treated like a serf, weren't exactly her idea of fun. Besides, sometime in those four days she'd hoped to see Geoffrey.

Then the full meaning of her thought struck her.

All day she fought a tug of war with her conscience. If she hadn't told Terry what was going on, at least until now she hadn't lied to him either. If he'd asked, if he'd noticed, she'd have told him the truth. To beg off the trip for any reason but the real one was to look Terry in the face and lie.

But four days could make the difference between confusion and finding some way to work this mess out. If Geoffrey's reluctance, whatever it was, could be understood and overcome, she and Geoffrey needed this time. If not, they could part without blame or bitterness. Either way, once she knew where things stood, she had to tell Terry.

Catherine did not fool herself that this plan justified deception, but if Mr. Big making employees jump was inconsiderate, what about Terry's "pack your bags," without even asking if she had other plans? He'd said he needed her in Egypt. She'd given up her work, her friends, her life as she knew it, to give him the companionship he's asked her for. Now, he was too busy for it. There was more than one kind of betrayal.

She sighed. Once none of this could have happened, but that time was gone. It had slipped away so slowly that neither of them had noticed. Now life offered her an unexpected gift of rare beauty. She had a choice. She could refuse this awakening. She could go back to the dulled existence of habit and safety. But wasn't that a betrayal, too?

She called Geoffrey. His phone rang four times. Then his voice answered, but tinny and speaking Arabic. He repeated in English, requesting the caller to leave name, number and time of call after the tone.

It was no way to deliver her proposition. Catherine hung up without leaving a message, but hearing his civilized voice touch even that innocent message with irony ignited a thousand fragments of fantasy.

Samira was vacuuming the bedroom. Catherine got out the hotel pamphlets she'd collected when she still hoped Terry and she would spend a weekend at the pyramids. Mena House seemed the most Geoffrey's style. It was tastefully opulent, with a romantic past as a royal guest house. Best of all, it lay in the very shadow of the pyramids.

As the vacuum played its noisy two-step at the other end of the apartment she tried Geoffrey again, left him a message to call her, then phoned the hotel. When despite the short notice she managed to snag a reservation she began to feel luck was on her side. Or, maybe, more than luck. "Fate," she tasted the word.

She smiled wryly at herself. But she went to the bank and withdrew enough money for the stay so nothing would show on the credit card bill, but she hoped that by then, either Terry would have to accept that she loved Geoffrey, or it would be over.

She paused. Which would be over? Was it possible their marriage was ending?

But that was trying to think too far ahead. This weekend, she needed to be open with Geoffrey as never before, and he with her. If he refused, well, that was an answer, too.

Catherine put her packing list in her shoulder bag. It was nearly time for Terry to come home, so she made one last try to call Geoffrey. His message had become so familiar she could recite it. Her hope sharpened to an anxious edge.

"I've got the weekend to myself. I'll be at Mena House from Thursday afternoon on." She paused. "Geoffrey, I want you to come." She emphasized the last word slightly, knowing he was too subtle to mistake it for a cheap innuendo. Knowing he would understand what she was asking.

When Terry came home he found her in bed. He stood in the bedroom door staring in dismay. "Don't get sick!"

Not when it might mess up your plans, she thought in irritation.

He took her silence for feeling too bad to give a cheery answer and came to sit on the bed. "Is it something you ate?"

"Maybe it's a bug. My head and stomach ache." The first lie.

"Don't give up on Sharm yet," he said gently. If you're not well, you might feel better waited on in a fancy hotel than here alone."

"Unless I'm better I don't think I can deal with a plane flight."

"I wish I could cancel." He sounded like he meant it. "Maybe Samira will stay with you."

His worry made her feel rotten. "I'll be fine. I just need sleep."

Frowning, he felt her forehead. She hated her earlier anger.

Geoffrey didn't call that night, but she didn't expect it. Wednesday she withdrew into herself, letting Terry and Samira think it was illness. When Thursday morning came, Geoffrey had still not called.

She could have pretended to recover, could have gone to Sharm with Terry after all. Reluctantly, Terry left for the airport. Repeating the claim to need sleep, Catherine gave Samira the long weekend off. "Maybe I'll join Terry and the Lyndore people later. Take your kids to the zoo, have fun."

Samira gazed at her dubiously, but only thanked her in a subdued voice and left.

Catherine phoned Geoffrey, got the same damned recording, and could only hope he wasn't out of town. As for Terry, she'd tell him she'd turned off the ringer to sleep, and of course she'd phone him. She packed the clothes and makeup on her list.

Without Terry, and maybe without Geoffrey either, she was going to the pyramids.

As her taxi crossed the Nile, between the modern buildings she saw for the first time the looming immensity of the Great Pyramid. Dark against the overcast sky, its contours blurred by haze, it overwhelmed even the tallest buildings of modern Giza. The angle of the road shifted, and the two other pyramids unfolded from behind the first. It was all she could do not to call out to the cab driver to look!—it was really them!

They were not identical. One pyramid had an apex of smoother, paler stone. One was smaller than the other two, though still huge. The driver smiled as she leaned forward. "Your first time?"

"Yes. Oh, they're wonderful. They're—" she searched for words, but could only find the certainty that Geoffrey would join her there. That they'd be there together. "They're the *pyramids*."

He grinned at her enthusiasm. "Welcome to Egypt!"

"Thank you," Catherine answered. "I think I'm finally arriving."

Mena House looked like a palace in India, with domes, pointed windows and archways. She was shown up stairs overhung by a huge chandelier cascading through an opening in the ceiling, along a thickly carpeted hall, to a little world from the *Thousand and One Nights*. The ample bed had many pillows and an ornate headboard. The closet door had decorative carving and the bathroom floor was polished marble. Before the dressing table stood a leather hassock. Patterned rugs overlay the already thick carpeting. Opening the window curtains, she was overjoyed by the spectacle of the pyramids, so vast the closest one filled nearly the whole view.

She considered hiking up to the desert plateau at once, but she wanted to share that experience with Geoffrey. Sitting cross-legged on the bed she gazed dreamily at the massive triangular slopes. "Please show up," she whispered, remembering the heat of his breath against her skin.

She finished reading Naguib Mahfouz and started Nawal el-Saadawi. Slowly the shifting light edged the pyramids. Though it was early for dinner, she bathed and put on a dress.

The sun consumed the horizon, then sank away, leaving the pyramids dark against a deep blue sky. Fearing Geoffrey was out of town after all, she had the switchboard operator dial his number. His phone ran four times, then five. She let it ring ten times.

So he'd turned off the answering machine. He'd gotten her message. And it was so unwelcome he'd switched off the machine to prevent her leaving more? Or he was on his way to Giza? She considered staying in and ordering room service, but if he arrived and she wasn't here, surely he'd look for her in the restaurant. Faking illness had meant going without much food, and hunger was making her irritable. She was not fool enough to imprison herself in a room all weekend with the pyramids outside.

In the lobby a wedding procession filed, accompanied by music and the women's high, tongue-trilled *zaghrouda*. As Catherine skirted the crowd an elderly lady invited her to watch. "Welcome!" she said warmly. Would Egypt never stop welcoming and evading her? Catherine tried not to sound bitter as she wished the couple luck and moved on. She'd thought she was hungry, but when her food came she could only pick at it. There were no messages for her at the desk. Back in the empty room she fought the urge to phone him again, and won.

Maybe he just did not want her. But that wasn't what the heat of his last kiss had said. She watched the stars brighten around the black silhouette of the pyramids, aching with longing for all she had ever lost. At last, she went to bed. The struggle against tears was bitter, but she won that too. For what it was worth.

 wenty-four

 riday dawned dreary, the kind of grey weather she'd imagined Egypt never had, until she moved here. Even indoors she needed her sweater. She phoned Terry at his hotel on the Red Sea, managing to reach him before he left his room for breakfast. Continuing to lie to him only made her feel worse. She forced herself to eat, then gritted her teeth and went out grimly to enjoy the pyramids.

As she trudged up the road from the gardens to the desert, the geometrical clarity of the nearest vast shape sharpened into individual limestone blocks, huge and raggedly stair-stepping toward the apex. Once, the surfaces of all three of these pyramids had been smooth, but medieval rulers had stripped off their facings and used the stones for their own palaces. Only the smooth cap at the top of the middle pyramid gave an idea of what they'd once been like.

But standing on the desert's edge with the sand stretching away, they looked so much a part of the earth and sky it seemed impossible that humans had built them, but they had. The myth that they'd been built by Hebrew slaves was as much a fantasy as that it was aliens from outer space. The laborers were Egyptians, working during the months when the Nile's flooding made farming impossible. Ancient Egyptian records documented the drafting of workers for royal projects, but they were paid, and they worked in the belief that they would share in the eternal life these imperishable tombs would confer on their king.

Whether hope, pay or the draft drove their labor, they had achieved a kind of immortality. Catherine tried to imagine the teams of sweating men heaving on ropes, dragging the massive stone blocks up ramps of piled sand. It must have been as dangerous as it was difficult. Crossing the rock-littered sand to the middle pyramid, King Khaefra's, she laid her small hand on an immense block and looked up. The stone slope towered vast, unfathomably ancient, as if in it time and infinity met.

"You ride camel? Twenty pound only!"

Contemplation shattered. Catherine turned to see a man in a dusty galabieh high atop a camel and leading another. "No, thank you," she said, but he did not seem to know those words. "*La, shukran*" meant nothing either. Evidently, 'no,' in any language, was not a word. He persisted so stridently that she had to walk away. He trailed her, insisting she was rude to ignore him.

At last he gave up, but soon a man selling fake scarabs approached. The only way to escape them was to keep moving at too brisk a pace to look at the pyramids. It was as if, having accomplished a mystery beyond understanding, humankind had an irresistible urge to spoil it with all that was the most petty. Though the brightening morning turned the pyramids incandescent, the magic was shattered. Catherine trudged back down to the hotel.

No message at the desk. Geoffrey had abandoned her, and she would never even learn why.

Catherine browsed the gift shops, went to her room and read, tried to eat lunch, then returned to her room and paced, trying to make sense of her life. From this vantage the picture was all too clear. She'd fallen in love with a man of dubious character only to be rejected by him. Even without him, her marriage was in serious trouble.

Wishing couldn't change that. But she did have a life, and maybe getting back to it was what she needed. California. Friends. The perspective she'd lost. But no, she had no job now. The tutoring program had another director. She had no apartment, only a bunch of possessions in an Oakland storage facility.

But there was still a place she could go. There was still a home and refuge, if only for a few weeks. Peace, far away from here, where she could think.

It was five in the afternoon Egyptian time, ten in the morning Eastern Standard. Her mother would be sitting down to her mid-morning coffee. Catherine picked up the phone. An assortment of electronic wheezes emphasized the distance, then she heard ringing. "Don't be gone, too," she begged.

"Hello." Her mother's voice was like waking from childhood fears.

"Hi, Mom," she tried to sound cheerful. "Guess what I just did. Walked around the pyramids!"

"Really? How exciting!"

Catherine thanked all the djinns of technology that it was a good connection with no lag. "How's Dad?"

"Your father's fine, but he's taken it into his head to build a fishing boat."

"With his own hands? Great."

"Maybe. If he finishes it, if it floats, how long will he haul it up and down I-75?"

Catherine knew her father. He'd lose interest, but till then he'd have fun. Thinking of the Kentucky River, even of I-75, made her throat ache with longing.

"How does Terry like the pyramids?"

Catherine swallowed. "Terry's on a business trip to the Red Sea." She tried to sound light. "We planned to see the pyramids together, but I got tired of waiting and snuck off."

"What's wrong, Cat?"

She fought for steadiness. "Nothing. Like I wrote you, Terry's swamped by office politics, and he's handling the stress by putting up walls." Trying to be fair, she admitted, "I'm as much to blame, I've put up walls, too." Saying more would be saying too much. "Mom, I want to come home for awhile."

There was a pause. Despite their disapproval of Terry's uncertain financial prospects, her parents were fond of him. "Think hard before you do anything drastic."

"That's why I need to get away. To think. Please?"

"Baby, you're always welcome here. You know that."

"Thanks." Catherine was more grateful for her mother's love than she could say. "I'll book a flight. I'll let you know from New York when I'm getting in."

She called EgyptAir and made a reservation that left in four hours. There was time to go by the house, get what she'd want, and call Terry. Easiest to eat dinner here. Descending, she saw another wedding party revving up. Men in embroidered finery clustered around a beaming young man, and young women giggled together. On the sidelines, tourists stood admiring the bride's lacy splendor. Behind them Catherine glimpsed a clear cut profile. Her heart contracted in disbelieving pain. As if he felt her looking, Geoffrey searched the crowd.

He found her. His expression was grim. They made their ways around the celebrating people, struggling toward each other, until at last they stood face to face.

"You got my message," Catherine said, hoping against reason that all was well.

"Yesterday morning," he answered. "I'm here to talk. There is a restaurant at the far end of the lawn. The outside tables will be quieter."

She didn't trust herself to answer. She nodded.

They found a table in an unoccupied corner of the patio. Colored lights drowned the stars, and an instrumental version of "The Shadow of Your Smile" seeped sentimentally from somewhere. She expected Geoffrey to make some cynical comment about it, but he only ordered rare steak.

She wanted the worst straight out. "What did you come to say?"

"Eat first."

"To strengthen me for the blow?"

He glanced quickly, the darkness of his eyes vivid. But he only said, "You look as if you need food and rest."

"You're tired too." At the best of times he had shadows under his eyes. Now they looked bruised with weariness. The food came. He cut his meat.

"You've only come to say goodbye."

"No."

Relief filled her, but another glance at him and her gladness was stillborn.

"I've come to tell you the truth about myself." Taking a small piece of the steak he'd cut up but not eaten, he startled her by leaning down. "Pusspusspuss," he called quietly. Only, it sounded more like "Basbasbas." From where he'd spotted it in the darkness a lean orange cat darted over, then stopped, flattening its ears. Geoffrey glanced at Catherine as if he wanted to make sure she noticed that.

"It's wild," she said. "Try tossing it something."

Geoffrey held out the meat, speaking soothingly to the cat. It eyed the food with yearning, but then eyed Geoffrey with alarm. "Perhaps it would rather take it from you." He handed her the bit of beef. "Did you know cats like being called by their ancient name? Or rather, that of the feline goddess, Bastet."

"Basbasbas," Catherine urged. The cat trotted eagerly to her and ate from her hand.

"Cats have a good deal of innate common sense," Geoffrey remarked. "At least, the sort of cat with whiskers and fur."

Catherine ignored that. "You're delaying."

"Eat," he repeated. Because it seemed the only way to get anything out of him, she tried. The cat mewed plaintively.

Geoffrey tossed it another piece of meat. It gave him a very wary eyeball before consenting to eat it.

"I've had enough," she said when she could stand the waiting no longer.

"Walk with me."

Without a word she stood.

 wenty-five

ou may not believe me at once," Geoffrey said as they strolled under the trees, "But I should like you to hear me out."

Puzzled that he thought she wouldn't, Catherine answered, "Of course."

He gave her a peculiar look. In the dim light from the hotel his eyes seemed very large. Ahead the nearest pyramid rose, a vast void pointing to a field of stars. Geoffrey paused by a palm tree, searching her face as if he could see it clearly. To her, his face was a paler smudge in the dark. His hair and sweater blended with the night. His eyes reflected the illumination of Mena House behind her. "Catherine." From his tone she thought he would touch her, but he did not. "I planned not to show up at all."

"Why did you want to put me through that?"

"Because I want you safe." He murmured. "But I also need you, and so I have come."

Catherine clenched her hands, whether in fear or anger she didn't know. Quietly she said, "Exactly why are you a threat to me, Geoffrey?"

"You have already guessed why. Don't claim you haven't." His eyes were too luminous. There was not that much light for them to reflect. "I need . . . I *crave* . . . blood."

Please, no, she thought, *of all things, don't let him be insane.* In the hotel the wedding party was in full swing with a brass band wailing wild desert ecstasies. If she had to scream for help no one would hear.

"If you're considering making a run for it," he strove for the familiar, detached irony, "I assure you there's no need."

She waited, tense but motionless.

"If you do run, I won't follow. I will do whatever I can to help you escape me."

His stance in the darkness looked weary, not threatening. Only the shine in his eyes was disconcerting. "If you're joking about the killings, I don't think murder is funny."

"Nor I," he answered. "If you can't believe me, will you try deferring your disbelief? Pretend to yourself, for now, that what I tell you is true."

More determined to discover if he believed it, himself, she nodded agreement.

He gave her a long look, but seemed satisfied enough to go on. "You know I was born in Wiltshire, studied at Cambridge, was married, and had a son. What you do not know is that those events occurred more than four hundred years ago."

"You're remarkably youthful for your age."

"Will you suspend judgment for the moment?"

"All right." She drew a breath to calm herself, and continued. "Four centuries ago. Queen Elizabeth I. Shakespeare. What a wonderful time that must've been! Pageantry, sophistication, glittering power games. I didn't take you for a romantic."

"Torture. Religious persecution. Extravagance and artificiality while the poor died of hunger. Fear," his voice tightened harshly, "and plague."

The wedding band finished. Only the scraping of the palm fronds filled the silence.

"If it helps to think of it as a fantasy, then do. So long as you hear me to the end," he said. "After a gentlemanly education and two years' travel on the Continent, I was in love with the idea of power. You're right, it did glitter in those days. More than your American corporate moguls imagine. Or perhaps it was only that I saw power differently then.

"The Harrows were an old family, but not important. I wanted to change that. I had an uncle at court and eagerly accepted his invitation to come see what I could make of myself. I rubbed shoulders with schemers far more experienced than I, scattered my family's income in the hope of favors, and won a strategic advantage. I managed to marry a cousin of Sir Francis Walsingham.

"My uncle opposed the match. I supposed he was jealous of the influence of my new relatives, but he told me he belonged to Mary of Scotland's party. He had brought me to court hoping I'd join their plot to assassinate Elizabeth.

"I wanted nothing to do with it. The risk was stupid, and my interests lay with the other side—politically, at least. Though I married a Puritan, I was never one myself. For my uncle's sake I remained silent about the Catholic plot. Nevertheless, it was discovered. My uncle and his cohorts were arrested. One of them suspected me of betrayal and he implicated me.

"They could prove nothing, of course. I'd done nothing. But the Queen was morbidly nervous of assassination, and I spent four days in the Tower. I expected interrogation, torture that would drive me to confess to crimes I had never committed, then execution. They came for me. But to my astonishment they released me. Walsingham had managed to convince the Queen I was not in the plot, but for my uncle's betrayal she banished me from court. I was fortunate, but it was the end of my hopes. I had little choice but to retire to Suffield Harrows and rebuild the fortune I'd squandered."

Geoffrey paused, watching her. As a fantasy, she could imagine him resplendent in a velvet doublet and hose, handsome, dangerous, as much at home parrying witticisms with courtiers as he was exchanging the intricacies of Arab courtesy with Yusef.

"Margaret resented my disgrace," he said. "Without the distractions of the court, we found we were—as we'd say these days—completely incompatible. To me, she seemed tiresomely proper and humorless, and she accused me of brooding and excessive secrecy. No doubt she was right."

No doubt, Catherine could have said. If it had been real.

"Like your own husband, I was too wrapped up in myself to see past her outward manner. I never learned until after her death that Margaret wasn't passionless, she was in love with another man. Perhaps her tedious Puritan morality kept her from taking him as her lover, or perhaps she was afraid of a duel. In those days I was jealous of my honor.

"Of our children, two survived infancy. Deborah died at the age of seven. Richard was a sturdy boy, but in those times men did not spend much time with their children. I regarded Richard as a diversion, and a spur to ambition. I went after the only power left open to me, wealth. Shipping was the most profitable occupation, so I bought into a trading company. I found a fascination in covering the angles and beating my opponents. It became my obsession."

"Not as glamorous as the first part of your script," Catherine remarked. "With your looks and talents, I'd rather the Queen had realized her mistake, made you her favorite, and like Essex you rose to power and fell from your arrogance."

"Essex was a fool. I survived," he answered grimly.

The breeze felt chillier than before. She shivered.

"Would you like to go back to your room?"

"I'd rather have tea, or else keep moving."

"I've another reason for suggesting your room. Considering the newspaper stories, I prefer the rest isn't overheard."

"Oh yes, you must be careful not to give yourself away."

His smile revealed his bitterness. "Do you still think I'm insane?"

"You say you crave blood. Two people were bled to death. Did you do it?"

"I will deny that — to anyone but you."

Her voice shook, not with fear but anger. "Yet you expect me to let you into my room?"

"I've given my word that I won't prevent or force you in any way."

"I should trust the word of a man who claims he's a vampire?"

His eyes were darker than the darkness. "Do you?"

She turned away from the honesty in them. In silence she led the way to her room. She entered first, keeping distance between them. As he drew the curtains she thought, *If the maid finds me murdered in the morning it's my own fault.*

Geoffrey settled in one of the chairs. Catherine took the other. Both pretended to ignore the bed. "We left you a successful Elizabethan entrepreneur," she prompted. "What next?"

"Margaret suffered a long, painful illness. Cancer, I now suppose. When she died, the end to her agony was only half my relief. The other half was freedom from obligation to her." He gazed at an empty spot on the rug, his left eyebrow slightly raised. Just when she imagined he was lost in his thoughts, he gave a small shrug. "A waste, but long past. My unhappy marriage doesn't reflect well on me, but I want you to know the whole truth. I suspect nothing less will convince you to disentangle yourself."

Maybe he was right. Despite everything, she'd made no decision. Otherwise, why was she still listening? "So," she deliberately pushed, "How did you get bitten?"

"I did not 'get bitten'." He sounded annoyed. "My condition can't be transmitted by biting or by any other means."

"Then how?"

"I mentioned plague."

"Yes."

"Everyone has heard of the Black Death, but other fevers also preyed on us then."

"Sweating sickness," she dredged up from her adolescent reading about the wives of Henry VIII.

"That was the most feared. It returned in cycles, but others spent their virulence and were never seen again. A few years after the accession of King James, we heard of a sickness that came on so swiftly that a person who was healthy at noon might be dead by evening. A form of sweating sickness maybe, but with no sweat, only a sudden, inexplicable melancholy followed by delirium. It broke, or else passed into convulsions and death."

He frowned, the fine creases between his eyebrows deepened by the lamplight. "I remember the soft, bright morning with the pear trees in bloom," he continued, "and the abrupt, utter despair that made a travesty of that beauty. When I began burning with fever my dread grew unbearable. I strayed into hallucinations that repeated endlessly, and the thunder of my heart was a torment I struggled vainly to shut out.

"Time doubled back on itself. I no longer knew the servant who tended me, or the room where I'd slept for years. My muscles clamped and my body began to jolt. Whether my eyes were open or closed I saw fluttering patterns of green and gold, like sunlight through leaves. The radiance grew until it overwhelmed me with loveliness. Time stopped.

"I floated without body or purpose, surrounded by light and at one with it. At peace. This is life, I thought. Pure, absolute existence. But into that bright peace swam a small speck of darkness. I had been content, but watching that single solid spot seep closer, I felt the vertigo of the formless light. Fear of its stillness grew in me. Like a drowning man I seized the solid patch. The thundering returned, and in mind-shattering terror I fought to let go, to regain the light, but the darkness entered me. The darkness *was* me.

"I was lying with my hands on my chest. Candles burned round the bed, which was unfamiliar, with high wooden sides. An old woman who had served the family since I was a boy sat by, dozing. The bed felt uncomfortably hard and narrow. With horror

I understood I was laid out in a coffin. I grasped the sides and vaulted out. Nan shrieked, and I drew my sword, as panicked as she was, until I realized that since I stood on my feet ready to fight, they were going to have a difficult time burying me.

"The servants feared me at first, but I'll never forget Richard's joy when he saw me alive. For the first time I realized how much he mattered to me, not only as my heir, but for himself. Fortunately, the parish priest decided my resurrection was God's doing rather than the devil's. I had been generous to the church for business reasons, so I received my reward beyond the grave."

"Didn't you say you were never buried?" she tried to catch him. "You don't sleep in a coffin or box of earth, I hope?"

"Would you do anything so unpleasant?" he asked, poker faced.

She glanced at his Italian sweater and tastefully snug pants, smiling despite herself at the notion of him sleeping in mold and cobwebs. The bittersweet musk of him returned to her memory, its sexuality vivid with life, not death. Even now she wanted to breathe it again.

"My strength returned quickly, but not my appetite," he resumed. "I fancied it an after-effect of the fever, like the way daylight had become painful. I thought I had better eat, but food nauseated me and afterward I vomited. At first I could sleep a few hours here and there during the day, but by night I was restless.

"Then, hunger began. I thought of red meat oozing blood. There was fresh venison in the house, so I woke the cook and ordered some, very rare. When it was brought, the charred stench sickened me. In desperation I sent for raw meat. I couldn't eat it but drank the blood. That tasted good, but I vomited again.

"Craving tormented me. I could think of nothing but blood." He stared at the floor unseeing. "Red rivers of it flowing through veins," he said in quiet, intent cadences, "waves of it washing salt-sweet to the rhythm of a driving heart, scarlet tides of it rolling from a wound. Not animal blood. Human blood, flowing from human flesh. I imagined its thick, wet heat spurting onto my tongue, dreamed of swallowing until it ceased to gush, then sucking what was left."

Catherine's fingers were cold. Uneasily she closed them around her upper arms.

Geoffrey glanced at her. "Yes," he agreed with her unspoken thought. "I believed the fever had driven me insane. I fought the urge for another day, and another. By then, though I did not know it, I was close to the feeding madness.

"An itinerant minstrel came to the house. I was so far gone that the man's being a sorry lute player seemed a valid excuse for what I contemplated. He was a wanderer. No one in the village would miss him if he disappeared. I kept him at his playing until the servants went to bed. By custom, wayfarers slept in the kitchen, but I told him not to wake the servants, to sleep in the unoccupied room next to my own.

"I smelled his blood even through the wall. I gave him time to fall asleep, then I silently opened his door. He sat up, hand on his dagger. With my new night vision I could see him clearly, but he stared, asking who was there. I told him I wanted another song. 'Can I play it tomorrow, please, sir?' he complained. I think he imagined I had other unwelcome intentions. But he hadn't been paid yet, so he sighed and reached for his lute. I leapt on him, clapped a hand over his mouth and forced him against the wall. I had not yet learned I have more effective ways to ensure a victim's silence."

"Such as?" Catherine tried to keep her voice steady.

From his glance, she was not succeeding. "Mere eye contact, when I wish it. The snake hypnotizing the bird, except that my ability is no myth. Some victims begin struggling when they feel sharp teeth in their throats, but by then it's too late. I was amazed at his feeble, slow movements. I didn't realize it was I who had changed. I felt the tendon of his neck taut between my teeth. By the pounding beneath his skin I found the artery, and bit.

"Blood filled my mouth, warm and rich. Ravenously I swallowed, and I felt strength and life pour into me. I couldn't stop until I had sucked him dry. It's always that way when I feed. I can't stop until I have taken all there is."

Catherine knew she should go. That the handsome man sitting opposite her speaking in his familiar, cultured voice was possibly the most dangerous psychopath she had ever met. Yet she could not bring herself to feel that. Controlled as his voice was, he looked sad beyond hope of comfort. The lines of suffering in his face were clear now. *What if it's true?* So seductive was his sincerity that this time she did not reject the question.

"Afterward," Geoffrey said, "I let the body fall, numb with disbelief at what I'd done. Yet the elation of new life pulsed through me. I bundled the corpse into a blanket and buried it in the forest, still half believing I was in a nightmare, then fell to my knees and begged God to let me wake. Except for a few stars the heavens were a black void, and the newly dug earth was cold beneath my knees. I was awake. I never slept again.

"Other changes came. My reflexes quickened, and I grew into almost a giant for that time. My neighbors marveled at it, and at my perfect health. I was forty-three years old, and as you'd expect in those days, my teeth were rather a wreck. Their condition improved." He smiled at his understatement, deliberately showing them to her. His canine teeth, though not particularly long, looked sharp. For the first time she noticed that the points of the upper and lower ones met exactly. Irrationally, she found herself doubting her disbelief.

Geoffrey watched her, aware how impossible she found his tale, but he added no arguments. As he said, he was only telling her, not trying to convince her.

Or himself.

Of all the possibilities, an elaborate joke or test of her feelings for him seemed too unlikely. If Geoffrey believed what he was telling her, there were only two possibilities. The first, that he suffered from psychosis, was at least credible. If he did, the question was whether he was dangerous. He had said, himself, that he was.

"Would you like me to go?" She heard the familiar mixture of reluctance and hope.

Despite everything, she knew that if she said yes he would walk out the door. "No," she admitted.

"More fool you."

Her uneasiness returned. "Why?"

"Do you imagine you are safe with me?"

wenty-six

She tensed. "You gave me your word."

"Oh, in that sense you are quite safe. You needn't fear I shall feed on you." His voice was disdainful, but his eyes searched hers, caring in them, and despair. Then, in response to something he saw in her, he hid the vulnerability. One side of his mouth lifted cynically. "Nor shall I fly into a lunatic rage and knife or strangle you."

"Then what danger am I in?"

"Before I tell you that, you must understand what you are dealing with. With caution, I managed to live a double life. Robbery was common on the roads in those days. I hunted disguised as a highwayman and the outlaws took the blame. They themselves were a regular source of nourishment, but since I must feed every five or six days, and that adds up, I often travelled. London was the best hunting ground."

"You talk as if it were a sport."

"A necessity," he corrected.

"And Cairo is even better?"

"It is easier to be discreet in any large city."

"I hardly call newspaper headlines discreet."

"Can't you guess why I let them be found? You didn't begin to suspect what I am?"

Her eyes closed. It was too horrible to face. "You killed two people because of me?"

"No," he answered sharply. "My need to feed has nothing to do with you. Only leaving them afterward. If you doubted me even a little, I hoped it would frighten you away." He leaned his head on the back of the chair, weary too. "The next is difficult to tell. But it's what you need to know the most."

"I'm listening."

As if forcing himself to return to battle, he raised his head. He considered the empty spot on the carpet, searching for words, his lowered lashes dark against his alabaster skin. "My neighbor and I used to hunt together —Stags, I mean, following our hounds. It was a fall day, pleasantly overcast, with a scent of decaying leaves sweeter than spring. We met on the rise separating our land. My party arrived first. Soon I saw my neighbor come cantering with his dogs and men, but on his most spirited mare galloped a rider I didn't recognize. She rode with a daring, lithe confidence, and her hair flowed golden as the leaves." He raised his eyes. "You will guess where this is going?"

It was too predictable. Any good tale needed a love interest. But under that intelligent, skeptical glance it was impossible to be patronizing. "What was her name?"

"Elizabeth Walker. She was my neighbor's cousin, widowed and free to do as she liked. King James' dreary court bored her, and she'd come to the country for a long visit. I felt drawn to her with an intensity that took me completely by surprise. Elizabeth was one of the most courageous, as well as clever, people I had ever met, and for a woman in those days she was astonishingly educated. We could speak of anything."

"A paragon." Completely irrational, the tickle of jealousy she felt.

"Hardly. As irritatingly stubborn as you are, but without your grace of quietly seeming to give way—though you don't really, do you? I knew I was still capable of feeling. More than before, to judge by my love for my son. But I thought desire for women was as lost to me as my humanity. I discovered it was not so. Yet, with my double life I couldn't marry. I withdrew, but she sought me out. I treated her rudely, but she called my bluff. Since I didn't want to give up her company I convinced myself no harm could come of our being friends.

"The trouble was that I'd never loved any woman as I loved her. I began to play with notions of marriage. After all, I'd managed to keep my need for blood secret from my son and servants for two years, and Elizabeth already accepted my other peculiarities, that I never took meals with others, and my aversion to sunlight. It would do Richard good to have a mother, I told myself. The chance I took with Elizabeth's future and mine alarmed me, but I couldn't stop myself.

"She agreed to be my wife but would not be my lover first. She said she would wait to have me honorably. I suspected her real reason was to sharpen our desire almost beyond endurance." He smiled in pain. "If so, it worked.

"We were married in the parish church. It still stands. That day it was filled with flowers…" He forced himself to resume. "By nightfall we were drunk on each other. Everyone knew it was a love match, and we found the bedroom filled with candles and the bed strewn with rose petals. As we made love, she gave me the sweetest mixture of tenderness and lust I had yet known. She was all I wanted in a woman, yet—" His wide eyes narrowed, as if with the memory of physical as well as emotional torment. "I scarcely need describe my limitation. You have sampled it for yourself."

Along with the lovely blazing of his desire, and the deep coursing of the pleasure he had given her. "It's always that way for you? You never come to orgasm?"

Geoffrey's eyes met hers in acknowledgement.

Events tilted, realigning. If that was so, then what he had given her was not the withholding she had thought but a gift. One he had known could bring him no satisfaction.

"I would have settled for that much," Geoffrey resumed. "Bedding her was not without pleasure. But I was a fool." His voice went cold. "Into the midst of my desire rushed a yearning so overwhelming, and so unthinkable, that it shook me to the bone."

Catherine looked back at him, waiting and knowing.

"It was not the feeding urge. It was nothing like commonplace hunger. In my love for Elizabeth, I thirsted for her essence, her self." Unknown depths resonated in his single quiet sentence. "I needed to drink her."

Heat flickered through Catherine. She was dismayed, but his eyes held hers, far darker than their mere color. For the moment she didn't care if she believed his story or not, only that she glimpsed passion beyond any ever offered her. Whatever he had said about disentangling herself, at last he was offering himself to her without reserve.

What if the impossible were possible? If he was exactly what he said?

He continued, "What I'd hoped would be the beginning of our happiness proved the onset of the most terrible isolation I had yet known. Everything depended on my pretending that all was as it should be, that my love for Elizabeth was ordinary love, though now I knew it was not. She did not discover my physical trouble so quickly as you did, but she gradually sensed something was very wrong, and that despite my attempt to play the contented husband, some obsession haunted me. All the while my thirst for her grew, until I no longer deluded myself I could control it. For her safety I must tell her the truth. I did not trust myself to stay away if she wanted me, but if she shunned me for a monster I could go. If the truth made her hate and fear me enough to denounce me to the priests, that was better than endangering her.

"It was easier for her to believe me than for you. My strange habits, the evil reputation of the forest, had begun to disquiet her. Unlike you, she believed in devils. But Elizabeth's reaction was not what I expected. She *asked* me to drink her blood. She said she did not want to be separated from me for eternity. If I was damned, she would be damned with me.

"As yet, I knew no other like myself. I did not fully understand what I am, but I did know my victims did not become like me. They died, and that was all. 'Whether I become like you or not, if I willingly let you have my blood, I will be outcast from heaven along with you,' she answered. I sensed it was unlike feeding, that I could drink from a minor artery and limit the amount. I could resist no longer.

"Drinking her was fulfillment. Not human pleasure, it is more absolute. It is an ecstasy coursing through every vein, but its center is the heart. It is physical, but even more than human orgasm it is far beyond the mere physical. We were one, at last. She was part of me, and I was at peace."

"But not for long," Catherine guessed.

His eyes unreadable, he acknowledged, "No, not for long. Having tasted that ecstasy, we both wanted more. We fought the desire, but far too often it won, and it was beginning to tell on her. We travelled abroad, seeking every alchemist or sorcerer reputed to cure demonic afflictions, but their potions and talismans were useless. My control during the drinking was slipping, and she was too much under the vampire spell to resist. She was growing too weak to travel. One night as I lay holding her, she began kissing me, urging me on. I told her I was afraid I'd kill her, but she smiled sadly and said, 'We both know you will, sooner or later. Do it now, while I still have the strength to want you.'"

Catherine didn't care if he'd done what he believed he had. Seeing him suffer like this was intolerable.

"The final consummation was..." He gave her a sharp look and stopped whatever he had been about to say. "What matters is that it did not last forever. It destroyed her." Bitterly he corrected himself. "*I* destroyed her."

"What are you hiding?"

"Nothing," he flashed out in such fury that she tensed, her heart thundering. Until she realized his rage was at himself. He did not have to say it. Elizabeth's death had been indescribable attainment. *The final consummation.*

"I buried her in the woods. As she had wished, I placed no cross on her grave. But I no longer believed the damned went to one place and the saved to another. God was evil, I thought. My grief and self-loathing were unbearable.

"When I had smoothed the earth over her, I fixed my sword in a tree and ran onto it. With my strength, I skewered myself to the hilt. It was agony, but I did not die. At length, passing out at times from the pain, I managed to free myself. The blood spurted faster then, her blood, and I hated myself for wasting it. I lost consciousness. When I awoke the wound was healed."

He rose, went to the window and put a tense hand on the curtains, but did not part them. "I was ravenous, but I did not want to survive and refused to hunt. But I was not given that choice. The feeding madness came over me." His hand clenched the curtain. "I don't remember starting for the road, or what cottage or village I found, but when the madness passed I was clutching the corpse of a small girl." He faced the shut curtains, refusing to turn. "It is the only time I have fed on a child."

Catherine gazed at his averted head, his soft hair, its high-lights shining darkly in the lamplight. She felt revulsion, yet it was devoured by a pity as terrible and avid as his own craving.

He did not turn toward her. Did not make her look into his eyes. "I swore that if I could not die, at least I would control my lust. I've taken care never to be overcome by the feeding madness again."

"But you're afraid that if you love again, you'll kill."

He wheeled to face her. "You still don't understand, do you? I *have* loved again. I struggle not to love, I sometimes win, but the love of my kind is not human love. It's not feeding, but it's as necessary to our existence." The blaze of his eyes muted now, he said, "It isn't always desire. It can resemble any of the kinds of love, but it is always fatal, Catherine. However I struggle against myself, I gradually drink the life from the one I love.

"1926 was the last time. In New York. Viviane, she called herself, with no last name, and as I often do I was using an alias, so she never knew mine. She was a dancer, experimenting with new forms and gaining notice. Though I was drinking her, I forced myself to abandon her. I moved to England and took a different name. My craving for her never ceased, but since human love is less constant than a vampire's, I thought she'd get over me. It took her nine years to find me. She'd been in and out of mental institutions. She'd scratched a living, but she no longer danced. She had never escaped my spell. There wasn't much left of the spirited woman I'd known, but I loved her as desperately as ever. She begged me to finish what I'd started. I did."

Catherine's head throbbed. She'd heard enough. The room was squeezing in on her, crushing her.

"From the first time I saw you in the museum, with that serious cat's curiosity of yours, you awoke a craving you can't comprehend. I hoped you'd disappoint me, that I could dismiss the thought of you, but each time we are together I want to be with you more.

"Of necessity, I am alone. You can't imagine what it's meant to hear your troubles and laugh with you, to find in you the surprises and strength that make you not potential prey or danger, but the rarest thing of all, a companion. You *are* rare, Catherine. Each time I attempt to push you away I only find myself luring you closer. For me, it is already too late."

She had to get out. Had to get away from him. She bolted to the door and groped for the knob. At last it jerked open. She was free. She shut it and ran.

wenty-seven

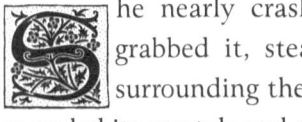he nearly crashed into a carved wooden rail. She grabbed it, steadying herself. It was the balustrade surrounding the cut-out where the leviathan of a lamp cascaded its crystals and colored glass down to a small lobby. The lobby was empty. There was no help.

But the door of her room did not open. He was not pursuing her. Mirrors reflected her endlessly as she sank down, leaning her throbbing forehead on the cool wood. Through the rail she saw two well dressed Egyptian women enter the lobby below. Choosing an elaborately backed divan, they lit cigarettes, too absorbed in their conversation to notice her. The universe pretended normality.

She wished she could disbelieve him. A few hours ago she'd pitied herself for the banality of a love affair gone sour. Now she gripped the railing in vehement longing to have her old troubles back. Whether he was what he said or insane, to stay with him now she would have to be insane, herself.

Elizabeth had believed herself doomed, and Viviane had yearned for death. Not her. It was craving for life that had drawn her to Geoffrey. She clenched the polished wood, closing herself off from pain, from all feeling. At last, armored in her numbness, she rose and walked with deliberate steps up the hall to tell him to go, and never look for her again. She opened the door.

Geoffrey turned from the window. Motionless, he waited for her to pass the sentence condemning him to his loneliness. His lips were shut, his face impassive. Only the anguish in his eyes escaped his control. She had shielded herself against her own pain, but his desperation tore through her barricade.

She refused to abandon him to that void.

Life, not death. She felt it in his nearness. She knew, at last, what she wanted. Who she was.

She closed the door behind her. "I'm no victim. As you said, I'm different from the women in your past. I trust my survival instinct. And I trust your word."

"I'll keep my word. That isn't the danger."

"Then there is no danger. Let me prove to you that whatever your love is, it doesn't have to be death." Heart pounding, Catherine went to the bed. "Let me give you peace."

His eyes widened. "To have that, I must drink you."

The cold tendrils that curled around her stomach were fear, but they were also indescribably sweet. "You're not alone," she told him. "Neither am I." His eyes darkened as the pupils expanded. She reached out. With a low groan he crossed the distance between them.

She closed her arms around him, breathing in his intoxication. As he drew her closer, parting his lips, she involuntarily tensed, but he kissed her, his lips warm and pliant on hers. His tongue greeted hers with delicate hesitation. She relaxed against him, for the moment just sharing it. Even in her arousal, the idea of having her blood sucked repelled her, but her longing to ease his suffering compelled her more.

He took her lower lip between both of his and sucked gently, but this time instead of insisting she surrender to the sensation, he paused, inviting her to answer it. She followed the sensuous bow of his upper lip. With the tip of her tongue she licked the slight deepness where the left corner, unlike the right, turned almost indiscernibly upward. In some inexplicable way the subtle upturn added to the sadness in his face. Tracing his fingertips lightly over her cheek he looked again into her eyes.

Hiding nothing now, Catherine returned the long look and watched his desire slowly gather from the deep places where he had imprisoned it to ignite like a thousand eager sparks. If she so much as touched him, he might do anything at all. But he held motionless, pausing not to restrain the intensity of his passion, but to share the fearfulness of what was happening between them. "Say no," he warned her, but he was already taking off her shirt.

Instead, she unfastened her bra, offering him her trust. He cupped both her breasts, looking at her as if the softness of her body wounded him, but she was stronger than he realized. She pulled off his sweater and shirt, and leaned to him, pressing skin to skin. Their mouths eagerly found each other again. They lay back, and he slowly pushed down her pants exploring the curves of her buttocks, then following the cleft to find her sex from behind. He coaxed as if he had discovered some small, shy creature in hiding. Though her legs were together she gasped at how open she was to him.

His hand trembled slightly. The last shred of sophisticated detachment was gone. His eyes devoured her, wide not with lust but alarm. Now, as she slid his pants down from the tender skin of his hips, was the first time he had been truly naked with her.

He had trusted her with his secret. She had only to reveal it to destroy him.

He pressed his erection to her thigh and she held him close. He had no guarantee she would not betray him. One moment of regret or panic was all it needed, and she could not promise what might happen. She kissed him, but as he stroked her neck she shuddered. What he wanted was gruesome, and even if there were bona fide vampires and he was one, every fear she'd had of some violent perversion was true, and more than true.

He felt her tenseness. "Not yet," he whispered. "Not until you're ready."

He closed his lips over her nipple, tickling with his tongue as he had discovered she couldn't resist. A second tremor passed through her, this time of pleasure, and wonder at how well he already knew her. Not all his beauty, or danger, or even his suffering, evoked such unbearable tenderness from her as Geoffrey himself, whoever—whatever—he was.

Lips enclosing her nipple like the calyx of a flower, eyes shut, he urged gently in his need not for sacrifice but sharing. Whatever he was, at this moment her love for him was absolute.

He kissed her other nipple with searching thoroughness, finally returning to her mouth, her eyelids, her ears, the depression between her collar bones. She realized he was tracing a slow spiral inward. Its center was her throat. Trying to stay relaxed, she shut her eyes, giving consent.

The two points of his teeth closed on her skin. They were sharp, but he positioned them gently. Catherine waited, motionless. He pierced her with a pain so sudden that she cried out, but as he lay with his teeth in her flesh he stroked her, comforting her.

Gradually he withdrew them, and instead she felt his tongue lapping in tiny, light swipes. It was for all the world like being licked by a kitten. Shocked to find the sensation not horrifying but delightful, she communicated it with a little sound of pleasure and closed her arms around him. In answer his lapping grew quicker and more eager, but stayed delicate. A shiver rose along the inside of her skin, unlike anything she had experienced before, at once thrilling with cool and hot as a fever.

Slowly it unfurled through her until the very beat of her pulse was a pleasure, and she pressed closer to the subtle delight of his heartbeat. He made a small sound of elated protest at her movements. His erection throbbing against her, he kissed and softly nipped, taking into his senses every angle, shape and scent of her, then eagerly returned to the ultimate intimacy of her blood. In a long intake of breath she whispered his name.

He raised his head, and she saw this was the abandonment to absolute passion she had longed for, and that no human act could ever be for him. "I love you, Catherine," he said. He lowered his head again. *"Love you."*

With his tongue he pressed her vein, coaxing the blood to flow more quickly. They moved together in an intimacy like ordinary lovemaking and unlike, sharing the glowing rapture of giving and receiving life. As he raised again to gaze into her eyes she noticed a drop of her blood scarlet in the soft hair on his chest. It was the most erotic sight she had ever seen. She shut her eyes, offering him her throat, but he kissed her mouth. Her blood tasted metallic on his tongue.

"Yes," she said in acceptance of the taste, and of him. Not what she had wished him to be, but what he was. She guided him into her, and he made love to her slowly, tenderly. Her climax came nearly at once. At its height he put his lips to her vein again and for the first time, sucked. The rhythm of their heartbeats rose like a wave and broke, merging into one. The ecstasy swelled so vast it swallowed the first. She ceased to be, yet lived with new splendor, her blood holding the obsidian flame of his soul afloat on its tide as on a limitless scarlet sea.

At last, he licked the puncture. This time his saliva was so cold she started. He raised from her, and in bemusement Catherine put her fingers to the bite. They came away clean. Somehow he had completely stopped the bleeding. He held her to him, and she lay content in the warmth of their oneness.

She felt a slight tremor go through him. Gradually she became aware that her neck was wet again, but not with blood. She stroked the slightly curling tendrils of his hair, and the warm solidness of his back, comforting him in his grief. Though she knew she should feel frightened at his certainty that eventually he would kill her, she felt only joy.

"There is only now," she told him, her mind drifting toward sleep. "Only the two of us here together. There is no past, and no tomorrow."

He pulled away. "Leave me."

She sat up in bed, but he would not turn to her. She knew what he was trying to do. "Geoffrey," she began.

"I've got what I wanted. You can get out now," he told her contemptuously.

Knowing he was trying to save her did not lessen the hurt of his closing against her. "No," she told him angrily. "You have no right. Not now."

"You're a fool," he said coldly. But it was a surrender. To her, to himself. When she put her arms around him he turned over, holding her with fierce protectiveness.

Protecting her from himself.

But what they had found was stronger than death.

She meant to love him and live.

wenty-eight

 rooster crowed in the distance. Catherine woke to find the first grey light surrounding the bed, but the mythical being beside her did not shrivel to smoke in the dawn. Awake, as he had been whenever she woke from her fitful sleep, he smiled.

In answer she touched the shadowy angle of his cheek.

"The pyramids are best at dawn," he said. "Shall we?"

The desert was gone. Where it had been was an uncreated world of floating white. Smelling of the Nile and of primeval mud, the fog wrapped them in its secrecy. Side by side they climbed the road that only yesterday had led to the Great Pyramid. Now there was nothing but a void swirling with particles of mist. Everything she'd believed clear had turned mysterious.

Geoffrey smiled, pleased with the shelter from the sunlight. Neither of them mentioned the impossibilities he had told her the night before, or what she had let him do. Catherine did not know how much blood he had taken, but not enough to make her feel faint. She was bursting with energy.

If the sun had been shining prosaically on a plateau full of tourists she might have gone back to doubting his sanity, and hers for letting him drink her blood, but in this softly altered world she knew better. She touched her throat and found two tiny raised places. Feeling as exposed as if she were naked, she turned up her collar to hide them. She remembered how Geoffrey's saliva had stung cold and stopped the bleeding. How could the reality she had thought she knew explain that?

"You're the only solid thing in the world," she told him.

"And you."

The paving ended, and they continued over sand littered with chunks of rock. Damp, the desert smelt heavily of limestone. A vague grey shape filled their sight, the pyramid looming alarmingly close. Catherine paused, but Geoffrey strolled on, silent as the fog. In his Italian sweater, his butt enticingly taut in those close fitting pants, he could be any handsome man visiting this place with his lover. She alone knew differently. She watched him approach a block of stone once dragged from the pyramid, but for some reason abandoned. He paused to examine its surface, then turned to her. The mist reflected as two white crescents in his eyes.

"What did you find, hieroglyphs?" Catherine joined him.

"No." With his finger he traced a ridged shell imbedded in the limestone, the outline of a fossilized sea creature. Reality gave another convulsion, turning the pyramid young beside the primordial beings whose bodies made up its blocks. And compared with these, the four centuries of Geoffrey's existence were the batting of an eye. Catherine took a deep breath, feeling she had dived into waters with no bottom.

"From sea to desert," Geoffrey mused.

"I wonder if you'll see a time when it's ocean again."

He didn't answer. The fog was thinning. Sand showed silvery as foaming breakers. The pyramid seemed to move toward them through the streaming mists.

"Come into the Great Pyramid with me," she said.

"You'll be disappointed."

She raised her eyes to the ascent slanting into the sky like a road to infinity. "Disappointed?" she scoffed.

"Oh, it's formidable, I grant you that. An admirable feat of engineering. But inside is only a plain, narrow passage. The farther you go, the more heavily the weight of the pyramid oppresses you, and the more foul the air from the generations of sweating sightseers. At last you reach an empty chamber. In it is a broken sarcophagus rather like an oversized black bathtub. That is all."

"Don't rain on my picnic, Geoffrey." A funny idea struck her, considering what he was. "You sound claustrophobic."

"No. Merely—aware."

"I'm going into the pyramid. I'd rather share it with you. But if you won't, I'll go alone."

Geoffrey regarded her in silence, lights flickering in his eyes as the pupils dilated for an instant. They were brighter than the sky they reflected. Knowing his secret didn't solve the enigma of him but added to it.

Dim as a ghost, a man emerged from the mist riding a camel. His head and neck were muffled in a grey wool scarf. He appeared not to see them. He passed and was gone, as if two realities had brushed, but not joined. "The first hawker on his way to work," Geoffrey said. "Soon a *ghaffir* should be here to open the pyramid for you."

The entrance was on the side toward them. Stairs had been built up to it. Geoffrey pointed to another portal higher up, framed by a pointed arch and blocked with stone. "That was the ancient doorway."

In unspoken agreement they climbed the stairs past the lower entrance with its padlocked steel door, and clambered among the big stone blocks to the higher recess. Graffiti scarred the surface around it, Arabic and Western scrawls, but also fainter Greek letters, and nearly eroded by the ages, neatly carved hieroglyphs. Geoffrey sat on a large stone, reading them.

Catherine perched beside him. The warmth of their touching thighs was suffused with the afterglow of their lovemaking. *The drinking,* she thought with a small shiver. Birds flitted in and out of stone crannies on either side of them, going out to their own business of mating and feeding. Below, the fog was melting except for a patch lingering thick as a wad of cotton along the river. The ruins of a small ancient temple emerged in the desert, and below the plateau, hints of the raw newness of Giza. Geoffrey took his sunglasses from his pocket and put them on.

"Is the light getting uncomfortable?"

"I enjoy the view," he replied.

Not what she'd asked. But obviously, he could look after himself. "You're sensitive to light, but it doesn't destroy you. And I saw your reflection in the hotel mirrors. You're not supernatural, you're only changed in some way medical science can't explain."

"Until about 1800 I was supernatural," he answered with a straight face. "Now I'm a mutation, if that pleases you better. In few more generations no doubt there will be yet another, even less gratifying explanation."

"I meant," she asked, feeling ridiculous, "you can't change shape, or anything?"

"Wouldn't that be convenient." He leaned back against the stone, musing as if seriously. "Actually, I never thought I'd care to be a bat. On the other hand, turning into a wolf might be some use." He showed his teeth in a smile, knowing it made him look like one.

Small at the edge of the plateau a man rode a donkey, swaying as if singing to himself as Samira liked to do. The Pyramids Road glinted with early morning traffic. Geoffrey asked her, "If I could give you any wish in the world, what would it be?"

"All I want is this moment. No pain for you, no confusion for me. Just the two of us sitting here looking out at the world together."

He considered her with Geoffreyan inscrutability. At last he said, "Your nose is peeling."

She rubbed it. "I suppose after four hundred years you've discovered the answers to all of life's big questions."

"Obviously," he answered with heavy irony.

"Did you mean what you said about believing God is evil?"

"I once thought so. It's been a long time since I believed in the existence of a god."

"Then, vampires being repelled by crosses is just another myth."

"Not necessarily. Some can't abide them, but I expect it's really their own guilt they can't tolerate. Since I no longer believe in right or wrong, I'm not bothered by their symbols."

"What do you believe in?"

"Staying free and rational. Not allowing myself to be encumbered by human weaknesses. My kind cannot afford remorse."

If she believed Geoffrey felt no remorse, she'd believe anything. But she only asked, "Free? From danger? When you've survived a sword through the heart, what danger is left?"

He glanced sideways at her, as if she might become a danger, herself. There must be some. Even if his body repaired itself as miraculously as he said, that would probably not save him from fire, or the gruesome beheading prescribed by folklore. "All right, I can imagine only too well."

"No, you can't," he answered coldly, "and neither can I, since I have never experienced the destruction of my body. We inhabit our bodies differently than you do. For instance, I feel heat and cold, but they don't trouble me. I have always suspected it's vitality we need as much as blood. One of my kind whose body is destroyed continues to exist, craving substance, until he or she can find a susceptible victim, gradually feed on the life as if it were blood, and steal the body. No end is possible, and no peace." He glanced at her. "Except during the brief times when we love."

It was not an invitation to offer comfort. What he said defied any physical explanation she could imagine, and his talk of possession and devouring made her uneasy. He saw it, but pretended not to.

"So there are other vampires. Why didn't you talk about them?"

"You needn't worry about them. Even if others were in Egypt—and they aren't—they wouldn't approach you."

"You sound very sure."

"They would not risk dealing with me."

"They're afraid of you, do you mean?"

"Certain strengths of mind determine dominance among us. Of the vampires still at large in the world, I am dominant."

This time she did hear pride. Whatever powers he meant, she suspected he had developed them over the centuries through the sheer force of his intelligence and will. "Like you said, the snake and the bird?"

"More than that. I can draw a victim to me, even compel actions at close range. I can do the same to other vampires, when I wish."

Fear breaking surface, she looked quickly at him. "Is that what you've done to me?"

"Not intentionally. Nor will I."

She searched for a sign he was lying, but found none. "I see," she said slowly, not relieved. "The 'vampire spell.' You think I'm obsessed against my will."

"Yes." His answer was sad beneath its harshness.

"We'll see." With a pebble she traced circles in the sand that had drifted onto the stone. "Relationships among yourselves, what are those like?"

"Nonexistent, so far as we can help."

"All of you are outcasts, alone except for each other. Surely there's more than hostility?"

"Perhaps so, once. I remember my excitement when after twenty years thinking myself alone, I ran across my first evidence of another. I couldn't rest until I found her. But she was only a poor wretch living like a rat in the London alleys. Despite our common condition, she was frightened of me. She was changed by a fever too, and knew no more of it than I did. But she'd heard a dockside rumor that a vampire hunted in Venice. I tracked him down. Gradually, my kind discovered each other, some two dozen, all told. Each had fallen ill of a fever, all had waked from seeming death to find themselves altered. Some were less fortunate than I and had to claw their way out of their graves."

"And any who couldn't escape their coffins?" Catherine asked. "Did they starve, or might they still be trapped?"

"If they are, they must be utterly mad by now."

She shuddered.

He looked at her, his face a barrier. "Now that you know the truth, if you wanted to be rid of me, what would you do?"

"Keep you in your body, yet stop you. " Then she understood. "Bury you alive? That's unthinkable! Sealed up but conscious, hour after hour, century after century, without even the relief of sleep?"

"And craving blood."

"Has it happened to anyone?"

"Several. We've managed to discover and release a few—not out of fondness, simply because no vampire can tolerate the thought. But those rescued after too long are no more than creeping, ravening human bats."

From his refusal to show any emotion she could only guess what horrors he had seen.

"Best not to think about it," he told her.

She doubted it was so easy. She saw movement below. "Someone's opening the pyramid," she said. "I know now why you're not thrilled with going in, but this is a tomb for the dead, not the living."

"The passage is very old. A single falling stone could block it."

"The pyramids will fall down on you? That's rational?"

He smiled, caught. But he still had the last word. "They will fall in time."

"Then, I challenge you to risk that they won't fall today. "Do you dare go into the dark with me?"

wenty-nine

nfair to say 'I told you so.'" Through the curtain of big brass and wooden beads the Giza plateau gleamed in the broad noon. The clink of silverware and murmur of conversation surrounded them.

"I said nothing at all," Geoffrey answered smugly.

"You don't need to. The very way you're sitting says it."

To do him credit, his description of the inside of the pyramid had understated the discomfort. A wooden staircase, cramped and uneven, ascended a steeply sloping ramp. A long, long staircase. They climbed and climbed. And climbed. After the first thousand stairs Catherine was sweating and panting in the stale closeness where hundreds of people had sweated and panted that week. Exasperatingly, Geoffrey remained light footed as a cat, not even breathing hard.

The voices of the other tourists echoed inconsequentially, and from somewhere below a guide's speech droned, but Catherine was more aware of the vast weight of stone suspended above. Instead of lessening as they climbed higher, it seemed to grow. At last they reached King Khufu's burial chamber. No electric lights illuminated it, only a man who silently held a huge, reflective sheet of metal. In one thing, at least, Geoffrey's dismissiveness was unjustified. Its starkness was majestic.

Its black granite walls rose to a corbelled ceiling in the gloom far above. No paintings or carved inscriptions softened the stately simplicity of the rectangular black granite sarcophagus, now broken at one corner, that once held the pharaoh's mummy. The black wasn't mourning, it was the night sky, the womb, the rebirth into immortality. Catherine's steps echoed as she crossed the stone floor, curious to look into the sarcophagus. Its lidless cavity gaped as if with unquenchable thirst.

The weight on her chest made speaking hard, and she turned to Geoffrey. He was still standing on the threshold beside the man with the mirror. Its reflection glistened in the damp on his forehead. He waited for her with impassive patience, but the sheen of sweat was not from the climb.

After she'd finished lunch they retreated behind the closed curtains of their room, she drifting between the pleasure of lying in his arms and the luxury of a midday doze, he quietly thinking...of what?

Toward sundown they sallied forth again, Catherine in her khaki desert pants and Geoffrey swathed in a Bedouin scarf from a gift shop. It made him look rather dubious, like a dark eyed T.E. Lawrence. When he put on his dark glasses too, she suspected the day's sun had told on him more than he let on. He would not admit to pain, but she saw him rub his temples. Still, he insisted she had to see the Sphinx before it got dark.

The sand felt warm through the soles of her shoes, but when they reached the plateau a chilly breeze rippled. At once they were besieged by the camel men and hawkers. This late in the day, tourist pickings were getting slim, and she and Geoffrey were the only prey in sight. Catherine despaired of ever shaking them when Geoffrey spoke. *"Seta gineh."*

A man tugged his camel forward.

"You're not going to ride that?" Catherine asked as the animal lurched to its knees.

"You imagine I am too old for a new experience?" With exquisite grace Geoffrey mounted the fringed saddle. Positioning his legs as the man instructed, he held out a gloved hand to her. She took it and climbed on behind. The camel stood with a double heave like a ship cresting a wave that made her cling to Geoffrey.

The ground was much farther away than from horseback, and the camel's walk rolled nothing like a horse's, but Geoffrey sat with relaxed dignity, adapting to the unfamiliar gait with the quickness of a skilled rider. Like when he'd handed her down from the carriage, it was a small sign of his origins in another age.

But his body was warm and solid, absolutely real in the circle of her arms. Catherine felt a flicker of memory from her own past, riding a motorcycle with a man she'd dated before she knew Terry, bodies molded together in the windswept night. But Geoffrey's body against hers aroused her far more. The plodding of the camel, led from the ground by the camel man, made her laugh at the inappropriateness of her glittering excitement. Geoffrey turned his head, smiling with her.

The Sphinx crouched with his lion paws outstretched. He was in a wide pit, his elbows and haunches below the surface of the sand swells. They approached him from behind, his feline back and tail toward them and his human head facing over the sand toward the green and brown of the town of Giza by the Nile. The camel knelt. They dismounted, paid, and strolled slowly along the rim of the deep enclosure.

"I never pictured the Sphinx in a hole," Catherine remarked, looking down at the leonine tail curved over the taut haunches.

Geoffrey gave her a quick glance. But his tone was casual. "He wasn't always. Drifting sand has raised the ground level. Do you see that carved stone between his front paws? A later pharaoh put it there to tell how the sphinx appeared to him in a dream, how he rescued him from the crushing sand. By the time Napoleon's expedition came, all was buried again, except for the sphinx's head."

". . . *Traum*," came a distant voice, like an echo from the desert. . . . *Dream*.

A group of tourists crested the horizon like a flotilla, trailing a dusty wake. A young Egyptian woman herded them to the far side of the Sphinx. With her scant German, Catherine caught only wisps of the guide's lecture, a longer version of the tale Geoffrey had told. A smothered god crying out to a prince for help. His reward, the crown. As the tourists reappeared from behind the massive stone, Catherine saw a dark head behind the blond ones, and a slender brown face with a strong, elegant nose and full lips.

She paused, staring. But as the tourists moved on she realized she must be mistaken. What would Mounir Abdel Razak be doing among a gaggle of German tourists? They trooped downhill to a vantage point from which they could frame the Great Sphinx's head between two pyramids in their camera lenses. The dark, curly hair bobbed beside a woman's canvas hat in conversation. Just a member of the group. Not the man whose love was gone forever. To feed Geoffrey's need?

"What is it?" Geoffrey asked.

She shrugged. "I stubbed my toe."

"Careful, the desert can be hazardous by twilight." His attention went to the ground. "There can be scorpions, too."

They made their way back to Mena House, Geoffrey guiding her around the stones he could see in the gathering darkness. Over dinner he made amusing conversation about old movies. She did her best to respond.

"Your mood is different," Geoffrey observed. "The realization of what I am is sinking in."

"I don't know."

"If we part now, we keep a dream that nothing can destroy."

"Can we part now?" Catherine searched his eyes. "Whatever you are, I love you."

When he had locked the door of their room behind him, he shut the curtains on the world outside. "Tonight, I only want to touch you, and lie in your arms."

"In loving you I love a killer. I wish I could hate you for it."

"I loathe myself enough for the both of us," he answered quietly. "Tell me how I can free you from me. Even now, I'll do it." His eyes were voids of naked longing. Not desire. Yearning simply to be human as she was, as he had once been.

In sorrow, she drew him close. She breathed in his bitter scent. He tensed, wanting to pull away from her comfort. But her blood sang at his nearness, and like an answer she felt the heartbeat in his chest. She kissed his closed eyes, and the curve of his lips.

"Leave me," he begged in a lost whisper.

"Is a tiger a murderer? Is a river?"

"I don't want your forgiveness. Fear me, Catherine. When the time comes, I'll kill you."

"When the time comes," she answered, unbuttoning his shirt. "I'll do what I must, for both our sakes. I'll abandon you to the loneliness you probably deserve. But not tonight."

Stripping the shirt from him, she ran her fingertips over the compact strength of his shoulders, the heat of his chest. The beauty of him kindled her tenderness and sorrow to an open flame, and in an answering rush he kissed her. His skin burned against her as if with fever. His tongue drew hers deep into his mouth. At last he backed away. "Undress for me."

She smiled, flushing with heat at his all-too-human request. Slowly, she did. He stood just out of reach, possessing every detail of her body without touching.

"Now you," she whispered. She saw the quick glint of his humor. He obliged. Never had she seen a man strip himself with such confident poise. Arrogance, she would have thought, had she not known the whole tangled web of his pride and self-hatred.

The contradictions of his mind and the equally fascinating counterpoints of his body, fine skin and hard angles, slenderness and solid strength, made him a complex and changing pattern, a kaleidoscope wonderful to contemplate, and sorrowful. As he draped his trousers neatly over the back of a chair the lamplight made a triangle of the slight concavity between the two halves of his rib cage and crescents in the hollows of his hips. The hair on his thighs was so silky-fine that from where she stood she could only see it where the lamp light gleamed on it.

He took her hands to draw her to the bed. "No," she told him, and pulled him down onto the thick carpets. "I'll have you in all the lowest places, where you belong." She kissed him, half dreading to taste blood. The cool freshness of his mouth blended incongruously with its heat.

His lips brushed her forehead light as a moth's wings, then opened her mouth. His tongue nudged in. She sighed, and he rocked her, stroking her tongue with the elusive touches of his. After a leisurely time he raised, not smiling, but with the last trace of hardness gone from his face.

They caressed each other without hurry, pausing to praise with a word or touch, feasting each sense on pliant skin, shadowed hollows, tender creases. His cock strained rigid, its flush dark. She took it in her hand and he moaned, almost too low to hear. To her delight a bead of clear fluid seeped from the tip. Inhuman or not, he desired this human loving too. She tasted the drop, letting its musk fill her senses like the pungence of a jungle at night, or the salt poignance of the sea.

He drew her up and entered her so quickly it took her breath. The intensity of the sensation stole a small sound from him. Such wild beauty shone in his face she would have loved him for that alone. She wrapped herself around him whispering how abhorrent he was, and how magnificent. "Yes," he moaned to her praises and recriminations, and plunged his hips in quick, short thrusts that split the center of her being like lightning.

Shuddering, he withdrew. She gasped as he sucked the eager tenderness of her nipples, and from her navel down to the damp cleft between her legs. His tongue found her clitoris and flicked over it. She would have parted to him, but he clamped her legs together with his knees, stroking in an exquisite lashing that made her writhe to open herself to him. "Geoffrey," she protested in intolerable frustration.

He raised from her, his face mock-polite. "Yes?"

She grasped him, meaning to perpetrate she didn't know what revenge, but he re-entered her in one deep thrust. She clasped his waist with her legs. Their need surged sharp and bright, binding them together as he sought fiercely for the release he could not have. She raised her legs to his shoulders to take in more of him.

He plunged deeper, but refused to relax his control. If he did, she realized, he would drink her. She suspected he was kneeling upright to escape the temptation of her throat. Yet, now that she knew the reason for his control, the self-denial and caring that it was, the awareness in his open eyes and his tense mouth were sweet to her. She looked into his eyes, giving him the mingled joy and sadness of the attainment he could not share.

He smiled. Leaning forward, he moved slowly now, urging her pleasure into echoes, each more subtle and delicate than the last until finally they faded. "Now you take me," he whispered. "However pleases you most."

She drew him down, rolling so he lay on his back. His cock still strained erect, moist with her juices and flushed to dusky rose. But when she closed her hand around it he took a quick, involuntary breath. She realized it was tender from overstimulation. Controlling her own desire, she moved down instead to stroke the dark thicket of his hair and gently cup his balls.

Geoffrey sighed, relieved to have the sensations shifted, so she turned her full attention to them . They were drawn up close to his body as if in their own fit of pique at his frustrated arousal. They were admirably aesthetic balls, tinged a lighter rose than his cock, making their veins look lavender. She tickled them softly with her tongue, breathing in that strangely intoxicating fragrance of his, the most definite here at his sex. Geoffrey drew up his legs, keeping them open to her.

"You're curling your toes," she said, smiling.

He uncurled them at once and opened his eyes, as if his toes had nothing to do with him.

With his hair disheveled his face looked astoundingly young. Or maybe it was that, if only for now, he was happy. His erection was fading, the head retreating into the foreskin. She took him very gently into her hand. He shut his eyes, his face relaxed while she stroked him as delicately as she could. And was rewarded by his soft gasp and the reappearance of the flared ridge of the head. She closed her mouth around it, urging him, then slowly, deliciously impaled herself on him.

She rocked her hips, keeping the sensations subtle, and in the reawakening anguish of his desire he cried out softly, but was content to have it so. The final shivering of her pleasure was as faint as a rustling of spring leaves.

She stretched out against him, feeling the simple happiness of a woman who has found the lover she has always dreamed of. Resting her head on his chest, she wrinkled her nose as the soft hairs tickled it. His hands drifted warmly, lazily over her. She knew that they were thinking the same thing: For good or ill, they were one, and would never be separate again.

Thirty

hen Catherine woke she heard the shower. *Al Ahram* and the *New York Times* lay on the table. The usual start to Geoffrey's morning, she supposed. She saw no reason to disrupt it by asking him to sit in the dining room pretending to eat.

"I'm going for breakfast," she called through the closed door. "Be back soon."

"Take your time. I may run an errand or two."

Maybe he wanted a few moments to himself. After all, he wasn't used to having to deal with someone else nonstop. So before she ate she took one last walk around the pyramids. Today they were as she'd always dreamed, golden in the clear morning light with the blue sky fathomless beyond.

I always knew you were magic, she thought to them, *but if anyone had tried telling me what I'd find here...* She shook her head. Life was beyond the limits of mere rational understanding.

In the restaurant she chose a table by the window. Outside were palm trees, and bushes blooming in pink and gold. Sunshine streamed through the curtain of brass bangles and big, onion-shaped wooden beads. Their glints and shadows fell over the tables.

Basking in the variegated pattern she sipped coffee and looped syrup over her waffles. Unbidden, the image of the tourist she'd mistaken for Mounir came between her and the sparks of sunlight. She didn't want to think of the compulsion that drove Geoffrey against his will. He had two choices, to control his need as best he could, or to refuse it and fall prey to the madness that would strip all restraint from him.

She could only hope Mounir had listened to her and was no longer stalking Geoffrey. If he, or anyone, threatened Geoffrey's freedom, she would protect Geoffrey with every means she had.

Knocking brought no answer. As she put the key in the lock Geoffrey came along the hall. No monster, no psychopath. A man forced into an existence he was not born to endure. An existence that could not last forever, and could not end well.

When they were inside he took her in his arms. His tongue stroked hers in a long, intimate tasting. "Sticky sweet. Let me see," he made his speculation an excuse to kiss her again. "For breakfast you had honey...and dust?"

"I walked around the pyramids."

"My morning was less strenuous." He handed her the paper bag he carried.

Inside was a silk scarf, pale green with deep lavender violets.

"It's lovely." But she knew what it was for.

In the mirror she watched Geoffrey wrap the scarf around her throat. His touch was soft as the silk. He'd known just what shade of green would turn her eyes emerald. Seeing their reflections together, as they must appear to others, she was struck by how opposite they looked, Geoffrey's pale and dark to her sunburn and gold-brown. His compact density made her seem startlingly fragile, yet they seemed whole together. In the angular structure of her own face she glimpsed the flow of shadow that fascinated in his, as if it were she who had his blood running through her veins instead of the other way around. "With you, I'm beautiful," she mused.

"You ever doubted your beauty?" He watched her reflection, ignoring his own.

She smiled, glad if this was how she looked to him.

"Your tall slenderness might charm any man, and your soft-spoken independence is provocative, but to me, you are a rare, rare beauty. Your skin is so translucent …"

He turned her wrist, showing her how the veins were revealed close to the surface. "This is as seductive to me as a glimpse of your breasts through a sheer blouse to an ordinary man." Turning her away from the mirror, he gazed at her. "Your quiet, clear depths are lovelier still, your humor, your understanding, the tender curve of your mouth." His lips caressed hers.

"But there is something else you will discover," he resumed. "The vampire glamour is on you now. All will notice your beauty. They will be drawn to you as if you, yourself, were a vampire. If you want a man, he will probably not be capable of refusing you." He stepped away. With a hint of cool amusement he added, "You should leave me while you're ahead, and go find Tom Cruise."

"Probably." She kissed him, a sweet, satisfying intimacy, and then again, as if despite the satisfaction of each kiss some spell did indeed keep pulling her to him.

"Have you noticed the time?"

She looked at his watch. "Noon," she said in dismay.

"Yes." He glanced balefully at the watch as if it betrayed him. "When must you be home?"

"Terry's plane lands at two-thirty. I'll need time alone before I can face him. We'd better go."

Reluctantly they abandoned the room that had been their secret haven. As they walked to his car a woman in a sun hat and clumsy makeup passed them heading for the hotel. Geoffrey's glance seized on her. Startled, Catherine turned, then saw it was the Polaroid hanging around the woman's neck that riveted his attention. "Pardon me," he swiftly bore down on her. "Might I ask a favor?"

The woman paused, uncertain at the purposeful intensity so at odds with his polite words. "Of course," she answered, as if bewildered to find she would have promised this darkly shining stranger the very moon.

"I want a photo. Would you be so kind?"

"A picture of you two?" She glanced enviously at Catherine.

"Only her. Move to your left, Catherine, and the pyramid will be in the background."

"You get in it too," Catherine urged.

"I don't like looking at myself. Stand exactly as you are."

She held still, looking at him. The woman took her picture, then started slightly as Geoffrey came to hover over the camera. As soon as the photo slid out he took it without waiting for her to hand it to him. "How long must it develop?"

"It'll be ready now," the woman stepped away from him, looking as if she'd like to move closer. Catherine remembered how that felt, and sympathized.

Aware only of the photo, Geoffrey carefully peeled back the paper and studied it. "Yes," he said at last. "I'll keep this." He stalked off with it, radiating possessiveness.

The woman stared after him, bemused as if some magnificent falcon had bowled her over with an accidental brush of its wing. Catherine saw her hurt. "Thank you," she told the woman gently.

The woman nodded with a puzzled frown.

Catherine went after Geoffrey, wondering why the snapshot was so important to him. It wasn't as if he'd never see her again. *I'll keep this.* To remember her by, after she was gone?

After he had killed her?

"You're wrong," she said, getting into the car.

He glanced at her, protected the snapshot between the pages of a book lying on the back seat, and started the car without answering.

"You are," she told him.

Traffic was heavy on the Pyramids Road, but she was glad of the extra minutes it gave them. She leaned back as the nightclubs and shops passed, watching Geoffrey drive with the brazen madness of a true Cairene, using his horn like an Egyptian and his brakes not at all. A long flatbed truck rumbled ahead, paper fluttering over its bundled load, which looked for all the world like stalks of uncooked spaghetti as long as the truck. The paper flapped again and Catherine saw that's what it actually was, a truckload of spaghetti.

She began to remark on it when, from a car next to the truck, a young man leaned out and snapped off a piece as long as a yardstick. She and Geoffrey watched the car swerve, the young man brandishing the pasta above it. Over the horns Catherine could hear him laughing with the other guys in his car. It dropped back and the spaghetti snitcher broke off some of his prize. He handed it to the driver of another car. Dropping back more, the young guys spotted Geoffrey's smoked glass. Edging their car close, they motioned him to roll down the window. Geoffrey did, and they gave him a stalk of spaghetti.

With a flourish Geoffrey presented it to Catherine. "My lady, I pray you, accept this token of my esteem."

"Thank you right kindly, sir," she played Scarlett O'Hara to his Elizabethan gentleman.

The young guys cheered them while the people in the surrounding cars shared the fun. Geoffrey rolled up the window and put on a burst of speed, slipping through the traffic to lose them all.

He looked at her as she sat holding the stick of spaghetti like some rare flower. "Catherine," he said in absolute seriousness, "Will you live with me?"

She was so startled the spaghetti snapped. She picked up the two pieces and laid them on the dashboard. Her longing to tell him yes was a sharp anguish. "You know I can't."

He paused, then gave her a bitter smile. "On second thought, what an idiotic question."

"That isn't what I meant. I'm not afraid of you."

"No?" he asked skeptically, but saw that wasn't it. "I see," he said. "You may be under my spell, but that is no reason for me to assume you want my company."

Ignoring his sharpness, she answered the hurt it covered. "My reason is Terry. I'm not sure I want to end our marriage. If I can't tell him the truth, at least I can tell it to you. I love you, but that doesn't mean I no longer love him."

Geoffrey was silent.

When they pulled up outside the apartment building, the curtains were still drawn. "Good," she said. "I'm home first."

Geoffrey regarded her, his jealousy a withheld fury.

"Geoffrey?"

"No, don't be afraid for him. I will not hurt anyone you love. Goodbye for now, Catherine."

Thirty-one

atherine sat at her mirror, humming the sweet, sad fragment of an Egyptian melody and remembering the warm dusky rose of Geoffrey's nipples. The aureoles were wide as quarters. Only the nubs at the center rose and tightened to a touch. Probably the women in his family had large nipples luscious as nectarines.

Long ago. All his kin were gone. So was the England that was his home. He was more alone than she'd imagined. What willpower had it taken to survive that way for so long? He was a victim as much as a predator. Yet, however unwilling he was, however great his suffering, it did not absolve him from the suffering he caused. Or did it? Knowing Geoffrey's secret and protecting it, was she not as guilty as he was every time he killed?

How much easier if she'd just been obsessed by his spell! If she'd felt no respect or caring for Geoffrey himself, she could've hated him for the pulsing in her veins. She shivered, her fingertips going to the two small marks that showed red in the mirror.

She wrapped the scarf around her throat. The green silk felt warm like his touch, and the violets complemented the paler purple of her long dress. In the two days since his return, Terry had said nothing about her inseparability from the scarf.

Terry's trip had gone well. When she'd phoned him from Mena House he'd enthused about Sharm el-Sheikh, the beauty of the blue sea and golden cliffs. For two days he'd talked about the mural he might paint there. He had tried to phone her at home, and he was oddly subdued about her failure to answer. Her explanation, that she'd switched off the ringer to sleep off her bug, was all too shabby. He had to suspect, Catherine reasoned as she loosely twisted up her hair

Please, let him suspect, pleaded one part of her mind. *Stop this farce. Let this, at least, be resolved for better or worse.*

No, dangly earrings were too much with the scarf, the other half of her mind calmly decided. Instead she slid an ornamented comb into her hair. "It's quarter till eight."

"All right," Terry answered from his studio. She heard him go into the bathroom and the water running as he washed the water colors from his hands. "The bucket's half full again. When's that plumber coming?" It sounded like an accusation.

"Tomorrow, the super says."

"*Bokra,*" Terry grumbled. The Arabic equivalent of *mañana.*

"*Bokra fil mish-mish,*" she finished the Egyptian expression. *Tomorrow when the apricots bloom.*

She saw him come in, or rather, his image in the mirror. Terry glanced at her reflection, looking troubled. But as he changed clothes he talked about their host. "Gawaz and Pete want each other's blood."

She glanced at him in the mirror, but he continued, oblivious, "Pete sees the mural's publicity as his baby. Gawaz believes it should be his. Judy thinks if he can't run it, he may try to sabotage it. You've got good people sense, I want your take on the vibes tonight."

He buttoned his royal blue shirt. Its clash with her violet and green was unlike him. "You look fantastically sexy. Is that a new dress?"

"I've had it a few years ."

"A new scarf, then. And different perfume."

She wasn't wearing perfume. She glanced sharply at him. "What do you mean?"

Terry came closer, nose wrinkling cute as a rabbit's. That was exactly it. Deceiving anyone as innocently well-meaning as Terry was like kicking a pet bunny. "No, I don't smell perfume," he decided, putting his arms around her. "But you do look delicious tonight."

"It's nearly eight. We'd better get a move on."

"I'd rather get a hard-on."

Gently she freed herself. "That might be arranged, in good time."

Even as she said it, the reluctance that crystallized in her startled her. She escaped to the solitude of the bathroom.

This won't do, she silently lectured her reflection as she smudged her eye shadow a little more. *Tell him what truth you can.*

Yet, some lies must now stand between them for the rest of their lives. That made her feel trapped as she had never felt in the grip of Geoffrey's arms and teeth.

The expensive living room was crowded and overheated. Catherine left the group she'd been chatting with and glanced at the clock, willing time to pass. As Terry had said, eddies swirled below the surface. Judy circulated, hiding an acute attention behind her thick glasses, while her husband Ibrahim, grey haired and professorial, watched with interest. Terry looked lost, keenly aware that he might be affected by intrigues that no one would let him in on. She only hoped Judy would keep them from running roughshod over him.

Pete Burge ambled her way, mild mannered and untrust-worthy as a bear. She expected him to nod vaguely and move on, but he paused. "Your glass is nearly empty, Cat. Wouldn't you like more wine?"

"Thank you, I would."

He smiled, took her glass, and took his time disappearing in the direction of the bar. Whatever schemes were afoot, she was being cordially treated. Maybe her uninvolvement made her safe. Pete returned with a brimming glass. The lamplight shimmered in its crimson depths. She imagined Geoffrey's sardonic sideways glance as she took it.

"I didn't know if you were drinking burgundy or zinfandel," Pete said. "I hope burgundy is all right."

"Fine, thanks. It's a lovely view, isn't it?"

He smiled, gazing into her eyes.

"The view." Catherine nodded at the picture window. The apartment, in a luxury tower in Zamalek, looked southwest. There, beyond the dark coil of the Nile, lay Giza. She could see a second, straighter river of light, the Pyramids Road where only a few days ago she'd ridden with Geoffrey, and he had asked her to live with him.

"Sure, it's a great view, but those big windows facing west are impractical. I'd like to see Gawaz's air conditioning bill."

She answered with a polite murmur, hoping he'd move off, but he stayed. "Have you joined some spa or gym? You positively glow tonight."

"Oh, I think Egypt agrees with me."

"Very much indeed." He searched for more to say. "Well, *hrm*." He made his way back into the thick of the party, smiling at her over his shoulder.

Pete had never noticed her before, except as Terry's appendage. She gazed out at the lights of the Pyramids Road, but the tug she felt was toward the opposite direction. Garden City. She wondered if Geoffrey was at home. The breeze flickering on the river was not so soft as Geoffrey's lips on her throat, or the supple heat of his tongue. She remembered how he had held her closer as he fastened his lips to the punctures and drank, his shivering as the ecstasy took them, and the small sounds of his swallowing. A ripple went through her womb. She raised her hand to touch the scarf over the two little marks. And quickly dropped it. To her embarrassment, her sex was throbbing and moist. Composing herself, she turned back to the party.

And almost bumped into a man standing behind her. Though the fault was hers, he excused himself. With his demitasse he gestured toward the window. "By day you can see the pyramids. But the night is beautiful too, yes? I'm Tewfik. You're on Gawaz's staff?"

"I don't work for Lyndore."

"Ah. So that is why you wander on the edges looking lonely?"

What was this? Several women here were prettier than she was, others were more elegant. This Tewfik, handsome as a young Omar Sharif, why was he buzzing around her?

"My husband's doing the mingling," she nodded toward Terry, whose ear was being bent by a two people at once.

"Ahh, Terry's wife," He sounded disappointed. "Your husband is a talented man. And a lucky one." He moved closer.

And Tewfik, Catherine thought, sipping her wine, was a man very sure of his own charms.

"Terry's neglectful, to let such an enchanting woman wander around bored."

"Excuse me, please." She slipped past him.

When Geoffrey had told her that she now partook of his allure, that men would find her irresistible, it had seemed absurd. How could obsession be infectious? As she picked over the dips and cheeses Judy came to forage beside her. "Terry's made a splash with Adil Rahin, over there," she said quietly. He's a bigwig in the Ministry of Culture." She reached for the brie and knife. "I, for one, will be glad when this party is over."

"Why?"

"Oh, nothing for you and Terry to worry about."

Secrets, secrets. Glancing around the gathering, Catherine saw in every face, every gesturing hand, a veiled portent. Each politely chatting person had some secret he or she guarded, fought for, lied for. What masks did she not see through, though they hung fragile as the silk scarf hiding the marks of Geoffrey's terrible need? Was it naïve to suppose hers was the only dreadful secret in the room? Maybe beneath these party-faces all was betrayal and guilt that could never be voiced.

"Wake up, Cat. Why are you so faraway tonight?"

She focused on Judy. "I'm sorry. Just a mood."

Terry made his way between the chatting groups, but caught sight of them and came to pause beside her. "Remember your promise," he whispered in her ear.

She frowned at him, puzzled.

"'In good time,'" he quoted her mischievously.

"Oh, that."

"Yes, that. " He smiled, waved his glass at Judy, and sailed off.

Catherine turned to see Judy beaming indulgently from behind her glasses, but then her eyes shifted. "Oh dear, there's Bernie sounding off again. I'd better grab his foot before he swallows it." She charged once more into the breach.

Catherine glanced at the clock. Time wasn't crawling, it stood still. She saw Tewfik smile hopefully at her and escaped for a moment's peace in the bathroom. What would these men feel if they knew what they were being attracted to a vampire by proxy?

Catherine found the bathroom, but at the end of the empty hall a door stood open on the dim bedroom where the wraps were laid on the bed. On the bedside stand stood a phone.

If she called Geoffrey, no one at this murky, interminable party would be the wiser.

She hesitated, hating her connivance. Common sense, too, protested. Only a few days had passed since she'd seen him. She'd warned herself their times together were a rare treat.

Which would not last forever. She wanted him now. She slipped into the bedroom, pulled the door to, and dialed his number.

"*Aiwa?*" Geoffrey's brusque Arabic *yes?* was less a greeting than a warning to keep a distance.

"You're so rude I think you need a licking."

His quickly indrawn breath delighted her. "Oh? Where do you intend to lick me?"

"Up the inside of your thigh."

"Tell me more."

She distrusted the urge that came over her to tease his blood lust, but it tempted her beyond caution. "I'm drinking burgundy."

His voice lowered, roughened to a whisper. "I want to share it."

She smiled. "You can get drunk?"

"Through you." She realized what he meant. If she drank wine, and he drank her.

"I need to see you soon, Geoffrey."

A streak of brightness swept the wall. Catherine turned to see Judy in the doorway.

"Thanks," she said casually. "Bye." She hung up, but Judy had already pulled the door closed. When she reached it, the hall was empty.

She replayed what she'd been saying when she saw the light of the opening door. Nothing to betray what Geoffrey was, but she'd talked love talk and used his name.

If Judy meant to tell Terry, trying to stop her could only make it worse. Especially if she hadn't really been overheard. The best test was to face Judy now and see her reaction. Catherine forced herself up the hall and plunged into the crowd. "Come on, Cat," said Terry's voice behind her. "Let's get out of here."

"It's early yet."

"I don't care. I saw those creeps pawing you with their eyes. What's with them?"

"We can beg off in a sec. I need to talk to Judy."

"She's on the phone to her babysitter, I think. Call her tomorrow." He fairly tugged her toward their hostess. Catherine stopped resisting, wanting to escape as badly as Terry did. During the ride to Maadi she heard scarcely a word he said. Judy was a busybody who liked knowing more than other people, but that was no reason to think she was malicious. Judy was fond of Terry, but Catherine didn't know her well enough to guess whether that would make her inclined to interference, or to discretion.

Terry clicked on the bedroom lamp. "It's been too long, hasn't it?" He found the tension in her back and massaged it.

"You've been busy."

His hands went around her, drawing her to him. "Hey, don't forgive me that easy."

She had to tell him. She'd waited too long, and now it was decided for her.

"I might wonder if you've missed this at all." He pulled the comb from her hair and kissed her, the full lips she had always loved coming down over both of hers. They were still as firm and resilient as a ripe, warm plum, only her feelings had changed.

"I wanted your reassurance," she said.

Terry was silent for so long she thought he had caught her inadvertent past tense. But he only said, "Egypt is all right, but I'll be glad when we get home."

Impossible, her pulse whispered.

His hand went to the scarf.

Catherine stiffened.

"What's this on your neck?"

"Just bug bites."

"Must've been one big, nasty bug." He reached to touch them. "Or else they're infected."

"No," she said, pulling back. She couldn't tell him about Geoffrey, not just when he'd found the marks. Though Terry had never taken the vampire scare seriously, how could he not wonder?

"Whatever you say, Queen Cleopatra." He kissed her again and continued undressing her.

She'd tell him tomorrow. Their marriage could survive if they both wanted it to. It always had. For both of them their marriage was the final security.

His scent was as innocently warm as a child's, but the insistent grinding of his hips seemed not sweetly childlike but only childishly selfish, unmindful that she did not share his mood. "Slower," she asked. Terry moved more gently for awhile, but as his arousal grew he pushed insistently again. She held him close, longing for their old connection, but every touch only emphasized how much had changed.

Afterwards he asked no questions. He held her gently, as if nothing were wrong. That was the hardest of all. When he slept she rolled to the edge of the bed, silencing her tears with her pillow.

hirty-two

hen she woke Terry wasn't in bed. The rectangle of sunlight from the window had crept halfway down the wall. Catherine sat up and saw the clock hands pointing to eight-thirty. "Oh no," she groaned aloud. "Terry?"

But the apartment was silent. He'd tiptoed off to work, careful not to wake her. She rubbed the salt of the dried tears from her eyes, only hoping he'd gone to the site, not the office, and that she got to Judy first. If her soundings confirmed the worst, she would swallow her pride, confide as much as she could, and ask Judy to let her break the news herself. Even if Judy guessed nothing or didn't consider it her business, Terry must be told tonight.

As she got out of bed she caught sight of herself in the mirror. She looked radiant. She shuddered. It had nothing to do with how she felt. Filled with anxiety, a leaden throbbing in her head, she pulled on her robe and went to the living room phone.

Ms. Bakhir was in a meeting, did she want to leave a message? She did, a request to return her call. She finished dressing just as Samira arrived.

"Good morning, Madam," It was the same polite, distant greeting each day now. *"Sabbah el-kheir, ya Samira,"* she returned as they avoided one another's eyes. A change must come or she would go mad. "I have a chore for you. It isn't fun, but it needs doing. The refrigerator defroster doesn't work. I'm afraid it'll have to be done by hand."

"No broblem," Samira answered.

Catherine did not correct her as she once would have. "When you break the ice, be careful of the electric wires. Let me show you." She led the way to the kitchen and opened the fridge and freezer. "You'll have to come closer."

Samira advanced a step, but still not near enough.

"Careful, or they could shock you. All right?"

Samira burst into tears.

"What's wrong?" Instinctively Catherine reached out to her. Samira backed away. *"I know."*

That she had a lover? But that was obvious. "Know what?"

"I know that one eats your blood."

Every muscle in Catherine's body locked.

"There, under the scarf, I saw where he bite you. That man in the black car."

"That's ridiculous—"

"Fawzy says, too. He says shut up stupid, or peoples will laugh and call us *beledi*. But that—" she searched vainly for the English word, "—*el-masas ed-demaa*, he eat your blood, Cataron! How can I shut up? Mr. Terry and the city peoples, they don't know what they see. City peoples laugh, but we *beledi* know." Samira took her by the arm. "Come to peoples who will help. In my street is a woman who knows the words, the…" She touched the amulet hanging around her neck. "She will break the trouble and hide you safe until he goes from you."

"That's silly," Catherine made an effort to reason with her. "Disapprove of my seeing a man if you want, but—"

Samira shook her arm. "I thought that, but it is not your fault! Please Cataron, let me help you!"

What if the village people did have some knowledge more ancient than Geoffrey? What if they could cure this obsession? She imagined her conscience clear again, her passions small and reasonable... The prospect was like gazing on a barren desolation of desert. "No."

"You must!" Samira begged.

Catherine looked at her, but shook her head. "I don't want to be free of him."

Samira clenched her arm tighter, then let go, making a small, shrill sound of pain that continued as she backed away. "I can not be where one that eats blood comes. I can not." She backed to the door. "*Rabena yeh miki, ya Cataron.* Allah's blessing on you!" Sobbing, she ran out. Catherine heard the front door slam and knew she would never see Samira again.

And that she had refused what might have been her only lifeline.

"Why? I thought you were happy with her work."

"I was." Catherine changed the phone receiver to the other ear, her head pounding. "I've put a glowing reference in the mail to her. But she wanted to leave."

"I thought the two of you got along," Terry argued.

"Not lately."

"Why?" he repeated.

"That's between Samira and me," Catherine answered. "I've decided I won't replace her immediately. Whatever the Burges say, I want to do without a maid for a while."

It was a moment before his voice came over the line. "All right by me."

Catherine set her jaw. She tried to phone Judy again, but after the meeting she had gone straight to the site. "*Ma'alesh,*" the admin assistant said with maddening brightness. *No matter.* The Egyptian comment on nearly every setback. Even had she known

Catherine's trouble, she might only have added that everything would work out, *inshallah*. As God willed.

But if not content with Egypt's brand of wisdom, Catherine had no choice but to acknowledge she was in its hands. At least, until Terry came home and she could clear up the grand mess she'd made.

"I'm glad you're home early," she told him. "We need to talk."

"Yeah, it's been a long time since we've had much chance. How about over Indian food? There's a good restaurant in Mohandeseen. That'll give us a chance to do another thing I've put off for too long. Before dinner I'll finally treat you to the pyramids. What do you say to a sunset camel ride for two?"

"No," she said. But he was trying to make her happy. Indian was her favorite food, not his. She took a calming breath. "Let's eat out if you want, but save the pyramids for another time."

"I thought you wanted to see them."

What a tangled web we weave… "I already have."

Terry looked stricken. "We promised to go together."

"Two months ago. I tried and tried to get you to go."

"I wanted to go, if there'd been time," he answered sulkily. He looked at her with his eyes clearer than they'd been for weeks. "Why are you so distracted, Cat?"

Despite her guilt, that was too much. "For two months I've done you the favor of not asking you that."

"Maybe I wish you had." He put his arms around her, holding her hard. "Maybe I don't want to go for Indian, or to the pyramids. Maybe I only want you. God, Cat, how can I have neglected you like I've done?" He tried to kiss her.

The spell. It was only the spell. She pulled away.

"It's like last night. You don't want me at all."

"Just now, I don't," she admitted. "I want to talk."

"Because you're seeing someone else."

The world stopped. Then she nodded. "Yes, I am."

"Not that guy with the skin disease?"

"What?" she asked, baffled.

"That Brit with the skin allergies, that's who."

After all the ways she had imagined breaking the news, this was too ridiculous. "Geoffrey has no skin disease." She searched his face. "Judy told you, didn't she?"

"No, I asked her. She didn't want to, but she's worried. She thinks Harrow is bad news." He ran his hand through his hair. In a small, stricken voice he asked, "Why didn't you tell me?"

A thousand excuses, and none valid.

"The blame isn't all yours," Terry admitted. "I practically pushed you into his arms, didn't I? But you don't need some handsome sleezeball, I'm here now. Completely. I've taken the rest of the week off. End it with him, and we'll go to Luxor, or maroon ourselves on a Greek island."

She shook her head sadly. "It's not that easy. I love him."

"We don't need outsiders. Not anymore. I won't let you down."

"I love him," she repeated.

"All right. I hear that. But isn't our marriage more important? We're in trouble, Cat."

"We were in trouble anyway."

"We weren't. This guy's got you lying to me, he's changing you in ways that scare me! You've got to stop seeing him."

"It's gone too far for that."

"This isn't like you!" His hands tightened on her arms. "Phone him. Tell him it's over."

She could only stare at him. "Listen to yourself. Ordering me around is no solution. We're going to have to work this out like we always—"

"No." Terry picked up the phone and pushed it at her. "Call him and tell him. Now!"

She marched down the hall, grabbed her shoulder bag and walked out the front door. Her last glimpse was of Terry standing with the receiver in his hand, utter disbelief on his face.

hirty-three

indling a faraway minaret, the sun reached out to the world's aching limitlessness. Through a taxi window Catherine watched the sky ignite. She was doing the right thing. The wrong thing. Wrong. Right. The taxi was weaving a thread through an unforeseen, yet inevitable pattern. Her heartbeat jarred her ribs. The shadows of the passing buildings lengthened like open doors.

Doors to the unknown. How many of those had she passed for years without noticing them? Portals glimpsed in the blue heart of a candle's flare. A bright gap between two forest trees. The suddenly dilating pupils of another's eyes. Back home, a creek ran through a steep gorge. Beneath tangled rhododendrons, it made a musical belling in that mist-heavy world. From what deep place in the mountains it came she didn't know. Now, in her mind she followed that shadowy watercourse upstream to where pebbles luminescent as moons lay on its sandy bed. She rode to join a lover whose mysterious impossibility had magnified all of life to splendor.

A lover who had told her he wanted her safe, but that he would be her death. She did not intend to die. Maybe in many years, when it was time, but not before. She was hungry to live, and she wanted the life she could have with no one but him.

In the shady, curving streets of Garden City, the noise of the traffic fell away. Catherine passed the venerable houses, the fanciful balconies leaning a bit, some of the ornamental details damaged or missing. Enigmatic houses enclosing unknown lives. She wished she'd phoned Geoffrey. Though he'd invited her to live with him, that might have been a moment's whim. She suspected he cherished his solitude as much as he hated it. Now here she came straggling, in her jeans and an old shirt, bringing nothing but what was in her shoulder bag.

Geoffrey's house showed through the leaves, a grey bastion behind its barriers of wrought iron and foliage. She hadn't remembered it towering so. She paid the driver and got out.

The gate was locked. Catherine saw an intercom and pressed the button. He isn't home, she told herself, half hoping it was true.

A buzzer sounded. Quickly she pushed apart the gate. As she went up the walk Geoffrey opened the door. "Come out of the light," he said as someone else might offer shelter from a storm.

Catherine stepped into the dim hallway. First she made out the arch of his brow, and the hollow beneath a cheek pale as bone. Involuntarily she stepped back. Then her eyes adjusted, and she saw the face she'd yearned for. "I've left Terry."

Geoffrey's eyes widened slightly, then his face transformed with gladness.

"So here I am, a waif on your doorstep."

"*Our* doorstep," he answered firmly. He took her in his arms and kissed her, welcoming her with warring delicacy and conflagration. Catherine seized both and gave them back. For moments, or days, they drifted through a realm of crystalline fragile gladness, darkly incandescent. But when Geoffrey withdrew to regard her, it was with a glitter of amusement. "You marched out with no belongings at all?"

"Not so much as a change of clothes." She smiled at her ridiculousness. "Later I'll get my things — "

"Bring only what you don't want to part with. I'll take the utmost pleasure in giving you whatever you want."

"I won't be showered with gifts like a kept woman."

"Not that. A fresh beginning for the life we'll lead, at once in the world and apart from it." His self-mocking smile negated the romanticism he'd displayed. He turned away, all practicality. "I'll show you the parts of the house you haven't seen."

She followed to a large kitchen with old fashioned glass-fronted cupboards and a massive bare table. The stove was old and looked cranky. "Everything is in working order," he said, "but there's no food. Are you hungry?"

"I'm too unsettled to eat."

He glanced at her as if apprehensive she might change her mind and go, but said nothing, only showed her a dining room with a long mahogany table and formal sideboard. "You won't have to keep all of this clean. A woman comes once a week. She is just clever enough to do as she is told. She knows no English, but I'll translate your orders if your Arabic isn't up to it."

On the right side of the front hall, what had once been a morning room was heavily curtained. A couch faced a desk stacked with paperwork and alphabetically labeled file cabinets. "Business," he dismissed them. With a slight, graceful gesture he invited her through another door to a larger room.

Books filled shelves of dark wood reaching from floor to high ceiling. A thick, patterned carpet covered the floor, and two wing chairs cushioned in velvet faced the fireplace, each with an ample foot stool. Between the tall, damasked windows stood a table draped with a tapestry of a hunting scene. Its colors were faded with age. "How long have you had this?" she asked.

He lifted his eyebrow in acknowledgement of her choosing it to notice. "It was at Suffield Harrows when I was a child."

Going to the table she touched the worn needlework. Stitches had been artfully replaced here and there. "You've cared for it with love."

"One does not love a piece of cloth." But she'd caught the trace of wistfulness in his face. "With careful treatment, things remain. Despite all care, people wither and vanish. Oblivion swallows them as if time, not I, were the vampire."

Catherine knew any attempt to imagine that ceaseless loss would fall short. Responding with protestations of love would be useless. The best she could hope for was to grow old and desert him, too.

She turned to the books shelved from ceiling to floor. Old first editions rubbed covers with paperbacks and slender volumes from small presses, no collector's museum but the treasure trove of a recluse thirsty for communion with other minds. English titles mingled with French, Italian, Spanish, Swedish. "In the evenings we'll sit here, two curmudgeons with our noses in our books, and each other close by," she said. "Yes Geoffrey, if I could roll time back to this morning, I'd choose you again."

They climbed the carved staircase. There were other bedrooms besides the one where they had made love, though none was furnished so exquisitely. Then she found his other lair: a room fitted with a large screen TV, two video decks, and walls of video tapes. "So you don't dream, eh? I've discovered your dreams."

Geoffrey leaned in the doorway. He crossed his arms, smiling. "Fair enough."

She looked at him posed there so elegantly, the sexual intent of his subtly outthrust hips too tempting to ignore. She let her gaze travel slowly over him, half invitation, half challenge.

He uncrossed his arms. "Watching a movie isn't what you have in mind, I take it."

She darted past him and down the hall, staying just out of his reach, though she suspected if he'd wanted he could catch her before she so much as lifted a foot. Their bedroom was as she remembered it, the crimson, the carved mahogany, the stained glass colors patterning the carpet. "Now this wonderful bed will be used, like it deserves."

He followed, letting her stay just beyond his grasp and no farther. "It's used. I don't sleep, but I rest. I stretch out on the bed, stare at the ceiling, and . . . " he paused, teasing her.

"And?"

"And I think."

She backed away provocatively. "What do you think about?"

Pace for pace he stalked her. "You."

"Now that I'm here, you'll never think about me."

"We shall see."

Laughing she fled, but he moved so swiftly she raced into his arms. "You are mine, Catherine," his whisper was triumphant. "I no longer have to share you with anyone." He lowered her to the bed and gathered her against his body as if trying to take her into him. "All mine."

She pulled away, meeting his eyes seriously. "Before you have a blood-orgasm from pure gloating, let's settle one thing. Say I'm possessed if you want, but I'm not your possession. I don't want talk about jealousy, or killing people who hurt me. I don't belong to anyone."

"You don't?" His eyes were wide and drowned in darkness. "I do."

Despite herself, she felt a streak of elation that such a wonderful being called himself hers. "Body, heart and soul?" she asked him skeptically.

"Served up on a silver platter to any recipe you wish." His tone was sardonic, but his eyes belied it.

Exultation filled her like the swelling of a deep chord. "The gut-level instincts hiding behind love can be insidious, can't they?"

"All love is insidious."

"What if I change your mind about that?"

His eyes went hard.

"Then I'll have to prove it."

He leaned away, opened the drawer of the bedside table and took out matches. When he had struck one he held it to the candle. A warm glow made restless bronze flickerings in his hair.

"What if love can save, as well as destroy?" she said.

"What if fish roosted in trees?" he dismissed the subject. He untied her sneakers and pulled off her socks. "How can you walk on such narrow feet?"

"It does take two of them," she agreed to forget solemnity for now. He took off his own shoes and socks and lay beside her. Slowly he unbuttoned her shirt, exploring with light brushes of his lips and tongue all of her that he bared. He dwelt on each tender place as if each was in itself the whole attainment. To him, she supposed, all human lovemaking was equally a prelude, the pleasure of cherishing and the pain of insatiable craving.

They devoured one another with gazes and touches, teasing with the suppleness of lips and tongues, tantalizing with teeth. Stroking his cock with her lips and tongue, she felt the head emerge from the foreskin, flagrantly demanding yet tender as innocence, the skin stretching fine over the rigid muscle. He begged for more with a low moan, and she knew her sucking awakened doubly erotic reverberations in him. She closed her teeth. He gasped and went harder, liking being bitten almost as much as he craved to bite. She nipped and sucked his balls and he shuddered, thrusting blindly. "Vampire," she accused.

"Sucker of blood. *El-masas el-demaa*," he agreed with an emphasis that was all the more poignant for its swarm of conflicting avidness and self-aversion. He kissed from her navel down, parted her legs with his hands, and then delicately parted the lips of her sex with his lips.

Despite his eagerness he forced himself to go slowly, tasting and savoring each fold and secret recess of her so intimately that alternating waves of denial and acceptance washed over her. She shivered uncontrollably, whispering his name in protest against giving herself so completely to him, and in joy that at last she could. When the wave of her pleasure trembled on the verge of breaking, he paused, looking into her eyes. Too far beyond words to plead, she was not even certain which she would have asked him for. But tonight of all nights there was only one way to seal their bond. She shut her eyes, offering her throat.

But when she felt his lips, it was on the tender skin between her hip and sex. His tongue tasted her skin, driving her heart faster. Then his teeth pierced her. Sudden luminous pleasure radiated along each nerve, turning her muscles so languorous she could not have resisted had she wanted. She swam in currents of burning, freezing chill with each sip.

Trembling with her, he pierced deeper and drank fast and feverishly. Yet on his own brink he pulled back, and returning to her sex, feasted on the juices that had gathered there as thirstily as if they too were blood. Quickly he brought her to her own edge, and she hovered intolerably there with him, but he moved to the punctures again, and urged her blood to flow as if it were pure sex. She no longer knew which was which, or whose vein was open to whom. The nameless beauty and terror of her thirst for him matched his for her. They soared higher into the depths, their hearts throbbing together as the room whirled and the night sang.

She moaned at the cold cruelty of his tongue freezing the bleeding. Even as he did he groaned, and his lips sucked in reflexive spasms. Drowsily she drew him up and kissed him. The furniture and window rotated slowly, deliciously around them. His heartbeat and tremors subsiding against her, Geoffrey molded his body warm to hers, preparing to hold her through the night. Though he would not sleep, this way of resting together seemed natural to her now. Nothing felt more right than the utter peace and oneness of their shared blood. She murmured, "You're sure having me around won't be a burden?"

"A burden?" he asked in a soft, dazed voice. "Only if too much happiness is a burden."

She smiled. Sleep swallowed her like a leaf in a whirlpool.

hirty-four

he woke to the aroma of eggs and toast. "Open your eyes, Catherine," Geoffrey said so firmly that this time there was no ignoring him. She did, and saw him standing by the bed with a tray.

She smiled. "You can cook?"

For some reason beyond her, he looked relieved. "Hardly. The yolks are both broken." He spared them a baleful glance.

"Their own fault, no doubt." She sat up. Geoffrey and the bed and the crimson walls spun.

"Catherine?"

It all slowly glided back into place and settled. "I'm all right," she said. "Those eggs smell delicious."

She drank the large glass of orange juice and began hungrily eating, proving she was fine, and better than fine. Geoffrey left but returned almost immediately, bringing the glass refilled with juice. "You're going to think I'll gobble you out of house and home." She looked at the nearly empty plate. "I did miss dinner last night," she added in defense of her piggery.

Leaning back against the pillow she stretched lazily. "What time is it?"

"Four-thirty."

"In the afternoon?"

"Yes," he answered the obvious with uncharacteristic patience.

She frowned. "I hope I'm not coming down with flu."

His expression was cold. "Last night I was careless. You are suffering from loss of blood."

Fear clamped tight claws on her shoulders. She fought them off. "Not necessarily. My throat's sore."

"The dry air."

"I've lived in Egypt long enough to tell the desert from a sore throat."

"Usually, but you're dehydrated."

Irritated, she answered, "You can't be happy unless you feel guilty, can you?"

He took the tray and left the room. Now she'd driven him away. He was mistaken, but she regretted her snappishness.

But soon he returned with a teapot and single cup on the tray. Beside the cup was a small pile of pills. She recognized a beige vitamin C, a school bus yellow B complex, a brown speckled multi, a little pink B12, and lurking beneath the others where maybe he thought she wouldn't notice, two hefty iron tablets. She was glad he'd returned, and vitamins would fight flu as much as anemia, so she accepted them without comment. Taking the teacup of cool water he offered, she set about the task of swallowing them all.

"I've an interesting murder mystery by a new writer from Yorkshire," he said as she poured herself some tea. "Would you like me to read the first chapter aloud?"

Better that than getting up and doing the dishes just yet. She was irked at herself for getting sick just as they were beginning life together but reminded herself they had time, now.

As if avoiding the bed, he sat in one of the claw-footed chairs. He read beautifully, the irony edging his tone perfect for the black humor of the mystery. His voice became a countryside where deep valleys lay between steep, stony slopes. She wandered there half awake until finally she rested by a hidden stream and slept.

The light glowed crimson. Sunset, filtered through the crimson curtain. Geoffrey sat in the chair. The book lay on the table beside him.

"I'm not that sick. You don't have to bore yourself watching over me."

His voice bit cold as steel. "We'll have no chance to get bored."

"You could try that game of driving me away once too often. It's not impossible to do, you know."

"Go, then." When she did not immediately leave, he added just as coldly, "At least, I will drive us both to our senses."

"I wish you'd come to yours. Last night was magnificent. You think I'd give that up yet?" She threw back the covers and got out of bed. "See? I'm not faint. Where did you put my clothes?"

"In the wardrobe." He watched her go to it. The room swayed, but she hid it as she dressed. "Bet I caught this bug at the Lyndore party."

He turned on the bright overhead light and approached, his menace a storm scarcely contained. "Look into my eyes, Catherine."

"I've seen your eyes." But to get him out of her face, she looked. The whites of his eyes were filmed with red. Shocked out of her aggravation, she asked, "What's happened to you?"

"I should think the answer is obvious. If you were to kiss me, you would taste blood in my saliva, too. Last night I had no need for blood. Nothing drove me but the lust you insist on calling love. You're looking at the symptoms of glut." He arched a brow at her reaction. "Not a pretty word, is it? And not a pretty condition."

His voice lowered as his fury increased. "Last night I surrendered to my selfishness, and afterward drifted in bliss like an utter fool. I did not even realize how severely I had robbed you until this morning I urinated. Or, what passes for that with my kind." With the cold precision of utter rage, he hissed, "Perhaps I should have dragged you from bed and made you watch me piss away your lifeblood, Catherine. Or shall I tell you what a part of me desires now, even as I fear for you?"

"What you piss is your own business. Leave me alone, I'm fine!" She stalked past him, hurried down the stairs holding onto the rail, and searched for an escape. Not the library. That was his territory. She remembered the back door in the kitchen. He was not likely to follow her, but she shut it after her.

Red light slanted over the garden wall. Parched weeds hissed in the breeze. Obviously, Geoffrey took no interest in gardening. Some previous owner had planted tamarind trees, a date palm, and against the house, jasmine bushes that now grew rampant. Beyond the dusty foliage Catherine saw a stone bench and made her way to it. She faced a small fish pool now dry. Beginning to feel dizzy again, she sat on the bench.

She should phone Terry to let him know she was all right. And that she was not going back. She couldn't have him coming after her. Sadly she remembered the new beginning they'd hoped to make in Egypt. Perhaps they could have, if things had been different at Lyndore, or if Terry had reacted to them differently, or if she had never met Geoffrey. If, if, if…

The sunset light was clearing her head. She felt her strength returning. This garden made a world of its own, its brightness separate and secret from the shadowy house. The high walls gave privacy from the neighbors' windows. Abandoned by the vampire, this forlorn garden seemed the most romantically vampiric place of all. The bowed legs of the old bench she sat on, carved like sea babies playing with dolphins, were cracked, missing an arm here, a nose there. The leaves sighed, throwing kaleidoscopic shadows into the empty pool.

She would fill it with water, and fish. Lotus blossoms should float here. She'd enjoy the work by day, and Geoffrey might like sitting with her by night, watching the moonlight reflect on the water. She would let the jasmines spread as disheveled as they wanted. That suited a demon's garden.

She caught sight of her hand on her knee, transparent as candle wax beneath her tan. The veins contrasted too vividly.

Her weakness wasn't flu.

The frightening thing was not the lost blood. It was realizing she'd been out of control. Swept by passion, Geoffrey could have drunk her blood until he killed her, and last night she wouldn't even have tried to stop him.

Every molecule in her cried out against renouncing such rare sweetness just when she'd found it, but for the first time it seemed real that if she wasn't careful she might die. She wanted to heal Geoffrey's pain, but not at the cost of her life.

Their happiness might last as briefly as a week before she had to go. Or might one more night kill her? She shuddered.

The only sensible course was to face it, talk with Geoffrey, and learn the truth.

She found him in his study. Invoices lay on the desk, but his back was to them. He sat staring at the closed curtains that faced the garden.

"If you keep drinking me, how long before I die?"

He was not startled to find her so near. Of course with his acute senses he had probably heard her come into the house as if she were a herd of elephants. For all she knew, he'd heard her in the garden through the stone walls of the house.

"Leave me and you won't die."

"That's why I need to know. Should I be afraid of you now, or next week, or next year?"

"It's a matter of weeks or months, rather than days," he admitted. "If we are careful."

"Then, before I'm forced to leave you to survive, I want to discover a way to survive with you."

His eyes were still tinged with her blood, but their expression was vulnerable. "Then we must abstain as far as possible — from the drinking, at any rate. When it defeats us and we must, if you feel dizzy or chilled, warn me at once."

"If I do, will you stop?"

"I give you my word I shall try with all my power."

She nodded, acknowledging his honesty. "Then I trust you."

"Trust my word if you like, but not my control."

"I trust my thirst to live. Can you?"

"Of course not," he answered so emphatically it was obvious he hated the temptation to hope.

Catherine stepped close to his chair. "Then trust in the love you fear so much." She put her hands on his shoulders, but he remained tense. "Trust that we are linked, that if destiny exists, ours are inseparable."

Geoffrey did not answer, but slowly, with reluctance and doubt, he let his head rest against her.

 hirty-five

ay and night flowed together, crimson through drawn curtains, amber from candles. The clock on the mantel punctuated hours that no longer divided time. They conversed, they made love, they read aloud and mused in companionable silence. Catherine had the garden cleared. She stocked the pool with lotus plants and Japanese goldfish. By twilight she and Geoffrey watched the glidings of the bulbous-eyed fish, sharing fragments of impressions and flights of fancy.

They tended Antiqa, Geoffrey's cavernous shop with its Bedouin needlework, silver tea services, Roman coins and medieval amulets against the evil eye, its ormolu pill boxes, its vases of tinted mouski glass with bubbles trapped in their fragile walls. In the back he kept his Ali Baba's hoard of real treasures, exquisite old Islamic ceramics of azure and leaf-green, antique carpets from Shiraz and Istanbul, trays embellished with the meticulous inlay for which Cairo had once been famous, and leaning against the back wall, carved wooden *mashrabiyya* screens that had once filtered and patterned the daylight in pashas' palaces.

Geoffrey's business hours were capricious even by Egyptian standards, and every so often someone wandered in, surprised to find the shop open. He said his important sales were made by appointment, but Catherine suspected he was neglecting business to be with her. She heard him returning phone messages putting customers off, and often Antiqa remained locked under the eye of his grim, pistol packing watchman while the two of them went to the movies or spent the day in bed. He drank her sparingly but gave pleasure generously.

When the sun shone too bright for him she worked in her garden or went out by herself since she still needed sunlight, but she drifted into sleeping by day, and found she wanted less sleep than before. Like Geoffrey, she was now the most alert by night. Though she was constantly a little dizzy and thirsty, a glowing elation sustained her.

Geoffrey brought a second tall mahogany wardrobe from a spare bedroom for her, lifting it as if it weighed no more than cardboard. He ferreted out merchants with European connections for clothing not to be found in Cairo's shops. Calling them Christmas gifts, he surprised her with crimson satin sheets, a rare rose bush with silvery lavender buds, and a Spanish guitar much finer than her playing deserved. She resisted such extravagances until she understood they were not recompense for the blood he took. His delight in giving was another of the secrets he vigilantly guarded. Pouring out a generosity long denied was a pleasure to him.

From her old life she retrieved little. Braving the Cairo traffic, she drove the Toyota to Maadi, choosing a time when Terry was at work, and brought back one load. But though she'd told Terry not to come to see her, she couldn't tell him not to call.

"I was a jerk the day you left," he apologized. "I don't know what got into me. Well, yes I do. I realized I was losing you. I panicked. I can cope now. I understand that you love this guy."

"Yes," Catherine answered, hating to hurt him but needing him to accept it.

"So, we need to figure out what to do."

"I have," she tried to be gentle. "Please, try to move on, too."

Her insistence that Terry not come to Garden City hurt him, but there was no help for it.

Catherine woke to twilight. The window stood open to the balcony where the scent of the night blooming jasmine ascended from the garden. She sat up, listening. The absence of footsteps or creaking boards meant nothing, Geoffrey never made those noises. She listened in vain for the faint sound of the television.

A nebulous misgiving seized her. Surely he did not need to hunt tonight. Yesterday the paleness of his face had held a faint flush of color, and his hand had felt warmer than usual. Though she tried not to think about it, she knew what those signs must mean. He had fed last night. It would be nearly a week before the need overtook him again. But the consequences could catch up with him even during his most innocent actions. If Mounir Abdel Razak discovered what Geoffrey really was, would he continue to merely gather evidence, hoping for an arrest and prosecution? Catherine doubted it. Mounir, and how many others? Geoffrey had the experience of centuries, but his two warnings to her had been rash. She must keep him from ever attempting another one.

She turned on the lamp and slipped out from the covers. On the other pillow a piece of paper lay, folded small. Puzzled, she opened it. The precise strokes of Geoffrey's handwriting, carefully free of old-fashioned flourishes, spelled out an odd little rhyme. Catherine frowned, at a loss until she realized it was a riddle. Its solution could only be an old chest of drawers, one with lion feet. Like the one in the spare bedroom. Slipping on her robe, she went there. Lying on top of the chest was a pair of fingerless lace gloves.

Mystified, she picked them up. Beneath lay another note. Its clue drew her downstairs to the library, where draped over an armchair she found a blouse inset with lace, ivory like the gloves, and on the footstool, a pair of silk stockings. Smiling, she lifted the blouse. It had a high collar with little buttons. Anticipating his fantasy, whatever it was, she gathered up the hose. One of the crimson garters encircled another little roll of paper. Its riddle took her to the back stairs where a pair of high heeled shoes was whimsically placed as though climbing two at a time, like she did. The toe of the left contained the next clue.

Aroused by this playfulness, she followed the foreplay of the scavenger hunt to her own wardrobe, where she discovered a long ivory silk skirt, impossibly demure except for a lace-edged slit to the hip. She found no further notes. She dressed in the fantasy costume, which included nothing to go under the provocative skirt. She put up her hair and imitated the circa 1930 movie makeup she thought would look striking with it. Last, she put on the gloves.

She checked the effect in the mirror on the inside of Geoffrey's wardrobe door, the only mirror in the bedroom. The style emphasized her height and slenderness, making her elegant and seductive. Charmed with this new guise, and with him for knowing it would suit her, she longed for his return. As if in answer, she heard the slight rattle of the garage door. She arranged herself in one of the carved-back bedroom chairs. The key turned downstairs, the tiny sound magnified in the stairwell. Catherine's pulse quickened.

She heard no steps, only the muffled sound of velvet. Geoffrey strode through the door furled in a black cloak. With a powerful grace movie Draculas only dreamed of, he turned to her, letting the cape flare, his eyes glinting in self-mockery and arousal. If the theatricality of his pose was oddly thrilling, even more the hint of real menace beneath. Then Catherine understood. This was not his fantasy but hers. For her, he dared ridicule his despair and give substance to the dreams he denied.

Catherine leapt to her feet. Mina to his Dracula, she swooned. As she'd trusted, he caught her before she fell. He carried her not to the bed but out to the balcony. Without a word, the embodiment of the darkness itself, he kissed her breasts through the silk, his lips and hands warm in the fervid night. Immersed in the perfume of the jasmine, silvered by moonlight, he parted her skirt, revealing her. Looking down at her, he undressed himself, all but the cape.

Prolonging each moment to an infinity, he bent to her again, caressing her with the powerful delicacy of his hands, the softness of his lips, the feverish heat of his chest and loins. He pierced first her sex, then shivering with a yearning even that intimacy could not slake, unbuttoned her high collar and closed his teeth in her throat. Their sharpness wounded her with unbearably sweet ecstasy.

With his lips and tongue he coaxed the blood to the surface. His cock was exquisitely insistent as he thrust to the rhythm of her blood pulsing against his tongue. She clung to him, voraciously devouring him as he drank her. As they shuddered together in the blood orgasm, the beating of their hearts and coursing of their blood flowed into the familiar oneness, a single luminous raptness in the throbbing heart of the night.

No time, no death. Bodies, yet no imprisonment in them. Nothing to separate him from her, or them from the swarming nearness of the stars.

Then a softness, his hair between her fingers, the tendril-ends clinging like smoke. He turned his head under her hand and stirred, thrusting one last time. She sighed in a pang as elusive and poignant as a scarce-heard echo.

"You forgot jewelry," he murmured.

Slowly, words regained meaning. "Oh? Did that interfere with your thrill?"

He raised to look at her, his eyes far blacker than the moon-silvered sky. "No." Luxuriously he stretched and rose. She loved the beauty of his body gleaming against the black velvet of the cape. She stood, fighting the dizziness that came over her. She was still clothed, her skirt falling together innocently, only her collar unbuttoned. "But," he continued, lighting a candle and carrying it to the dressing table, "had you remembered, you would have opened your jewelry box."

She lifted the lid while he held the candle for her to see. In the tray opposite her discarded wedding band lay a ring set with a burgundy-dark garnet surrounded by jet and topaz, deep fires throbbing in the flicker of the candle. Taking her left hand in its fingerless glove, Geoffrey slid the ring onto her finger. Its rich hues and obvious antiquity fascinated her. Or was it that it was his, and his spell coursed through it as her blood did through him? "Lovely," she whispered. "But it must be valuable. You don't mean for me to wear it?"

"I had it made in 1606," he answered. "Modern, by Egyptian standards."

"You shouldn't give it away."

"It was Elizabeth's. I have never wanted anyone else to wear it, until you."

Tears came to her eyes. Too many emotions conflicted too sharply. Then it occurred to her that considering what he thought the end of their relationship would be, he might not regard it as given away. "I'll wear it," she promised, "but when I go I'll give it back."

"Throw it in the Nile if you like. Do you really suppose a lump of metal and stone means more to me than you do?" His pain wounded her, and she held him close.

When he did not return her kiss she guessed she had hurt him more than she knew. He was such a complex and fragile predator, and she loved him more for each subtlety she discovered. She licked the now familiar taste of blood from his lips, and he suffered it as though this, too, were pain, letting her tongue wash the blood from his.

He wrapped the cloak around them both, against the warm night breeze. His kiss was another drinking of her, savoring and greedy by turns. At last he stepped back, moonlight sliding like quicksilver over his cheek to outline the sculpted bow of his lips.

"You are my match, Catherine. I have never known anyone who could take me to the edge of intolerable ecstasy and hold me there as you can. Never known anyone who could satisfy me in the necessity of my unsatisfaction as you do."

"You satisfy me," she answered. "Utterly."

"No. That is yet to come."

She shivered. "Don't talk like that. Just hold me."

He did, gently. She felt the beating of their hearts in unison. "I won't let you kill me. I'm going to live, Geoffrey."

"And how will you stop yourself?"

Not *how will you stop me,* she noticed in hope and despair. *How will you stop yourself.*

hirty-six

he nights grew cooler, but the fragrance of roses lingered. The scents of marjoram, coriander and roasted melon seeds mingled in the streets of the spice market. Shopping with the evening crowds, she and Geoffrey strolled through lanes of vivid colors and multitudinous sounds, beneath balconies like black lace against the thick stars. An insistent throbbing of desert drums from one window clashed with the wistful flutter of a Nilotic flute from another. Like a vampire, Cairo lived the most intensely by night.

The luminescence in Geoffrey's eyes reflected it all. Though he and Catherine rarely touched in public, her blood ran through them both, one secret within the thousand mazes and enigmas of the city. "Jaffiry and Cataron, haunting the Cairo nights," she said, "drinking the scents of cinnamon and dates until we've swallowed the whole city, and it becomes ours, and is us."

"To drink Egypt with you is intoxication," he agreed. "But tell me, would you rather haunt the Paris nights? Or Rome? Any city in the world can be ours, if you wish it."

Possibilities flowed through her mind, the Thames lapping the misty banks of London, the shadow plays of Bali, crepe myrtle in the old quarter of Savannah. Yet none seemed as charged with wild sorceries as Cairo. "You've made Egypt my home," she said. "After I've left you, we can meet now and then in Venice or Istanbul. For now, being with you here is the universe."

Pausing at a stand piled with vegetables she picked out a lovely fat white garlic.

"I would rather you didn't buy that," said Geoffrey.

"You're not serious." Moving closer with it, she teased, "If I wear a wreath of this will I be safe from you?"

He took it from her. "Eating it taints the blood with an unpleasant flavor," he answered too quietly for anyone but her to hear.

"Mmm," she murmured, breathing in his scent. She spotted a heap of *golgas*, tubers creamier than potatoes. "No garlic, then. Just these and cumin." Reaching for one she felt a small stab in her finger. A splinter from the wooden stand had lodged in her skin. It came out cleanly, but her blood welled scarlet. She smiled mischievously. "Geoffrey."

When he saw the drop of blood the pupils of his eyes expanded. Catherine laughed in giddy pleasure.

He took her by the hand, holding her finger so that none would spill. It was the finger with his ring. He led her to the entrance of an alley. The ring cast garnet and amber reflections, then dark swallowed them. In a shadowed doorway Geoffrey raised her hand to his lips. His tongue swept warm over the cut and she shivered.

Geoffrey tensed. "Let us be sensible," his whisper rasped. His hand closed hard over hers and he pulled her back out to the lane, into the colored lights and shoppers.

"What is it?"

"We were unwise, wouldn't you say?"

He hadn't lied. Hadn't said *nothing*. But what had put him on his guard that he didn't want her to know about?

Glancing behind, Catherine caught a flick of red, a cigarette tossed aside. Beyond the smoker, a man in drab clothes strolled away.

It wasn't Mounir. He wasn't slender but stocky, and his hair was greying. From the back he looked like an aging boxer or professional soldier. Or a thug. "Police?" she asked quietly.

Geoffrey gave an almost inaudible sigh. "I didn't want you alarmed. Yes, I am being followed. I have been for some time now. And yes, that is a policeman. But he has nothing to do with the Antiquities Service or the regulation of international trade. My police contact told me he is a homicide detective."

She gave a small cry.

"I'm not part of any homicide investigation."

"Can you be sure?"

"I have my information from two separate sources. Telling me the truth has proved profitable to them, and they know it will continue to be. If you want to know, I think our rather substantial shadow is working on the side as a private investigator."

"For who?"

Geoffrey's eyes narrowed. He suspected someone, that was clear. "At first I thought it was a certain European syndicate who don't like my independent trading. But I now think that unlikely. Nor is it religious extremists targeting a wealthy Westerner."

"Then, who?"

"Mounir Abdel Razak."

"Geoffrey, let's leave Egypt."

"It's the same everywhere. As threats go, our friend Mounir is predictable. I don't know why he suspects me, but he plays by the rules. He merely watches, hoping for evidence. He won't get it."

She dreamed of being chased, she and Geoffrey, through the eucalyptus woods on the UC Berkeley campus. They dodged among shadowy trees but couldn't shake the pursuers. Legs heavy as if the eucalyptus sap were a sea of molasses, they struggled, couldn't run fast enough, searched desperately for shelter. She opened her eyes. Geoffrey sat on the edge of the bed, frowning at her in the candlelight. "Whatever you dreamed, it called me," he whispered. "I wish you wouldn't. I find it disturbing."

"They were trying to catch us."

"Who was?"

"Mounir. He thinks you killed someone he loved."

"You knew that?"

"He told me long ago." She burrowed into the pillows, miserable. "I betrayed you. I didn't tell you. But it was only because I wanted to protect him. Then, when I didn't see him again, I hoped he'd given up."

"It's not important." But he sounded sad. "You are human, Catherine, and you're good. What should I expect? And after all, it makes no difference. Believe it or not, I see no reason to harm Mounir. Actually, I rather like him."

She raised her head, startled.

"He warned you off me quite early, did he? Mounir Abdel Razak is a man who cares about others. That's a weakness. He's village-bred, as I am. So probably he's a hunter, a man shaped in a world where people take matters into their own hands. Yet, he has educated himself. That's a weakness, too. He can't see what I am because he can't bring himself to believe in it."

"He's obsessed." she warned. "He wants justice."

"Prison? Execution?" Geoffrey shook his head. "I've played this game far longer than he has. Unless Mounir brings himself to realize what I am, he's no threat."

Geoffrey lay beside her. He could almost be mistaken for a sleeping man, except the muscles in his jaw were tense, and every so often a slight tremor passed through him.

"You want me and you're fighting it," she said.

"We must both fight it."

The wardrobe door was ajar. In its mirror she caught sight of her reflection glowing, translucent in the crimson light. Her cheeks were hollower, her eyes larger and more radiant than they had been. She glanced at the table where the she had arranged little bottles of perfume he had bought her. "Mask the scent of my blood."

"You do it. I must leave the room."

But she needed him too fiercely. She leaned back against the pillow, letting the sheet slowly slip from her breasts. Geoffrey cursed and rose.

Seizing the most exotic and overwhelming of the scents, he stripped the covers from her and pulled her to her feet. With one finger he touched a drop to each pulse at her throat, then with two smoothed it down the curves of her breasts, into her wrists, and with lingering strokes, behind her knees.

"There," he said. "Now even I can detect only the one thousand and one nights, all the mingled spices of Arabia." But he brushed the sensitive bluntness of his fingers down her throat again, following the lines of the tendons. Lowering his mouth again, he kissed her throat so gently that she did not realize he had pierced the skin until she felt a warm wetness creep down her neck.

She would have protected herself from him. Or else, she would have begged him to fasten his lips to her. But she only looked into his eyes. They glittered as he watched the thin trail of blood slowly roll down her breast, her ribs, her stomach, the hollow of her hip. It trickled into the corner of the hair on her sex, gathering there, then coursed a narrow, glistening path down her thigh, and her knee, and the inside of her calf. When it reached her ankle he put his lips to her throat and stopped the bleeding.

Kneeling, be bent to her foot, gathered the blood with the supple heat of his tongue, and moved upward, sipping slowly, diverting to linger over whatever softness or hollow drew him, but returning always to the rivulet of crimson. His lips centered over her heart. Pressing to her, he held her, his lips thirsty on her skin. She cried out softly to him.

"Catherine," his moan resonated low. The piercing of his teeth was a spear of ecstasy through her.

Thirty-seven

The twilit pool mirrored their dark shapes, her kneeling on the edge, Geoffrey on the bench reading by the light of the half moon. Below their reflections the fish drifted, shadows caught in torpid, watery dreams. She saw one wake and circle among the roots as if searching. Or was it the slow whirl of a sunken leaf? A page rustled as Geoffrey turned it, and she smiled over her shoulder at the strangeness of him sitting there reading in the dark. "What does the night look like to you?"

"A blue transparency, rather like looking through stained glass, except for the night colors."

"Which are those?"

"They have no names. Your eyes can't see them, and my kind has never invented words for them. The pool deepens to sapphire at its bottom, but a vivid darkness like a cold flame shines from the eye of the smallest goldfish, the one with the forked tail. It thinks itself well hidden among the roots, but its gills pulse, showing a color that is not scarlet. There is a subtle tint along the limbs of the tamarind tree, just at the edges of the moonlight, rather pale and incandescent."

"I wish I could see it."

"The night is beautiful to me," he answered as softly as the murmur of the leaves. "I wish I could photograph it for you."

"When you had your fever, everything turned radiant, you said. You floated in nothingness. Do you think you died?"

"Am I dead, do you mean? What a flattering question to be asked by the woman I love." He opened his book again.

"If the shoes fits. But no, it was a real question."

"You fancy the notion that you make love with a walking corpse?"

"Stop being difficult. You did say you inhabit your body differently than I do."

"Certain accounts from people revived from clinical death interest me," he admitted. "The light, the sensation of bodiless freedom. But none who returned to ordinary life have described anything like the darkness that engulfed me and the others of my kind."

"You seized it and held on. You could have chosen not to. You might have stayed where you were."

"I chose darkness over light? Yes, it's occurred to me. If so, I wasn't aware at the time. It was a blind choice."

"An instinctive one," she countered.

"Show me how to reverse it and I'll waste no time."

She hated that answer. "You chose without knowing what it would mean, but what about me? I chose you with my eyes open. What does that say about me?"

She heard the book land on the bench with an exasperated thump. "You persist in making it a moral question. It was a disease. I am now its carrier. You are its victim. My inability to resist entrapping you is the only deliberate choice in the whole matter, if you wish to cast blame."

In the silence the lights of an airplane pulsed across the sky.

She imagined Geoffrey dead. Really dead, gone from her, gone from the world. At peace. "You must've tried," she said. "I don't mean suicide. You did try that. And I realize you can't live on synthetic kool-aid blood like a movie vampire. But if you must kill, just hunting randomly…"

"I see," he answered quietly. "Turn my need to the good of humanity? Feed only on murderers and thugs, remove the oppressors from the world? Become the judge of others' worthiness to live." His voice harshened. "A self-appointed god."

But his fury was not directed at her. A realization struck her. "Your kind tried to do exactly that."

"Would I be such a fool?" he snarled.

"I can't see you starting it, or leading it. Someone else did, but however reluctantly, you allowed yourself to hope. Even now you can't forgive that."

"Hope? Of course I hoped when I discovered I wasn't alone. I hoped for companionship, others to whom I need not pretend."

"Others who wouldn't die and leave you."

"That did present possibilities. Imagine the wealth and control a few talented people could acquire in two centuries. Not only for the sake of power. For security. No more existing as fugitives, no more being the hunted as much as the hunters. I could have made us so strong no one could have threatened us."

"What went wrong? No, start at the beginning. Tell me about the others."

"The first rumors of another hunter reached me during the war to overthrow Cromwell and restore the king. As I told you, in the end I discovered only a ragged old half-wit. Or perhaps, being forced to exist as she did had deprived her of her wits. But her mumbled tale of another like us led me to Venice.

"My family had connections there. I'd visited Venice as a young man, but now I saw it as never before. At night, the water sparked with blue luminescence below the bridges, it slid like phosphorus against the stones of the houses. They were crumbling even then, the water licking with the soft, ceaseless insistence that will sooner or later dissolve that magnificent city to nothing.

"The delicate, trembling reflections, the echoes. They were so haunting, and so exquisite, that I was beguiled into carelessness.

A sword split the air right before my eyes. I scarcely had time to draw and counter. Not since my change had I met a match for my speed or strength. There was joy in being tested, really tested. I prevailed. I let him stagger back, dazed. Orlando was his name. He, too, had once fallen into a fever, seemingly died, and was 'resurrected.' So he chose to put it.

"Nor was he the only one. Some dozen had found one another. They had a leader. Orlando described him as a man of extraordinary vision. Before his change, Johann von Berchin was a young philosophy professor at Heidelberg. 'He has the learning to comprehend what has happened to us, this Johann,' Orlando promised me. 'He is discovering the way to cure of us of our deadly curse.'"

"Did you believe in a cure, at least at first?"

"Not really, though biology was a largely uncharted science at the time, and who knew what might be possible? No, what I hoped for was cooperation between my kind, but in that I was entirely disappointed. The scent, the very presence, of a vampire is repugnant to another vampire. I didn't foresee how difficult controlling that animosity would prove. Von Berchin believed it could be overcome. If any could have achieved that, it was he. Blond, magnetic, benevolent, had I not known what he was I might have called him angelic. But that was the effect of his spell. He needed blood as much as any of us.

"I did not foresee the power his spell would exert on his own kind. He thrived on hopes, but they were false. The more so because he believed in them, himself. Johann prated compellingly of Galen, Plato, Plotinus, and of what he called a 'Chymical Wedding.' 'Alchemy?' I scoffed. But he smiled and said he had no interest in transmuting lead into gold.

"These were just symbols, he said. So was the vague self-perfection sought by human alchemists. No, he said, Alchemy's highest purpose was the transformation of our kind. We would become immortals with no need for blood. He had Orlando working on an elixir, but that wasn't enough. We must achieve worthiness. We must be the enlightened guides of mankind. He founded an academy for that purpose. He named it the Society of the Golden Lion. Ostentatious twaddle.

"Yet, I saw a use for the academy. Some of our kind needed education and polish, if they were to exert influence. Others must learn to control behavior that endangered us all. If they couldn't, then we needed to control them. Johann could call the Society anything he liked, so long as it provided these things.

"But as fast as I accumulated resources, von Berchin spent them. Had it been greed, I'd have known how to handle him. But anyone in need, vampire or human, inspired his generosity—with my money. Oh yes, Johann was the stuff saints are made of. His mercy was as boundless as his guilt."

"But it sounds like he tried."

"Ceaselessly. I can't remember Johann without his books, maps and diagrams. Orlando slaved over sulfurous alchemical fires at his bidding. He urged the Society to hunt only evil prey, never the innocent." He smiled. "Deciding who deserved death and who did not provoked endless quarrels. From killing to killing, many clung to a hope that each would be the last. That Johann would find the elixir. He shored up their despair by claiming that their suffering could confer the wisdom to become worthy advisors to mankind. To whom, he insisted, we owed a great debt.

"At last, he discovered the elixir. His explanation even seemed logical. The transformation required one vampire and one human. Their blood, mingled with this elixir, would produce the antidote. He had a volunteer, a gullible young man who loved and believed blindly in him. Johann had greater strength than any of us. He could resist drinking those he loved, and his lover might have lived had he not been ensnared in Johann's false hopes. Orlando meticulously performed the process. Johann and the young man bled into a chalice, he added the elixir, and they drank the result.

"Johann vomited and was otherwise unaffected." Catherine heard the catch in Geoffrey's breath. "For mercy, we tried to kill what was left of the young man. In the end we were forced to bury it alive. One only hopes that perhaps it eventually died. That was too much for Johann. It broke him.

"His believers turned on him. They waited until I was gone. Whether they betrayed him to the men who captured him or merely stood by and refused to help him, I never learned, but I should have foreseen it. Perhaps I did, I don't know."

"What happened to him?"

"It took me half a century to discover where he was buried. When I unsealed the pit, I found what had been Johann. But I couldn't turn it loose on the world. I had no choice but to seal it up again."

She couldn't put her arms around him. She had no other comfort to offer. There was none.

"It is still there, beneath the mountain," he said. "Mad, hideous. Ceaselessly, it craves blood."

T hirty-eight

 atherine dreamed of candles. The eyes of candles, blinking, flickering. Thousands, filling the jasmine air of the bedroom with smoke. Phantom shapes scintillated before her, the candles' eyes watching her. The shallow hammering of her heart woke her.

Through a narrow crack in the curtains, sunset splashed a long streak down the red wall. Chilled despite the sweat beading her forehead, she sat up. The room spun slowly as she stuck her feet into her slippers and made her way to the wardrobe to dress.

As she opened its door, light flashed, but the inside of the wardrobe door was dark. A scar gashed the wood, and jagged shards glinted, held in place by the brackets. The rest of the mirror lay shattered on the carpet.

She didn't wonder what had happened. Geoffrey had struck at the reflection of himself.

Yet, the noise hadn't waked her. She slept so soundly these days. She did little, but slept the heavy sleep of exhaustion. She stepped back from the splintered glass, glad she had her slippers on. The room floated for a nauseous moment and she steadied herself against the bedpost.

Geoffrey was right. She had to go, or he would kill her.

Despite his love.

Because of his love.

What would he do then, loathing himself as he did? How much longer could he cling to his desperate control? Empty despair filled her.

Down the hall the phone rang. And again. She lifted her head, but it stopped. "Catherine," Geoffrey's voice called. It sounded oddly neutral.

Pulling her silk robe around her, she went to the video room where the upstairs phone was. Geoffrey handed it over without a word, then left the room.

"Yes?"

"Cat," Terry's voice was strained. "Is everything all right?"

"Why shouldn't it be?" She'd asked him to give her space.

He didn't answer at once. She hadn't intended to hurt him, but the last thing she could deal with now was Terry trying to argue her into going back to him.

"I think you should know this. I wouldn't've called otherwise. I just had a weird visit. Do you know somebody named Mounir?"

The room spun. Catherine gripped the arm of the sofa. She had to think clearly. "Geoffrey has a client named Mounir."

She pictured Terry frowning, rubbing the skin between his eyebrows. "I don't know whether I should warn you about Harrow, or warn you both about this Mounir guy. He showed up out of the blue, telling me to get my wife back home because Harrow is under investigation."

"What investigation?"

"Could this guy be undercover, maybe not a real client at all? He hinted, acted like he had weight to throw around, but he wouldn't say who he was with. He just said you're considered an innocent bystander and advised me that Lyndore can't afford you being connected with 'it.'"

"What did you say?"

"I asked him for his identification. He wouldn't show me any."

"Because he's faking. Mounir Abdel Razak has approached me, too. He doesn't represent anybody. He's just a man with a grudge against Geoffrey."

"Maybe so, but I don't like this. And whatever's between these two guys, I don't like Harrow dragging you into it."

"He didn't. Listen, did this Mounir strike you as quite rational?"

"Well," Terry considered. "Yes. But he wanted you away from Harrow, and it wasn't just consideration for my mural, or Lyndore. Why should he care where you are?"

"Like I said, he's trying to get at Geoffrey."

"Then Harrow should call the police. This guy isn't all talk. That's just my gut feeling, but it's a strong one. He means business."

"I'll tell Geoffrey." She changed the subject. "I saw the Lyndore from the Cornishe yesterday. Your mural is coming along. I saw pale green, and shapes starting to grow in amber and blue."

"It's happening," Terry conceded. "That is, whenever I get enough breathing space from the reporters and documentary crew to work."

"It's beautiful, like a breeze, or a wing. Are you happy with it?"

"I like what I'm painting. I'm not happy. How could I be happy?

That was unfair. Deserved. It was her fault. His. Hers. How could she know?

"I can wait for you, Cat. I *am* waiting for you."

She thanked him for the warning and ended the call as gently as she could.

What did Mounir think he was doing, trying to scare Terry into dragging her away from Geoffrey, like some caveman hauling his wife home by the hair? Had he given up on proving anything against Geoffrey and resorted to this desperate attempt to 'save' her? Or did it mean Mounir and his homicide detective were closing in?

She found Geoffrey in the library. He looked up from his book. "Mounir Abdel Razak is becoming a nuisance."

She tensed. "You could hear me?"

"From here? Actually, no. I was referring to his hired help. His moonlighting policeman is parked in the street, staking out the house. Again."

She sank into the wing chair opposite him. "Because they've got nothing on you. Mounir's getting desperate. He tried to make Terry think the same he originally had you thinking, that he's some kind of government investigator. He tried to scare Terry into forcing me back to him."

"How very Bedouin of him. Terry, being a civilized man, consulted you."

"You act like he shouldn't have."

"He shouldn't." Geoffrey went back to reading his book. "Mounir wants to save your life," he added without glancing up.

The big box clinked as Geoffrey set it down on the old Kashan rug. "I bought these some months ago at an estate sale. Would you like to help me sort them?"

Catherine sat beside him on the antique shop floor. All day they had behaved as though yesterday's phone call and conversation had never happened, but she could feel their time running out. Soon she must leave him. And he must leave Cairo, at least for now.

He cut the packing tape and opened the box. Glazed fragments gleamed with cobalt and apple green leaves, pale aquamarine waves, peacock patterns on white. "Wall tiles, centuries old," Geoffrey said. "Made in Cairo, some of them, but most probably come from Damascus. I doubt we'll find many whole ones. The owner sold off the best as her fortunes declined, but some of the fragments may be worth—" His strong fingers burrowed deftly into the glistening colors and extracted a corner with lines of azure suggesting a windblown bloom heavy on the stem. "—a collector's interest. Beautiful, isn't it?"

Pushing thoughts of parting aside, Catherine took it from him. "Very. I wonder what the whole tile looked like."

"Keep looking and we may find out. I'll get some empty boxes to sort them into."

He, too, was acting, pretending all was well. Catherine watched him go to the back room. Antiqa, this haven and treasure trove, was sheltered from the glare of the street by wooden shutters that could be lowered and locked or raised to make awnings. Daylight didn't penetrate, and she could almost believe that time didn't, either. The topaz light from the lamps on tables and suspended from the ceiling could almost be the light of oil lamps, as ageless as the shop's scents of incense, leather, old books, and a hint of Sahara dust.

Geoffrey returned with some empty cardboard boxes. "Put the whole and nearly whole tiles here. Particularly eye-catching fragments here." Sitting close to her on the rug, he pointed at the other two boxes. "Fragments not worth bothering with. Everything else."

They turned over the glazed pieces, some crumbly and fragile, others vivid as if some seventeenth century craftsman had just pulled them from his kiln. "In my youth I saw tiles like these framing a fireplace in London," Geoffrey remarked. "They stirred my curiosity about the wide world."

Catherine fingered a ragged edge. "A shame they're mostly broken."

"Nothing lasts. But artists reuse the smallest fragments in mosaic work."

They lapsed back into quiet, the only sounds the clinks of the pieces, the sounds of traffic outside, their murmurs as they showed each other especially pleasing finds, and in the long, cavernous space, the ticking of the clock.

Geoffrey was still absorbed in the task when Catherine began to flag. The dim beyond the lamp teemed with floating particles, and the dust from the old tiles dizzied her. Geoffrey paused. "You're not well. Shall we go home?"

She hated giving in to the weariness that now seemed always to hang like a cloud over her. "I'm fine. We've still got half the box to go."

"At least you must rest and eat. I'll go round the corner and get some *shwarma*. Or would you rather have *béchamel*?"

"I could eat." She paused. "*Béchamel*, if it has red meat."

Geoffrey rose, dusted his hands, and went out. Catherine thought of resting on a nearby divan, but getting up was too much trouble. Cross-legged on the rug, she listened to the never-and-always-changing throb of the traffic. When she closed her eyes she could feel the pulse of this crowded, gritty, haphazard city, always on the edge of desperation, always optimistic.

The bell on the door tinkled. "That was quick." Catherine opened her eyes.

Against the amber and green glass of the door was silhouetted a slender man with curly hair. Mounir Abdel Razak.

He came forward without a glance to either side, as if he knew very well Geoffrey had gone out. "He had Yahya Hafez pulled off the case."

Catherine tensed. "He?"

"Geoffrey Harrow. Who else could have done this?"

It was news to her. Encouraging news. "Yahya Hafez is your police detective? Good."

"Not good. Without Yahya's access I could never have identified the owner of that car that left the Shubra street so soon after Nefissa was last seen. That car that had no reason to be in Shubra."

"Definitely a crime," Catherine murmured.

Mounir's fingers swept anxiously through his hair, but his voice was quiet. "You're very clever, for a dead woman."

"And you've been watching too many movies."

"Yahya's captain forbade any private detective work. It makes the police look bad, he said. Yahya thinks he got orders from above, but he refuses to help me anymore."

"That's why you went to Terry?"

"You're in danger!" Mounir glanced at the door, but the footsteps he'd heard passed by on the sidewalk. "Your husband is angry, his pride is hurt, I understand that. But doesn't he care about you at all? He doesn't even bother to see this state you're in! Look at you, like a ghost! What is Harrow doing to you?"

Catherine slowly pushed her pile of tile fragments to the side. "I can take care of myself." Her heart was pounding. She took a long breath to calm it. "If Geoffrey pulled strings to stop your harassment—what else can you call it? Following us, staking out our house—then, can't you count yourself lucky and walk away? He has the influence to turn the police against you, to hurt your career. Must you push until you leave him no choice?"

"Leave him alone? Let him get away with what he's done? He's a killer. If I don't stop him, he's not going to stop!"

Catherine reached for a piece of tile, but her hand was shaking. "Go now, Mounir. Unless you want to tangle with him in person."

"Maybe that's exactly what I want!" But he strode out, banging the door shut. The bell jangled.

Thirty-nine

ou've blocked Mounir," Catherine said. "Might that be dangerous?" The fire Geoffrey had built in the library hearth crackled warmly but her hands still felt icy.

"Mounir is a young man without means or influence," Geoffrey answered. "It was his homicide detective who was beginning to concern me. He was making awkward inquiries."

"How do you know?"

"What nefarious spy network do I have in place?" He smiled briefly. "The Rotary Club. A fellow member warned me."

Catherine looked at the book in her lap. Borges' *Labyrinths.*

> *Time is the thing I am made of. Time is a river that sweeps me along, but I am the river; it is a tiger that tears me apart, but I am the tiger; it is a fire that consumes me, but I am the fire.*

"Her name was Nefissa," she said. "She grew up with Mounir, in his village at Amarna. They were in love, engaged to be married.

Nefissa worked in the poor neighborhoods. She was in Shubra one evening, about nine months ago. She was never seen after that, but a man was seen getting into a car. A black Toyota with two of its license plate numbers matching yours." Catherine closed *Labyrinths*, turning to him. "There isn't even proof that Nefissa was murdered. Maybe she had reasons of her own to disappear. Maybe something else happened to her."

"You're asking whether I killed her."

"She was tall, slim, she wore a striped headscarf, blue and white."

Geoffrey gazed into the fire. Its flickerings played over his face. At last, he answered, "How should I know?"

"You can't remember? Whether or not you killed her?"

"It was nine months ago, you say."

One among many. He couldn't even remember. Catherine couldn't look at him. She left him sitting in the library with his book on his lap. The chill in the hallway penetrated the cores of her bones.

She woke to a sweetness that swelled like a deep chord, its bass reverberating though her loins, its high notes shining filaments of delight. Part of the pleasure was a sheltering, cradling weight. Geoffrey held her, sipping her blood.

She pulled away, but he drew her to him and fastened his mouth on her throat. Starting fully awake, she twisted, fighting to free herself, but moaning entreaty, he pinned her arms. His strength was terrifying. In mounting panic she tried to ram his face with her head, to jab him with her knee, but his reactions were too swift. Blocking her barely disturbed the thirsty working of his lips and tongue, drawing the life from her flesh in hot rushes of terrible, abhorrent pleasure. "Stop," she hissed in utter terror. "Killer!"

He raised his head. In the dusk the blood glistened on his perfectly sculpted lips. "Don't, Catherine—" He lowered to her again.

As he tasted her she felt his grip loosen. With a desperate explosion of all her strength she propelled herself sideways and free. Rolling from the bed she ran to the next room. Panting, heart thundering, she locked herself in.

The room was cold. Its antique bed was as fragile as a museum piece. Or a funerary bed in an ancient tomb. Wetness trickled down her throat. She touched it and held out her hand. In the darkness her fingers were smeared darker. He'd had no chance to close the wound. Trembling, she pulled the case from one of the pillows and sat on the bed, pressing hard.

The door made a small sound as he touched it.

She tensed.

"Catherine." His voice was raw with anguish.

The lock was no barrier to him. He could wrench the door from its hinges.

"I lost control. Let me seal the wound."

"A shame to let the blood go to waste, you mean? Like carelessly spilling good wine."

"That is not what I feel."

She pressed the pillow case to the wound. "Tell me, Geoffrey. For your kind, is there any difference between what you just did and rape?"

"Rape, is it?" In a voice colder than a dead star he said, "I could show you rape. If I loved you less, I could render you unable to move and take whatever I liked. Is that what you want to hear?"

"It's the truth." She was shaking so violently she could hear it in her voice.

"The truth is that when you so much as leave the room, I can hardly stop myself following you. I can scarcely leave you for an hour. You looked so distant in your sleep that I couldn't bear it. But I would not have killed you."

"Not yet," she corrected bitterly.

"True," he admitted. She imagined his mirthless smile, equally bitter. For a long moment she heard nothing else.

"And if I could control my need indefinitely?" he asked at last. "All too soon you will age and die. Like all the others, one way or another you will abandon me."

His desolation sent a shudder through her.

Self loathing filled his voice. "You may as well go back to your own bed and sleep. Lock the door if you like. I won't come near." She heard a small sound as his hand left the doorknob, and his bare feet retreating, deliberately audible so she would know he had gone downstairs.

She lay tensely under the bedspread, sleepless and shuddering.

Slowly she resurfaced. She had not meant to sleep. It was dusk. She heard nothing. He was not watching a movie, or talking on the phone. She was not very dizzy as she got off the bed, only exhausted in body and will.

Geoffrey was right. She could trust herself no more than she could trust him now. Was he in the house, or could she go downstairs? This room looked down on the driveway, but when she parted the curtains it was empty. In the gathering dark she saw the garage door gaping black.

He never left it open like that. He wanted her to know he had gone.

For good? But of course not. It was she who must take advantage of the reprieve he'd given her. It was she who must go.

She went to their bedroom and quickly dressed, then climbed the back stairs to the disused third floor, once servants' quarters, where Geoffrey stored odds and ends. The bare floor creaked and dust rose, but she found what she'd remembered seeing when she'd first explored. A suitcase.

It was the old fashioned, handled kind, but no matter. She dragged one downstairs and stuffed her clothes and toilet articles into its gaping maw. She carried it and her shoulder bag down to the first floor. Against the carved knob of the banister a white oblong was propped. An envelope. It was not sealed. Inside was an airline ticket to New York in her name.

Tears blurred her vision. She put the ticket in her purse. A crimson spark caught her eye. Her hand shook as looked at Geoffrey's ring. The eager fire of the garnet. The topaz like light through fall leaves, and the jet like his eyes. She went back upstairs to leave it for him. And a note, so he'd know survival drove her away, not the bitterness of their last words.

There was a pad of paper in the video room, so she detoured for it, reached into her purse for a pen, and paused as she saw one lying by the pad. Scribbles filled the paper. Geoffrey often doodled when watching television or on the phone, mostly abstract shapes like these. A curve, a forcefully drawn square. Inside the square was a stick man. Then she saw what it was. The curve was a hill, and the square beneath the hill had thick, black sides. There was no opening. No way out. An underground cavern or tomb, and trapped in it, a vampire.

Himself, buried alive.

The car's motor sounded, turning in at the driveway. She'd lingered too long. She had to get out the front door before he came through the side door from the garage. Catherine ran downstairs, grabbed the suitcase and let herself out just as the car's motor was magnified in the hollow of the garage.

She waited for it to switch off, for him to cross the pavement to the side door. Then she could reach the street unseen. Kasr el-Aini wasn't far, cabs were always there.

Geoffrey's motor was still running. Odd.

Maybe he couldn't bear for her to use the ticket after all and was about to waylay her. She ran down the walk to the gate, let herself out, and hurried along the sidewalk, glancing furtively down the driveway. The garage door still stood open. Inside, the car was still running. Its tail lights were on.

The car door was open. In the dim twilight she made out a darkness on the ground, and another darkness slumped over the steering wheel. Dropping the suitcase, she ran up the driveway. The black on the ground glistened in the lights from the car. Geoffrey wasn't moving. As she reached him she saw the whiteness of his still face against the wheel.

orty

eoffrey did not move. Even his eyelids never flickered. Blood pooled dark in the car and on the garage floor. Smeared red footprints showed that he'd tried to get out before losing consciousness.

A high, anguished sound filled the garage. For a moment Catherine didn't realize it was coming from her. A hospital was impossible. The blood she stood in was not scarlet but dark. Its pungence smelled unlike the iron tang of human blood.

Without decision or thought, she switched off the ignition, shut the garage door and locked it from the inside. Pulling Geoffrey back as gently as she could, she opened his drenched jacket and shirt. A wound as big as the palm of her hand surged like a subterranean spring with each rhythm of his pulse. His face did not look unconscious. It looked dead.

He'd been shot, maybe through the heart. The car was undamaged except for the blood, he hadn't been inside when he was hit. An ordinary man would have died before he could get back to it, let alone manage to drive home. Whatever agony it had cost him, he'd done it. That was enough to ignite her hope.

He'd said he couldn't die. Yet, he did need blood. If she couldn't halt the loss, he might never regain consciousness. Or worse, the feeding madness would overcome him. Somehow, she must stop the bleeding and get him into the house.

From a story she'd once read by a Kentucky mountain writer, a desperate idea came to her. Grabbing a box from the garage shelf, she dumped out its contents and snatched her trowel from its hook. Behind the garage she dropped to her knees and dug. The desert soil, fine as talcum, blew into her face as she clawed it into the box. Running back to Geoffrey, she pressed handfuls of it hard into his wounds, front and back. It made a muddy mess, but she mounded on more until the black paste grew thick enough to seal the wounds. She pressed it there, willing it to harden.

At last, panting, gritty sweat blurring her eyes, she dared to lift her hands. The mud stayed in place. But she couldn't get him out of the car, weak as she was. She could drive the car, there was no help for him anywhere. No help, and no hope. She bowed her head over his unconscious body, giving way to a grief sharper than any pain.

She woke from her exhaustion. Her shoulders were cramped. Geoffrey's chest spasmed with a sharp intake of breath, and she realized that was what had waked her. Fearful of what it might mean, she caressed his bloody forehead. He gasped, eyes flying open, teeth bared. His agony exposed all four canine teeth. For all their sharpness they seemed small, pitiful weapons now. With abrupt, relentless clarity she saw her self-deception, and his. He was as much time's creature, as doomed, as she. Nothing escaped its inevitable end. It was only a matter of when. She gripped his hand.

He shuddered. Slowly, with forced deliberation, his lips shaped her name. She put her ear to them. "Rifle. I think. ...Was Mou…" He clutched her, trying to pull himself up.

"We need to get you in the house," she told him. "Can you?" His answer was only a gasp, but she had to take it for a yes. She braced under his weight, and he responded with enough of an effort that she managed to pull him out, staggering when he fell against her. Each step felt like the last she could manage, and at every weight shift an anguished sound escaped him. Crossing from the garage to the house took an eternity, every moment a terror that some passer-by, even Mounir himself, might see them.

At last she got the door open and they stumbled through to lean gasping against the wall. The nearest place to lay him down was the sofa in the study. That was up the hall, but now they had the wall for support. As she finally lowered him onto the sofa, he lapsed into unconsciousness. A little blood oozed from the mud-packed wounds. She ran for a blanket, covered him, and tried to think. She couldn't give way to shock now. At any moment Mounir Abdel Razak might arrive.

She washed the blood from her hands and hurriedly locked the doors and windows. At each she peered out, but few cars went by, and the only parked cars were familiar ones belonging to neighboring houses. Nothing moved in the shadows of the garden, or beside the house. Not that it meant they were safe. Mounir, the desert hunter, had managed to evade even Geoffrey's night senses.

As sharp as they were, and as fast as Geoffrey could move, Mounir must have shot him from a distance. If he'd fired, seen Geoffrey fall, and cleared out before he could be caught, Mounir might think he'd killed him. If he did, Geoffrey might have time to heal.

Because if Mounir knew, he'd keep coming. Catherine felt that in her bones.

And it would be her fault.

Mounir had lost his hope of gaining the evidence to stop Geoffrey, and first Terry, then she, had destroyed his last hope of saving her from Nefissa's fate.

Catherine had known she'd have to leave Geoffrey anyway. If she'd only left Antiqa with Mounir, all three of them would now be safe.

Geoffrey's breathing was shallow. His pulse beat fast, as if he was struggling. That his body could heal itself was the only hope. She'd gotten him to what safety she could. She could do no more.

Except, think clearly. The blood stains must be cleaned from the hallway, the car, and the garage. Mounir wasn't the only danger. By now the police had probably taken blood samples from the scene of the shooting. How long for the lab to do its work? Geoffrey might be the victim of the shooting, but that wouldn't help him once his blood was analyzed. If the police traced him here, she must convince them no wounded man was in the house.

She rolled up the hall carpet and hid it in a closet, scrubbed the blood from the floor, but the wall paint had absorbed some of the blood. In the end she dragged a table to conceal the worst of it. Then she showered, put on clean clothes, and buried the bloody ones in a garbage bag in the back of an upstairs closet.

The car and garage still needed cleaning, but her strength was gone. She was so dizzy she was nauseous, and her head throbbed. She sank into the chair near Geoffrey. Oblivion still had him, but that was better than agony. She watched his sunken eyelids and shallow, irregular breathing.

Sometimes his breaths deepened. Twice he moaned. Through the drawn curtain the dawn bathed his face in muted amber, making it seem an alabaster effigy, as ancient, yet ephemeral, as Mounir's shabti. The one Nefissa gave him.

Geoffrey turned his head, muttering faintly. In his weakened state even this gentle sunlight hurt him. Catherine opened the drapes only enough to close the wooden shutter. The street was quiet. One car passed by, but the woman driving it didn't glance toward the house.

Geoffrey's face looked more strained, not less. His open lips revealed gums nearly as white as his face. He must be dehydrated, but she didn't dare give him water. She'd never once seen him drink any. She knew perfectly well what he did need. As if her thought penetrated his coma, a tremor ran through him. He needed strength to heal, and she could give him that strength.

If he could control himself with anyone, it was her. But would he recognize her, or only take what he desperately needed and discover his loss afterward? She remembered his tale of emerging from the feeding madness to find himself clutching the child's corpse.

She prowled another circuit of the house, angling to peek between the curtains without moving them. Children were playing a few doors down. A cat lazed on a porch. Why was it so quiet?

If only she dared go out for a newspaper. Maybe the shooting was in it. A corner shop a few blocks away carried the English language *Egyptian Mail*, but she couldn't leave Geoffrey defenseless.

Catherine went back to the study. When she took his icy hand it was heavy, completely bereft of grace. "Geoffrey, I need you conscious."

His labored breathing was shallower than before. He was not getting stronger but weaker.

orty-one

he touched his wasted face, but wherever he wandered, he was unaware of her. In the parlor the clock struck sounds that might mean some hour, though this was like no passage of time she had ever known. Geoffrey stirred under the blanket, moaning in a delirium not of fever but cold.

She imagined, or else sensed, that she was only glimpsing what had always been. He lay stretched on the rack that had tortured him for centuries. Murder, guilt and compassion denied, were slowly wrenching away all that was human in him: all that he strove desperately to be rid of, yet could not. In the end, this struggle would consume his reason, and he knew it. She remembered his doodle of a vampire buried alive. As Johann was. As Geoffrey would be if he was taken and it was realized he could be destroyed no other way.

Her eyes, already swollen, burned with tears she could no longer suppress. Thunder rumbled in the distance. Her throat clenched as if gripped hard. Forcing down her despair she checked the mass of mud and blood on his chest and found it still hard and dry. No blood seeped out.

The growl of the thunder came again. She raised her head. Odd. In all her months in Egypt it had sprinkled a few times, but it had never stormed. As the deep roll vibrated again, she realized it wasn't thunder. It rose and fell in volume, but it was continuous, and in it she heard distant shouting, and a rumble of motors, or was it something more ominous?

Pushing past exhaustion, she climbed the stairs to the TV room. The screen brightened into President Mubarak's massive, hard face. He sounded stern, but she couldn't understand enough Arabic to follow his speech to the gathered press.

Radio. She switched it on, and yes, BBC World was reporting about Egypt. Security Forces conscriptees had revolted against the poor conditions in their camps. These were military support laborers, and the tourist guards she'd seen patrolling innocently holding hands, young men far from their home villages and serving under duress. Rumors they'd be forced to serve six instead of three years had ignited their frustrations. Blaming the foreign support that kept the regime in power, they'd attacked Mena House and fire bombed two other Giza hotels. It was all under control now, Mubarak's stony voice assured the press. But the distant noise said otherwise.

A ring like breaking glass sent Catherine to her feet. Then she realized it was just the phone. She considered not answering.

If there was more trouble, a threat more immediate than the danger of the spreading riots, she needed to know about it. She lifted the receiver and spoke as firmly as she could. "Hello?"

"Harrow isn't dead." Mounir's flat voice sounded devastated.

Time. They needed time. "What are you talking about?" Maybe he knew Geoffrey was here, but maybe not. She stopped trying to control the shake in her voice. "What did you do?"

"I shot him. I saw him fall down. I don't miss. But he got up and staggered away. Allah save us, I shot him with my hunting rifle, straight through the heart, and he *staggered away*."

"Where did he go?"

Silence.

"You shot a man, maybe killed him! You may have thrown away your life, and for what? Is revenge worth that?"

"Not revenge. It's too late for Nefissa. He's killing you, yet you still protect him. Until now I didn't understand. How can such a thing exist? Even after the drained bodies turned up, it's against all reason. It can't be. But you know what he is."

A vampire. Even now he couldn't bring himself to say it. Maybe he still didn't quite believe it. She saw no other hope. Anything like police protection would be in Giza or Tahrir Square, in the uprising on one side or the other. All bets were off for ordinary law and order. If Mounir came for Geoffrey, who would stop him? "That's crazy," she tried desperately.

"If he's not there, you must go before he returns. Please, for your life, Catherine!"

"You shot him, he went off to die, and I don't even know where to bring help! Where is he, Mounir?"

The line went dead.

She had to get Geoffrey away. Her ticket to New York was no good. The airport was closed, and even if it reopened she'd hardly be allowed to drag an unconscious gunshot victim onto a plane. She's have to drive. Alexandria was a big city, they could hide there. Maybe the crisis hadn't reached that far.

She couldn't carry him, and there might be roadblocks. He had to be conscious.

In his tremors Geoffrey had knocked off the blanket. His skin looked shrunken against the bones of his face. He twisted in another spasm and his eyes opened. They were empty. She knelt by the couch. "Geoffrey."

No flicker of recognition.

She held her wrist to his white lips. "Drink."

His eyes receded deeper into his bloodless flesh. His chest heaved as if he struggled from a deep well toward her voice. "No," his whisper rasped. "Must hunt. Help me up."

"You can't. Mounir knows. We've got to get away." She gripped his arm, hoping the pain would focus him. "Keep us both alive, Geoffrey."

His lips contorted, baring his teeth in a naked snarl. "Bullets," he gasped as his consciousness sharpened, "—are—kinder than your trust."

"Too bad." Holding his cold hand in hers, she pressed her other wrist to his mouth.

His fingers gripped hers in helpless fury at her as his mouth opened spasmodically, against his will. She felt the stab of his teeth. He drew the blood weakly, his trembling making him lose his grip, but she leaned to him, fighting surges of fear, holding her wrist steady for him. She felt her blood leave the small wound as the force of his drinking slowly grew stronger. "Yes," she whispered, gripping his hand. "You've fought and survived four centuries. You can survive now."

Despite the morning, the light through the curtains was going oddly somber, and at the edge of her hearing a faint ululation rose, like Arab women at a wedding or funeral. Were the rioters coming? Or was it the rushing away of her blood? Geoffrey's hand closed over her wrist, holding her to him. His life was hers. He belonged to her as she had never thought to possess anyone. A high, trembling thrill quivered like light reflecting on water, spilling into the darkness that gathered around them in deepening throbs.

Against her closing eyelids she saw leaves arching in an endless roof of green, and gold sunlight sparkling into bright fragments. A tunnel opened before her, with leafy branches and emerald moss. Mating dragonflies careened giddily in the rippling reflections of a stream, blood flowing toward a vast, echoing cavern. Stalactites glistened like stars and the blood of the earth welled silently, endlessly, its luminescence turning the darkness crystalline.

Her arm was wrenched and she was flung backward. She landed hard. With a shock she remembered to breathe, but her lungs filled with nothing. Struggling, she opened her heavy eyelids, and burst into air.

Geoffrey sprawled on the couch above the floor where she lay. He was panting, pale, but he managed to sit up. "Let me seal the wound."

She was too dizzy to rise. She swam along the rug toward him. His clasp was firm as he guided her wrist to his lips and she felt the familiar little stinging chill. He released her. His eyes closed. "No one asked you to carry my existence on your shoulders."

"Then help me with the burden. Let's go." But nausea washed over her, and the air glittered with specks of light. She laid her cheek on the rug. Its soft prickles pleased her as her sight ebbed.

 orty-two

 ubies tumbling, glistening against one another, scarlet lights trembling. She basked in the jeweled splendor of nothing, on the verge of everything.

"Catherine, can you hear me?"

She moved her lips, but her tongue was too large. It blocked her answer. She opened her eyes.

Geoffrey leaned over her, haggard. Behind his head the ceiling was at the wrong angle. Then she realized she was lying on the couch, not the floor. "You made a bad bargain," he told her, "but let's see it through."

She freed her dry tongue from the roof of her mouth. "Couldn't let you run wild in the streets," she whispered.

Gently he helped her sit. "I'm nearly healed, and the strength you gave me will last for some hours."

"How long did I sleep?"

"You fainted. Not long. I let you rest while I caught up on the news."

"Can we get to Alexandria?"

"The bridges are closed, and traffic is backed up on the main roads between here and Tahrir Square. That includes Kasr el-Aini and the Cornishe, but we may be able to thread southward by back streets, head north to the east of Cairo instead of crossing the Nile, then cross the delta westward to Alexandria."

"Then we have to go now. Mounir called. He knows what you are."

"You're right, I understand Mounir. I doubt if he'll waste time trying to convince the authorities. He's a hunter, as I am." He helped her to her feet. "The revolt will soon be quashed, probably brutally. Martial law will follow, curfews, road blocks. If we can get out before Mounir realizes it, he may be stuck here."

Catherine was dizzy but could walk without help. "Your suitcase was outside the garage. I fetched it," he told her as they spread the blanket over the car seat to hide the blood. He got into the driver's seat beside her and they backed out of the driveway. "Mounir drives a white Mira."

Catherine saw no white car, almost no cars at all. People who didn't have garages had probably hustled their vehicles out of sight behind the houses in case the riots spread to this affluent neighborhood.

Distant sirens and a muted roar sounding like heavy machinery reached them from the direction of Tahrir Square. Otherwise, the morning seemed preternaturally silent. Its brightness was subdued by the tinted windshield. Geoffrey looked exhausted. He focused on the road with an effort. Every now and again a shudder went through him. "The blood I gave you wasn't enough," Catherine said. "You need more."

"I'll cope."

They wove through the shady streets of Garden City. The familiar, sprawling old houses and apartment buildings pulled at her as they passed, as if she'd never had another home, each configuration of balconies and wrought iron, each tree shading the streets, almost as cherished as the geography of Geoffrey's body. She looked at his strong hands on the wheel.

"I wonder if traffic is moving southward on Kasr el-Aini," Geoffrey began, but broke off, his attention on the rearview mirror.

In it, she saw, not close, but following, a nondescript mini truck, the kind driven by thousands of Cairo odd jobbers. It was too distant to make out the driver's face, but he was slender.

"Not a white Mira, but..."

Geoffrey gripped the wheel. "Damn!"

As the road curved, she saw cars ahead. They were sitting still, blocking the way. People craned out of open windows as if they'd been stuck there long enough to be impatient.

Another tremor went through Geoffrey. He didn't have time, they had to get out of this. He threw the car into reverse, looking for a place to turn around, but another car rounded the bend behind, trapping them. Geoffrey blew the horn sharply, but the mini truck pulled up behind the car. The truck's driver was Mounir.

"On foot?" Catherine asked. "Catch a taxi? Surely he won't shoot at you in front of so many people."

"I doubt we'll find a cab."

"Back to the house?"

He switched off the ignition. Hand trembling, he threw open the car door and got out. "Don't follow me. If don't return in half an hour, get out of Cairo as fast as you can. Go and keep going until you're in America, or wherever you want to go."

"Geoffrey!"

Pulling a wad of money from his pocket he stuffed it into her shoulder bag and shut the car door.

"Wait—"

But he was striding between the milling people who'd left their cars. He disappeared into them, toward Kasr el-Aini Street.

Behind, the door of the mini truck opened and Mounir Abdel Razak got out. Heading in the same direction, he neared her car. Not knowing what to expect, she locked the door. He glanced at her through the tinted windows, but moved quickly past.

Catherine opened the car door. If she could catch up to Mounir, divert him with promises to leave, maybe he would focus on getting her to safety and abandon whatever he was planning. She slammed the door loudly. "*Ya* Mounir!"

But horns were honking. He walked on and was lost among the bystanders, following Geoffrey. Catherine followed.

orty-three

ebilitated as Geoffrey was, and close to the feeding madness, he might not be able to defend himself if Mounir attacked, or found police or military officers. In this disturbance, any accusation might lead to an arrest. Though she was in little better shape than Geoffrey, Catherine hurried to catch up. Geoffrey was no longer in her sight, but Mounir's head bobbed into sight between the people who had gathered on the street corner.

As Catherine neared Kasr el-Aini Street, she saw why so many had left their cars. The broad street was jammed with traffic at a complete standstill. People listened to car radios, shouted at one another, or sounded their horns as if they thought that would do any good. To the north, smoke rose into the blue sky, and Catherine glimpsed what others were watching, men in uniforms standing along the sidewalk. The sun glinted on carbines. Maybe they were only posted along this main thoroughfare to prevent rioting, but the people around her kept anxious eyes on them.

She made her way between the onlookers, losing sight of Mounir's curly hair and tan jacket until he stepped into the street, threading his way between the stalled traffic. On the other side, for a moment, she thought she saw Geoffrey's profile against a shuttered shop window. She plunged between the stopped traffic.

Anxious faces stared through windshields. Some yelled at her, a Western woman on her own making as good a target as any for their fear of getting caught up in violence. Mounir stepped onto the opposite sidewalk. Catherine saw him hesitate, perhaps puzzled, as Geoffrey strolled calmly ahead, in the direction of the smoke and soldiers. Cautiously Mounir followed through thinning numbers of onlookers. An acrid smell of burning came on the breeze, and the deep rumbling again. Catherine wondered if it was tanks.

On the corner ahead, Geoffrey paused briefly, glancing up the side street. Mounir stepped into the shadow of a shop awning, but Geoffrey turned the corner and was gone.

"Mounir!" Dry from dust and fumes, she could hardly shout. She had to get closer. She couldn't let Mounir catch up to him, but he too turned the corner. She reached it. The side street was straight and short, with apartment buildings close to the sidewalks. They lacked the age and charm of those in the Garden City, but they looked just as barricaded against trouble, their wooden shutters mostly closed to protect the glass, and their iron balconies empty. So was the sidewalk, except for Geoffrey walking far ahead, and Mounir, following.

What was he hoping to do, lose Mounir? And then, go toward the disorder? She knew what he needed. At what looked like a narrower crossroads, Geoffrey seemed to consider for a moment. Then, without a glance back, he turned the corner to what couldn't be much more than an alley. If he knew these ways, if there were other outlets ahead, he might lose Mounir yet.

Not if Mounir could help it. He'd quickened to a run. "Mounir!" Catherine shouted again. He must have heard, but he slipped into the alley. She ran after them.

The alley was narrower than she expected. Dusty stucco walls, the backs of apartment buildings, were punctuated by the corrugated metal of closed garage doors, and utilities boxes clinging like barnacles. Its end was a dirty buff blank, a dead end. Other than an old VW bus parked a little ahead, she saw only nameless litter and greasy urban desert dust. Then Mounir stepped cautiously from the cover of the bus, his back to her, his hand to his jacket pocket. Metal glinted there.

A corrugated door plunged upward, a pale hand gripping it. "*Ya* Mounir!"

"No!" Catherine screamed at the same time.

The young man whirled, knife flashing, but Geoffrey moved too quickly, blocking Mounir's right arm with his left. His right fist gripped Mounir's shoulder, turning him. His command was quiet, and utterly cold. "Stand still."

Mounir's free hand went to his head. He shook it as if dazed. Geoffrey looked past him, meeting Catherine's eyes. Then he bent his face to Mounir's neck.

"No!" Catherine cried again, falling against the wall, but Geoffrey was shuddering with his need. Catherine saw the familiar sideways tilt of his head as he bit.

Mounir's knife clattered to the pavement as Geoffrey pulled him closer, eagerly clamping down on the throbbing artery. A hoarse cry echoed in the alleyway, utter terror from some fathomless place in Mounir's soul. He struggled, but clumsily, as if his body warred with some other controlling force. Their harsh panting mingled, Geoffrey's quickening as he crushed his victim to him, taking what he needed. Locked in the throes of his feeding, he no longer seemed aware of her, or his surroundings. His body jolted obscenely with each swallow.

Mounir began to convulse. Avidly Geoffrey arched against each spasm. From the small motions of his head he no longer swallowed but sucked out the last trickle of life. Mounir went slack. His arms dangled.

The world reeled. Catherine clawed at the grimy wall, pulling herself up, and toward the brightness of the street. She had imagined him hunting like a tiger, stripped down to feral, animal magnificence. Not even her darkest imaginings had conceived how ruthlessly he enjoyed besting his opponent, or the rational intention in his eyes as he met her gaze for that steady moment.

How utterly himself he was when he killed.

Just as, sweetening it with romance, with sex, with a love too sincere to be denied, he would suffer when he knowingly, consciously, took her life.

She stumbled into a run.

orty-four

he Nile flowed wide and slow, translucent as jade. On the far bank a green stripe of farmland was tufted with palm trees. Behind them rose desert crags, barren, high and massive. The highest, shaped like a pyramid, was called the Horn, but the pharaohs had called her She Who Loves Silence.

A fine view. White sails of feluccas drifted gracefully on the river. Fields glowed emerald against the immense backdrop where ancient tombs were hidden. The hotel garden faced it like an audience facing a stage. Onlookers came and went. Leafy shadows slipped across the tables and wicker chairs, and beds of roses released perfume that masked the arid dust.

Sipping fruit juice against her dehydration, Catherine watched the light change. By early morning the heights glowed coppery pink as if softly floating, their recesses faintly lined in lavender. As morning advanced, the shadows flattened and color slowly drained away, leaving depleted white bones lying in the stark noon. With afternoon, the ravines went dark, then the hills. Gradually the desert haze obscured all but their silhouette. At sunset it loomed darkly vivid, a deep crimson against an unearthly scarlet sky. At that hour Catherine withdrew to her room and shut the curtains.

She had escaped very nearly too late. Her strength, almost used up, was returning only slowly. But the face in the hotel room mirror began to be a little less pinched, and strolling the shady garden path no longer made her dizzy. She began to wake in the mornings and feel sleepy at night.

She wasn't sure how many days had passed. Her memories of her escape were confused. Helwan Street, its traffic moving. The black and white of a taxi, the driver telling her that trains were running. Buying a ticket, no matter where, so long as it was not Alexandria. Well-meaning faces floating above her, telling her in Arabic mixed with English that she had fainted, that she was ill, she shouldn't travel by herself. That drove her back to her feet. A stuffy train, incredibly slow. The long vertiginous darkness of night.

She barely remembered arriving at the Luxor station, had no memory at all of getting to this hotel, but the wad of cash Geoffrey had pushed into her purse was more than enough to hole up with until she grew strong enough to leave.

The revolt in Cairo was over. Nothing had come of it but summary shootings of the leaders, fear among the citizenry, and mutual recriminations between opposition groups that weakened the chances of further resistance. It might be years before the Egyptian people united to throw off Mubarak's regime. *And then what?* Geoffrey's cynicism echoed in her mind. *Another just like it?*

Airline schedules had returned to normal, and there was nothing to stop her leaving Egypt as soon as she felt up to it. Up to making a new life in America. Not in Oakland, or Kentucky, or any place where people knew her. Not anywhere Geoffrey could find her.

Here in Luxor, the future seemed far away. Tourists filled the hotels, crossed the Nile on a gleaming white ferry each morning to visit the tombs of ancient kings and queens, bought souvenirs in the bazaars, and rode along the evening streets in caleches jingling with bells. They made music and laughter in the garden at night, but they and the hotel staff seemed as unreal as ghosts.

Yet, people were safety. If Geoffrey stepped suddenly from the shadows her cries would draw a crowd. At night she locked her door, and her third floor balcony door, and made sure the phone was in reach. If Geoffrey wanted to find her, he could. The law had required her to register her passport at the hotel, and he had the connections to trace it. But her precautions were common sense only. She no longer felt the panic that had driven her onto the train. She no longer felt anything.

Not even when she saw Mounir dying against the red of her closed eyelids.

Or Geoffrey's last look into her eyes. Its meaning was clear. Mounir had avoided the soldiers in easy reach, soldiers enough to overpower Geoffrey but the forces of an untrustworthy government. The shock of what Geoffrey was had pushed him to a desperate reliance only on his hunting skills, and an older, more ruthless hunter had seized on that mistake. Geoffrey had meant for her to follow them. He'd seized on his one last chance to provoke a horror so violent it would turn her love into revulsion. He'd known hatred was the only thing that could free her from his spell.

If she'd left him earlier, Mounir might still be alive. Maybe she did not deserve to survive, but she must carry through, or Mounir had died for nothing.

Jasmine twined the eves of her hotel room balcony, its scent infecting the night with a sweetness as insidious as memory. Each morning she brushed away the shriveled flowers she found fallen like dust.

Still shaky, she took a first real stroll, along the Cornishe— Luxor had one, too. Cruise boats were moored below, and the river glistened in the evening, silhouetting their paddle wheels. On the blue twilit bank stood Luxor Temple. Stone pharaohs flanked the entrance, and an obelisk stood like a stone needle. Just one, an imbalance. The other had been carted off to Paris. Once, exploring Luxor Temple would have interested her, so she bought a ticket.

She walked through the gates in the tall pylons, up a row of towering columns. Electric lights illuminated them, and the night concealed the temple's ruinous vacancy, making it look almost alive, as if its priests and musician-priestesses might come at any moment with their incense and bronze chimes. The walls were carved with mysterious rituals. The floodlights picked out the figures making offerings or going about enigmatic activities, but their colors had drained away.

Broken statues of gods gazed straight ahead, inscrutable, given an illusion of their lost gilding by the yellow spotlights, and the abyss above, studded with stars, seemed a ceiling set with gems. But it was only a dream, a beautiful illusion. On the walls of one chamber a queen performed a sacred marriage with a god. The two of them, mortal and immortal, embraced for eternity. Catherine turned away.

Tendrils of soft, dark hair slipped through her fingers. His musky scent stole around her. Weeping with joy, she caressed the smooth glide of his muscles beneath his supple skin. The darkness of his eyes was luminous, and he bent, his soft lips grazed her inner thigh, seeking the faint blue branchings beneath the skin.

Heart slamming against the cage of her ribs, she woke. Her loss was too terrible to endure. The close darkness throbbed with menace.

Geoffrey had been honest with her. He had warned her he was evil. His suffering was real. His love was as genuine as human love. But if she went back he would kill her. It would increase his self-hatred, perhaps enough to destroy his sanity. Or he would continue to murder for another fifty years, or two centuries, until he battled love again, and again committed the ultimate betrayal of killing the one he loved.

But not her. She had escaped. She took a long, steady breath, making her mind a blank and her heart a hard, sterile knot. The curtain across the balcony door stirred. It was only the draft from the air conditioner that moved it, not a strong, pale hand. Its print of ancient Egyptian dancers showed against the lights from the garden, swaying gently.

She was safe.

Catherine sipped guava juice. Soon the other guests would return from their excursions to the Valley of the Kings, Hatshepsut's temple, or Karnak. Then, the raucous music and German beer parties that filled the hotel's patio every night. For now, the garden was peaceful. Empty.

A tall, slender man with blond hair and a honey colored tan crossed from the patio. Her gaze brushed him without interest. At first she did not even recognize him.

"Cat!" Terry hurried to her table. But he stopped just before stooping to hug her. His expression was aghast.

"You found me," she said.

"You're sick." He threw himself into the chair across the table from her. "Have you seen a doctor? You're—"

"I'm getting well. How did you find me?"

"The American Consulate traced your passport."

Terry needed no connections in high places for that, of course. He was still legally her husband. But if he could, Geoffrey could. That he hadn't so far only meant his resolve to help her escape still held. But that was no guarantee he could control his need forever. Behind Terry the rose bushes stirred in a puff of Nile breeze. Their motion attracted her gaze.

"You're still angry." Terry pushed his hair back. "You've left him, though. When I called during the uprising to make sure you were all right, Harrow told me you'd gone."

She frowned. "When?"

"Five days ago. It took that long to find you. The Consulate was trying to evacuate Americans. They've been swamped."

"Geoffrey was still in Cairo?"

"Why? Are you afraid he'll come here and bother you?"

"Bother me?" Catherine tried to smile. It almost worked.

"Well, he wasn't exactly taking good care of you, was he? Look at you! What was he doing to you?"

"Nothing. Want some juice or tea?"

Terry let an exasperated sound escape. He searched for what to say. "You don't even seem like you," he ventured at last.

Why had Geoffrey not left Egypt? Staying in Cairo endangered him. Mounir's police detective would suspect who'd killed him. Even if Geoffrey had made Mounir look like a casualty of the riots, a burned body in an incinerated car for instance—that white WV van for instance—

Catherine stopped herself. "I'm not me," she said. She even thought like Geoffrey now.

"That's bullshit, Cat. Look at me. Talk to me."

"I'm leaving Egypt."

"Going home to California?"

"I don't know where."

His relief vanished. "Listen, I understand that you're hurt. Believe me, I've learned how much it's possible to hurt." He didn't reach for her hand, didn't force on her the touch he clearly wanted. "Take your time. Heal. Soon I'll be home, too."

"No. Finish your mural."

"It's nearly done. I told Pete it's the last."

"Don't throw away your future for nothing."

His clear eyes clouded with anger. "Don't call what we had nothing."

She shook her head wearily. "No, it wasn't nothing." Behind him a white sail hovered on the gleaming Nile. She remembered them sailing in the felucca, the morning sun on the gold of his hair. "I'll phone you when I land in New York."

As soon as she promised it, she wished she hadn't. Easing his pain now would only make it worse in the long run. Even if she were still the woman who had loved Terry, she couldn't draw him into a future that might expose him to Geoffrey's enmity.

"Terry," she roused some semblance of fierceness. "If you care for me, don't blow your chance with Lyndore. Go back to Cairo and tell Pete you'll paint the Red Sea mural. Play Judy's publicity game. Enjoy the success you've earned."

Moisture glistened in his eyes, but he refused to use his pain as a weapon. "Go away, you mean," he said quietly. "All right, I will. For now. But you've left him, and you'll get over him. If I paint another mural, it's for you. You can't stop me from hoping. I won't stop trying to get you back."

She wished she could give him some small shred of comfort. "It's time for you to go."

He turned away so she would not see his face. To cover it he leaned over and picked a rose from the bush nearest the table. For a moment he looked down at its crimson petals, then he gave it to her. Standing, he bent and kissed her. She shaped her lips to his, knowing it was goodbye.

"Promise you'll call when you get to America?"

"Yes."

Turning was hard for him, and walking away harder.

Holding the blood red rose, she watched him go.

orty-five

El-Orouba Road, Cairo
March 1986

rimson blossoms flowed past the taxi window. Violet and saffron flowed like honey, purple and amber streamed by too fast for shapes, throbbing rhythms against the green. But between the leaves, the desolation of sand and rocks stretched like bleached bones to the sky. Relinquishing Egypt, where time flows in more than one direction and the desert floats on the horizon like a dream persisting on the mind's edge. The minarets and high rises of Cairo fading into dust, like all mirages that we call our lives.

A sign in Arabic and English warned that the airport was near. Two hours until her flight. In case he sensed her nearness, in case he came to stop her leaving, she'd go through security at once, mingle with the crowd until boarding time, think no thought that might draw him closer.

The taxi turned in at the entrance. Airplanes shimmered on the runways, white as ghosts.

Not ghosts. Survival.

His staying in Cairo might not be hope she would return. There might be another reason. She knew why she did not want to face it. Maybe, at last, he had run out of the will to survive. Maybe he waited for Mounir's murder, for all the murders, to catch up with him.

Because, she knew, he craved as much as feared the nightmare he had doodled. The vampire buried alive, imprisoned in torment but no longer killing. No longer burdened with sanity. Johann had despaired and achieved that obliteration, but in Johann's era many people believed in vampires. Whatever myths existed, they had discovered how to stop him. What would this era think of to do with an anomaly like Geoffrey?

That was why her survival must be her final gift to him. As soon as she landed, before she phoned Terry, she would phone Geoffrey and let him know. Maybe her survival would give him the strength to survive, too. It might be the only thing that could.

As long as she lived, neither of them would be free of craving. Always a thread of hope would bind them. Hope that they might meet again. Fear that they would. But Geoffrey would continue to be clever and careful because he'd know she wanted him to. Eventually, her lifetime would be over and he could grieve without remorse, as other lovers grieved. Nothing could ever deprive him of the knowledge that he had not destroyed her. It might be enough to make his existence endurable.

An existence that destroyed others. But she could no longer dwell on right or wrong, or the darkness of which love is capable. She must learn to keep her nightmares to herself.

"Here we are," the driver said. "International terminal."

This one act. Boarding a plane. Then, nothing else. Only to live until she died.

The taxi driver looked back at her. "*Ya* madam? Broblem?"

"*No.*" The low fierceness of her voice filled the small space.

He frowned. His big moustache and wrinkles made him look like a walrus. He was irked. A foreigner talking nonsense was not what he needed at the end of a long day. "You have suitcase? Bassbort?"

This silliness, humanity, is what I want to avenge and protect?

Catherine smiled. "Yes." *This, and every other ridiculousness, kindness and longing that is human.* "Take me back to Cairo."

He sighed in heavy exasperation. "You sure?"

She gave him Geoffrey's address.

The shapes of Cairo's skyline appeared faintly. They grew, dreaming in their dusty haze. Abruptly, with no warning, the setting sun ignited them.

The Khan el-Khalili wafted by, the spice lanes of the Mouski on the verge of their evening waking, the gaudy movie billboards and the far more vivid warmth of friends strolling hand-in-hand on the Sharia' Champollion. The taxi crept through the dusk traffic along the wine dark river of time, and hope, and necessity. From her shoulder bag she took Geoffrey's ring. Its garnet and topaz flamed as she slid it on her finger.

Finally, she saw the whole web of her own deception. Her failure to phone Terry would alert him to her disappearance. Her odd behavior made sure the taxi driver would remember her, and she'd given him Geoffrey's exact address. If Mounir's death didn't lead the police to Geoffrey, hers would.

No more deceptions. She would seduce him with his own destruction as irresistibly as he'd lured her with hers. However many times he had loved, however many lovers he had killed, it was she who would be his last. She would possess him as absolutely and finally as he lusted to possess her.

Love lay open with its core revealed, a wellspring darker and more cruel than she had imagined. One truth glittered there like a black opal. Geoffrey deserved love.

Tahrir Square spun, a whorl of hooting traffic sheathed in gold. Catherine laughed softly at its dazzle, as eternal as the sun, as ephemeral as a bubble. The taxi plunged past the American University into the leafy, curving labyrinth of Garden City.

Above the mimosas a lavender sky was flushed with rose.

Each turret and ornamented doorway glowed incandescent in the sunset. Each palm frond and blade of grass gleamed fresh and vital as if newly born. Light refracted through the windows of parked cars, turning her skin iridescent.

With a quickening pulse she anticipated the winglike curve of Geoffrey's upper lip. The precise austerity of his lower one. The small dueling scar at the corner of his mouth. The thought of his breath hot on her throat seized her with a shiver tender and glistening as a butterfly's wing.

Oh, his fragility, and the jagged edge of grief she suffered for him!

At last the house came in view, its balconies veined with flame, the glass of the windows ablaze. Her heart contracted with fierce tenderness. She had never loved him so infinitely.

She paid and got out, taking her shoulder bag and the overnight bag she'd bought in Luxor, but leaving her plane ticket on the back seat. Her name was on it. The driver steered away without noticing it. Not yet.

The gate stood closed, its spikes forbidding entrance, but she took out the key and swung the iron bars inward.

The front door opened. Geoffrey stepped out. His dark hair was scarlet light, and the planes and hollows of his face glistened with molten radiance, but he endured it. In a clarity deeper than sorrow or joy she climbed the steps.

"I felt you coming," he said.

"Yes," she acknowledged the mystery that even now eluded understanding. He stood back, letting her in. The scent of old wood and books, familiar, home, made an undercurrent to the pungence of his blood musk.

Swiftly he took her in his arms. His kiss was soft, luminous, voracious. His tongue was hers, and the lithe solidness of his chest, and the demanding vulnerability of his erection. All hers. Tenuous as the faintest breeze on bare skin, the first shivering of mingled chill and inferno as his heart ceased, then began throbbing to the beat of hers.

As if scorched, he broke away. "I don't want you dead."

"No. You only want my death."

He shuddered. But his smile was faintly ironic. *"Time is a river which sweeps me along, but I am the river; it is a tiger which mangles me, but I am the tiger; it is a fire which consumes me, but I am the fire."*

"Consummation," she agreed.

His eyes acknowledged, their depths magnitudes brighter than light.

"Come upstairs," she said. Heart pounding, she started up the steps. A wild impulse seized her to run out the door, to escape, to live. On the landing she turned.

He paused, hand on the carved banister, craving one last moment before it must begin. His face, pale in the dusk, was more beautiful than she had ever seen it before. Through their approaching oneness she felt, as much as saw, his desire, his grief, the finality of his despair and limitless love.

He climbed the stairs to her.

Photo (with Ogygian, his no-eye side) by Laura Battles

Beth Tashery Shannon worked with the Egypt Exploration Society's excavations at el-Amarna and contributed to *Amarna Reports* IV and meetings of the American Research Center in Egypt. Her experimental short fiction has appeared in *Pushcart Prize* III and IX, *Chicago Review*, and *TriQuarterly Review*. Her story in *Pleasures: Women Write Erotica* (Doubleday) was a basis for an ABC TV movie. Coincidentally, in 2009, *Twilight* actor Edi Gathegi performed her prose poem "Bons" with WordTheatre.

Her novel *Tanglevine* was published in 2012 by BearCat Press, as was *The Sun and Stars*, a murder mystery set in the court of Henry VIII, under the pseudonym Elizabeth Adair.

Shannon's literary criticism includes an essay on *Salome* in *Approaches to Teaching the Works of Oscar Wilde* (MLA Press). She has taught university creative writing courses and edited fiction for a publishing house. Currently she works as a freelance graphics artist and editor.

She lives in Georgetown, Kentucky where she writes and volunteers as a tour guide, researcher and back-scratcher of elderly stallions for Old Friends, a retirement facility for Thoroughbreds.

onts

I love fonts. They're the soul of book design. Because the mood of *Dark Wine* matters so much to it, the print version with its beautiful type is the only one that really feels like *Dark Wine* to me.

The text is in Arrus Bitstream. Designed in 1991 by Richard Lipman, this font produces a clear, modern typeface, yet graced by subtle decorative touches.

The floral caps are Romantique Initials. Like Geoffrey Harrow's, their history is long and a bit mysterious. Their origin is in the initial caps found in early sixteenth century editions of *le Roman de la Rose,* like the 1503 copy from Lyon in the Library of Congress (digitized images: lccn.loc.gov/48041318). These printed caps evoke illuminated letters in medieval manuscripts, and in turn they inspired modern renditions like the beautiful Vampyres Garden, designed in 1997 by "Black Box." I'd long wanted that font for *Dark Wine*, but technical issues prevented it. I was ecstatic to find the almost identical Romantique Initials in public domain, credited on the Fontspace site to "Character," 2007. The style and similarity of these two modern renderings makes me wonder if both might be redrawings of a late nineeenth or early twentieth century typeface. I would be interested to know more about it.

Beth Tashery Shannon

Dark Wine took shape in my imagination some years ago, but I wasn't completely pleased with it. I might never have got it right had it not been for urgings from my publisher at BearCat Press. I owe her many thanks. What possessed me to write *Dark Wine* in the first place? I like ghost tales, vampire stories and other fiction about the paranormal, and I enjoyed recapturing my impressions of Egypt in the mid-1980s when I first spent time there. But where did the obsession that ensnares its characters come from? I don't know. I can only quote from the one vampire story that ever really scared me, "The Room in the Tower" by E. F. Benson: "It came out of the dark, and into the dark it has gone again."

Beth Tashery Shannon

www.ingramcontent.com/pod-product-compliance
Lightning Source LLC
Chambersburg PA
CBHW030654260626
47157CB00007B/2649